Badger
Game

Badger Game

Michael Bowen

ST. MARTIN'S PRESS · NEW YORK

BADGER GAME. Copyright © 1989 by Michael Bowen. All rights reserved. Printed in the United States of America. No part of this book may be used or reproduced in any manner whatsoever without written permission except in the case of brief quotations embodied in critical articles or reviews. For information, address St. Martin's Press, 175 Fifth Avenue, New York, N.Y. 10010.

DESIGN BY DEBBY JAY

Library of Congress Cataloging-in-Publication Data
Bowen, Michael.
   Badger game / Michael Bowen.
      p.   cm.
   ISBN 0-312-02864-4
   I. Title.
PS3552.0864B33   1989
813'.54—dc19   89-4082

First Edition

10 9 8 7 6 5 4 3 2 1

To Harold J. Bowen and Judith Ann Bowen, who
have to accept some of the responsibility.

Badger
Game

Badger Game: An extortion racket in which a man is lured by a woman into a compromising position and is then confronted with and blackmailed by the woman's accomplice, posing as her husband or brother.

—*Webster's Third New International Dictionary*
(Unabridged 1981)

Thursday Afternoon and Friday

Chapter 1

Bliss was it in that dawn to be alive,
But to be young was very heaven!

— Wordsworth, "The Prelude"

At 10:42 P.M. on March 2, 1962, Katherine Colleen Ferguson arrived at the corner of Broadway and Seventh Avenue in New York City. She arrived there after a journey of 128 feet, straight down.

In the tenth-floor hotel room where Mrs. Ferguson's last trip began, the police found no luggage and no suicide note. They did find an olive green leather purse with a shoulder strap, and an oxblood Diplomat model Dunhill attaché case.

The purse contained: a wallet with just under forty dollars in currency and change, a Diners Club card, and a handful of department store charge cards; a compact; a pale pink lipstick; a small plastic package of Kleenex tissues; a silver Cross fountain pen; a Parker T-ball jotter ballpoint pen; a combination pocket calendar and address book; a small pack of business cards; a set of keys to an apartment in the low sixties on Central Park West; a Kennedy-for-President campaign button; a palm-sized white leather pouch holding a rosary with ivory beads and a silver chain and crucifix; a tortoiseshell case containing thirteen Pall Mall cigarettes; a slim black-and-gold Cartier lighter; and some lint, crumbs, and miscellaneous jetsam.

The attaché case was empty.

Not quite eight weeks later, when Thomas Andrew Curry and I walked out of the United States Courthouse in Foley Square, we didn't know anything about Mrs. Ferguson's death in early March. Neither of us had heard about it, and we wouldn't have thought much of it if we had. The name meant nothing to either of us. On April 26, 1962, our minds were on an appellate argument I had just made, based on a brief Thomas had helped me write.

"Can I offer you a ride back uptown?" Thomas asked me.

"For what I'm paying you on this little project, you certainly can."

His car pulled smoothly up to the curb. He opened the rear door for me. Holding onto my hat to keep the car top from knocking it off—I have a lot more experience with taxis than limousines—I ducked into the inviting gray suede interior. Thomas climbed in after me. He wasn't wearing a hat.

I caught a warm glint of professional satisfaction in his green-flecked brown eyes as he settled in beside me. I had argued effectively because I'd had the sense to learn his brief thoroughly and follow it closely. He knew it.

Thomas's face was tanned and radiated with sun glow while mine was still winter-pale. He had a light brown mustache that emphasized his face's angularity: prominent cheekbones, long nose, and a blunt, emphatic jaw. There was a slight curl to his brown hair, which spilled very slightly over his ears—a little long for the era.

He was six feet tall and weighed about 175. He was in basically sound but by no means outstanding physical condition. He was the kind of person who played basketball or tennis or handball whenever he could, but who couldn't stand just working out for its own sake. He enjoyed rich food and strong drink and it showed.

He smiled easily, showing off-white teeth. He had lost one of the front teeth during an intramural boxing match at Princeton, but the false tooth that replaced it was a near-perfect match. The smile was firm but sometimes superficial, designed to keep you from getting below the surface. His mental toughness was like his physical toughness: You had to get to know him rather well before you realized it was there. There was absolutely nothing flashy about him, but if you'd wanted to capture the real Thomas Andrew Curry on canvas you would have had to skip pastels and rely on bold, primary colors.

Thomas's three-piece suit was the same shade of gray as Robert E. Lee's uniform in all those pictures of his surrender to Grant. He had on a white shirt and a blue tie with tiny white dots—what he described as the kind of tie old men in Boston wear when they take their fathers to lunch. I'd told him once to dress conservatively when we went to court, and to Thomas "conservative" and "dull" were synonyms.

He glanced at his watch. "I promised to pick Sandy up at three-fifteen," he said. "Will that be a problem?"

"On the contrary, it will very likely be the highlight of the trip."

"Alfred," Thomas said then to the driver, "the public library and then Mr. Furst's office." The limousine pulled away from the curb and purred down the street.

"How do you think the argument went?" I asked him.

"I think you should have used the limerick."

"Thomas." I sighed, exasperated and amused at the same time.

"I mean it. It summarized our basic position perfectly."

"That's hardly the point." Even back then, people said I was stuffy. I prefer to think of myself as serious. Business clients expect their lawyers to be serious people. Especially European business clients.

"Instruct me," Thomas said. He said it affectionately; the smile warmed up a few degrees. "What is the point?"

"Thomas, this was the United States Court of Appeals for the Second Circuit. It's the greatest court in the world. There are at most two members of the current Supreme Court who could sit on the second circuit without being embarrassed by their relative mediocrity. The ghosts of Augustus Hand and Jerome Frank and Benjamin Cardozo are walking around in there."

"So put the limerick in Latin."

I laughed in spite of myself.

"You're thirty-two years old, Thomas," I said then. "You apparently want something besides—besides—"

"Besides four million dollars."

"Well, yes. I mean, I know why I do this, Thomas. I do it because I've got a wife, an ex-wife, and five very acquisitive children to support. I'm not sure why you do it. But whatever the reason is, it's apparently important to you, and since it's important to you, you have to play by the rules they make. Sooner or later, you have to drop the clever undergraduate routine and get down to the dull, serious, tedious, conservative business of being a grown-up."

"You make it sound so appealing."

I sighed again.

The limousine was coming up to the main branch of the New York Public Library. That building is one of my ultimate defenses of New York City. Say what you want to—crime, traffic, corruption, whatever—any city that can produce something like the New York Public Library isn't all bad.

There is a stone lion on a pedestal guarding each end of the broad steps leading up to the library's main entrance. Sandrine Cadette was standing just in front of the farther lion. She was holding an old-fashioned brown leather briefcase upright between her legs while she read through some four-by-six note-cards and waited for us.

I said she was standing just in front of the lion. She wasn't leaning up against the pedestal, as most people would have done. She was wearing a beige jacket-and-skirt suit, one of only three outfits she owned that she felt comfortable wearing to the office. It had to be dry-cleaned, and dry-cleaning it cost sixty-five cents. If she could save sixty-five cents by standing up straight instead of slouching, she'd stand up straight.

Her hair was blue-black. Beehives were fashionable for women back then, but she wore her hair in a kind of short, no-nonsense cut, like a close-fitting helmet. I'm never confident of my estimates of women's heights, because I don't take proper account of whether they're wearing heels or not, but if I had to I would've guessed her height at five-seven or five-eight. Her complexion was deep brown, as prototypically Mediterranean as anything you'll ever see. Her whole face, in fact, evoked southern France—until you got to her eyes. Her eyes were where the Norman blood showed: royal blue and, in certain moods, as cold and bracing as deep spring water.

Sandrine at twenty-four was physically attractive but *jolie*—cute and pert, with a kind of jovial prettiness—rather than beautiful. While she was seldom the most fetching woman in a group, however, she was almost invariably the most striking. The main reason for this, apart from those Viking eyes coming at you out of her smooth, brown, Latin face, was the expression of wonder and delight that she wore much of the time.

People tended to take this for naiveté, but it wasn't. It was astonishment of an entirely different order. The United States of America was simply unbelievable to her. She once told me that she didn't fully appreciate Surrealism until she came to this country, and she meant it.

As soon as the limousine stopped, Thomas clambered out so that he could hold the door open for Sandrine. She stepped into the car and smiled at me. She smelled of soap that made me think of Monet's water lilies. She didn't use perfume or hairspray and she never smoked before 5:00 P.M., so the clear soap scent dominated.

"The debate went well?" she asked, a lilting accent coloring her voice. She spoke English well, but not perfectly. Her modern language in school had been German.

The two aspects of English Sandy was least comfortable with were swearing and idioms. I only heard her swear twice the entire time I knew her—there was a convention back then that well-bred men and women didn't swear in each others' presence, absent extreme provocation, unless they knew each other very well—and both times she used the all-purpose French *merde*. With idioms, though, she just plunged bravely ahead and left her listeners to figure out her meaning.

"It went rather well," Thomas said.

"Thomas thinks I should have used a limerick," I said.

"Leem-ah—?" she questioned.

"Short, humorous poem."

"What was the subject again?"

"Res judicata," Thomas and I said at once.

" 'The thing adjudicated,' " she translated. "That has what meaning, please?"

"The conclusive effect of prior judicial determinations," I said.

"One kick at the cat," Thomas said, more helpfully.

"One bite at the apple," I chimed in.

"What was the leem-ah—what was the poem?"

"It goes like this," Thomas said. " 'Round three of a tiresome rift/Found the judge exceedingly miffed./He said, "You just gotta/Plead *res judicata*/'Cause the *res* here is not to the swift." ' "

"Mr. Furst," Sandrine said to me, "how could you possibly pass up the chance to say something so *drôle?*"

"A life of iron discipline," I answered.

"Talking of discipline," Sandrine said, "is there anything at the office that compels my attention this afternoon?"

"Nothing that can't wait until tomorrow morning, I think," I said. "Why?"

"I believe that Thomas may have a new case for you."

"Why hasn't Thomas told me about it?"

"Because he does not know about it yet," Sandrine explained patiently. "It only came up this morning."

"Perhaps we could begin with this morning, then."

"This morning, affirmative. I spent an hour or so in the Museum of Modern Art this morning. While I was there, Harrison Tyler—the painter, have you heard of him?"

"Vaguely," I said.

"Nope," Thomas said.

"In all events, Harrison Tyler came up and said that he had noticed the Curry and Furst firm name stamped on my briefcase. And he asked if Thomas Andrew Curry was the Curry in that firm. And I said no, that was his father, but that Thomas Andrew sometimes did franc-tireur work for the firm."

"Franc-tireur brief-writing, for example," Thomas said.

"To make a long story one word, he said he might be able to use Thomas's help on a matter, and I said that I would see if we could see him this afternoon."

"Well," Thomas said. "That settles that."

The limousine stopped in front of the medium-sized, utterly undistinguished midtown office building where the discreet and unostentatious law firm of Curry & Furst did its work.

"Thank you for the ride, Thomas," I said as I got out. "Thank you for the potential client, Miss Cadette. Have a pleasant afternoon. And if you decide that I should take this case, please remember to get a retainer."

About three minutes later, when I got up to our modest suite—essentially half of one floor, with corner offices for two partners, window offices for six associates, the odd, internal cubbyhole, a switchboard operator who doubled as a receptionist, and a six-woman typing pool—Thomas Graham Curry greeted me with what had become his standard question.

"Afternoon, Furst," he said. "How did the argument go?"

"Afternoon, Graham. It went well enough. I expect it'll come out all right."

"Good. Glad to hear it." He turned to go into his own office.

"Your son did a good job on the brief," I said to my senior partner's back. "It was a richly nuanced issue, and he turned in a first-rate piece of work."

"I understand you had to take a bawdy limerick out before you could send the brief to the printer."

"It wasn't bawdy," I protested gently. "He only put it in a footnote. And he wouldn't have put it in if he hadn't been sure I'd take it out."

"Hmph."

T. Graham Curry went into his corner office and closed the door. I walked toward mine to do the same.

In 1929, when I was twelve, my father told me about the German Army marching into Brussels in 1914. He hadn't been there—he had left Belgium for the United States in 1910 and never gone back—but he could recite almost verbatim the rather poetic press accounts of the event: rank after rank of field gray uniforms marching past with impeccable precision all day long and into the night, the heelplates on the soldiers' boots striking orange sparks from the cobblestones as twilight gathered.

I realized then that the occupation of Brussels was a kind of dividing line for my father. He dated things by whether they happened before or after that event. The day the kaiser's army occupied Brussels was the day everything changed, the day that Then stopped and Now began. Nineteen thirteen and before was when things were the way they were supposed to be. After that was when things were different.

My dividing line is November 22, 1963, and my last normal year is 1962. I don't know why that is, really. After all, I've lived through the depression, World War II, Hiroshima, the cold war, Korea, McCarthyism—all in a way more momentous, more world-changing than the assassination of President Kennedy. I just know that, looking back on it, that's the way it seems to me: Before then, things were distinctively one way, and since then they've been distinctively another way.

Thomas Andrew Curry and Sandrine Cadette were two of my favorite people. If it was three forty-five on Friday afternoon, and there wasn't any work that couldn't be put off until Monday morning, and I wanted to go out with some good friends and swap war stories over something alcoholic for a couple of hours, I'd include Thomas and Sandy every time.

This is their story, not mine. I was in and out of it, but I got most of the details later, one piece at a time, sometimes by talking with someone else involved, often just by sitting down and figuring out how certain things had to have happened, reconstructing what people must have said. Putting it all together was a bit of trouble, but I enjoyed it and, anyway, telling that story is the best way I can think of to recapture what was special about the way things were Then.

Chapter 2

Marxism is the opiate of the intellectuals.

—Raymond Aron

In late September, 1951, T. Graham and Thomas Andrew Curry had a talk over lunch in the Bowler Room of the Crab Club in Princeton, New Jersey. Thomas later on occasionally referred to this conversation as the Chat in the Hat. That was about the funniest thing to come out of it.

The talk came about because of Thomas's intimate romantic interest in a young woman named Emma Schwartzman. T. Graham pointed out that Miss Schwartzman was a Communist. Thomas pointed out that she had a magnificent pair of breasts. T. Graham noted that the United States was at the moment at war with a Communist state. Thomas noted that Miss Schwartzman had a bottom for which the term *callipygian* might have been invented.

The conversation went downhill from there.

T. Graham ultimately informed Thomas that unless he severed the unsuitable attachment, funding for Thomas's education would end, thereby affording the army an opportunity to teach Thomas a useful trade. Without another word Thomas, who had broken up with Emma Schwartzman three days before, stood up, dropped three of his last five dollars on the table, and walked away. He enlisted in the United States Army. He didn't see his father again for almost nine years.

Chapter 3

. . . you choose your enemies,
you don't choose your allies.

                Raymond Aron

T he first thing you noticed about Harrison Tyler was the hook,
a surgical steel prosthesis at the end of his left arm. In case you
didn't notice it on your own, Tyler made sure you noticed it
by tapping his forehead with it in a casual salute while he shook
hands with you.

Tyler's apartment was almost indecently spacious for the Village, taking up the entire second floor of a building that housed
on its first floor a magazine and tobacco shop, a small grocery,
and a coffeehouse. To reach Tyler's apartment, you had to go
into the coffeehouse, out a side door into a tiny hallway, and
up a flight of grimy stairs.

Tyler was a couple of inches over six feet tall, large-framed,
and ostentatiously robust, as if he should have been out in
Montana or someplace and couldn't quite figure out what he
was doing in New York. His appearance seemed at first to fit
right in with the coffeehouse downstairs, but Thomas decided
after about five seconds that Tyler looked like a bohemian in
the same sense that John Wayne looked like a cowboy in *Red
River*. It wasn't a complete imposture, in other words. The
image wasn't totally divorced from the reality it alluded to. But
the Tyler Thomas and Sandy saw seemed calculated to provide
the thrill without the threat, not a genuine beatnik but a Bronx-
ville matron's idea of a rebellious artist, just as John Wayne was

a twelve-year-old boy's idea of trail boss. The real thing would have had sharper corners and more grime around the edges.

His brownish red hair was long and pulled straight back from his forehead, as if he couldn't be bothered to comb it; but it was clean and it didn't stick out strawlike from his head. His khaki work shirt was sweat-stained, but it didn't reek. Under his fingernails there were flecks of dried paint, but no dirt. He had shaved that morning. The room he led Thomas and Sandy into was messy but not filthy. Everything about him suggested affected casualness, but nothing was slovenly or foul.

"We might as well start by showing you the painting," Tyler said. "We can talk about the problem, but it won't make any sense until you've seen the painting anyway."

He led them into a long, sparsely furnished room with white walls and a hardwood floor. He stopped in front of an eight-by-fourteen-foot canvas on an easel braced against one wall. He briskly pulled away a bedsheet draped over the canvas.

"It's called *Badger Game*," he said.

"I fail to grasp the title," Sandy admitted. "Is it American slang?"

"Yes," Thomas responded. "That much I can help you with. An allusion to Raymond Chandler and mean streets, seductive women enticing timid accountants into compromising situations and that kind of thing. Am I right, Tyler?"

"Look at it with your eyes before you look at it with your mind," Tyler said, smiling ambiguously. "We can talk about the title anytime."

Tyler withdrew from the room while Thomas and Sandy obeyed his injunction and turned their attention to the canvas. It was about 80 percent complete. A metallic gray line ran bladelike from a spot four feet from the top of the left side to a point four feet from the bottom on the right side. Beneath this line, Tyler had slavishly copied a painting called *Wisdom*, along with its frame and title plate, right down to the artist's initials in the lower right-hand corner of the canvas.

Wisdom depicted a rather Olympian woman dressed in a flowing white Grecian robe. Over the robe she wore a buckler.

A spear rested against her right shoulder and a shield leaned against her right leg. A close-fitting helmet covered her head, though not thoroughly enough to hide her abundant blond hair or conceal the beatific gaze in her eyes. With her left hand she raised a shell from which to drink water she had presumably taken from the stream at her feet.

Above the gray line, Tyler had painted a different woman. Instead of a flowing white robe, this one wore olive-drab combat fatigues. Instead of a helmet from the Trojan War, a G.I. model rested on her head. Instead of a shell, she drank her water from a hip canteen. From her eyes came the thousand-yard stare familiar to anyone who has been in combat. And instead of a spear, she carried a Garand M-1 United States Army infantry assault rifle with a fixed bayonet. She carried it butt-upward, held by its sling on her left shoulder. Its bayonet pointed directly at Wisdom.

"You see what he has done," Sandy said.

"Well, roughly, I suppose, yes. But I thought you told me on the way over that Tyler was an abstractionist who was always getting into rows with people who think that an angel should have wings and that the average person has fewer than three eyes."

"Yes," Sandy said, "I think that is exactly the point."

"I must be overlooking something, then."

"The bottom is hyperrealistic, a photographically accurate depiction of its subject."

"Which I thought was just the kind of thing he didn't like," Thomas said.

"Precisely. Because you see, its subject is not taken from life or from the real world. The subject is not mythological merely, it is a painting of a mythological subject. Tyler has done a photographically realistic painting of a bad painting."

"Okay. Sort of an ironic commentary."

"Yes. Especially when you consider the painting in the upper part of the canvas."

"But that one isn't abstract either," Thomas protested.

"No, it is not. But it is also not realistic in the photographic sense. Not repeat not. One can tell at a glance that it is paint on canvas. It is representational, but it does not just copy reality, it creates reality. You see how much more alive and vibrant and so forth the painting on top is?"

"I'll take your word for it."

"He is saying, *'That* is painting. I can do that whenever I want to. I paint abstractions because I can express myself better with them than with recognizable objects. But hyperrealists paint objects with exactitude because they have no artistic ideas to express.' "

"Are you entirely sure that he's saying all that?"

"Well," Sandy murmured, smiling up at Thomas, "it is a big canvas, no?"

"So," Tyler's voice boomed then from the other side of the room. "You see the problem, I take it?"

"Indeed," Thomas said, glancing over his shoulder. "You're liable to get some people cheesed off."

Chapter 4

If you call your adversary a Nazi and you're not dead sixty
seconds later, you have refuted yourself.

—André Chamson

Tyler's study was a cubicle off the studio that a GS-11 would
have regarded as cramped. A modest collection of middlebrow
books lying in casual disarray on a scarred, wooden desk made
no particular impression on Thomas or Sandy. Neither did the
answering machine on his telephone, although those were still
rather rare in 1962. The pistol, on the other hand, got their
attention.

It was a .45 automatic, mounted on a two-inch-high plate
of polished maple. A small silver tag rested on the base of the
plate. On the tag was engraved "July 5, 1952," and below that,
"*Angeilion Dakadaimonois.*"

"My uncle gave that to me," Tyler said, following Sandy's
gaze.

"Your uncle?"

"My uncle and your uncle. Uncle Sam."

"I see," Sandy said.

"What do you know about art?" Tyler asked then, aiming
the question at Thomas.

"The usual Ivy League stuff," Thomas answered. "A mile
wide and an inch deep. Let's see: Delacroix, George Caleb
Bingham, the major impressionists. That about covers it, I
think."

18

"What about your girl?"

"Miss Cadette isn't my girl," Thomas said as Sandy sent an ice-blue glare in Tyler's direction. "She and I free-lance for the same firm. Right offhand I'd assume that she knows practically everything."

"It doesn't matter," Tyler said, waving his one hand impatiently. "You don't think you know more than you know. That's what's important. I asked you to come here because you're an attorney, and you're supposed to be a little bit more creative than the general run of that breed."

"I hate to be tiresome," Thomas said, "but we might as well get it right. I'm a lawyer, but I'm not an attorney."

"That distinction's a little too subtle for me."

"I have a legal education. I know a fair amount of law. But I don't enjoy the legal privilege of practicing law."

"Can you do any good for someone like me?"

"Theodore Furst is an attorney, and sometimes asks me to work with him on particular matters."

"I get the picture. You can do the work as long as he signs off on it."

Tyler swung his legs out from behind the desk, crossed them at the ankles, and rested his feet on the top of an olive-green footlocker with black metal hasp and corner braces. A solid-looking Master padlock held the footlocker tightly closed.

"Tell me what you thought of *Badger Game,*" he directed.

"It looks to me like a piece calculated to make something of a splash," Thomas said, "have a big impact, attract a lot of attention—and make whoever it's aimed at rather angry."

"Good. Then it's successful."

"If that is so," Sandy said, smiling and with a glimmer of mischief playing in her eyes, "you may need a bodyguard more than a lawyer."

"I can take care of myself in that department," Tyler answered, perfectly serious and apparently unconscious of her gentle mockery. "I want help from a lawyer because I've heard rumors that if *Badger Game* is ever publicly displayed, a sniveling little crypto-Fascist shit here in the Village who has the unbelievable pretension to imagine that this work is aimed at him is going to sue me."

"You want a lawyer so you can keep from getting sued?" Thomas asked.

"No. I don't need a creative lawyer for that. I've already gotten very solid advice on how to minimize my exposure, as you cats put it. I don't want to do that. I'm not interested in compromising the integrity of my work just so a lawsuit never happens." He paused and looked directly into Thomas's eyes. "What I want is to get sued—and win."

"A rather tall order," Thomas said, "even for me. The legal equivalent of not just outdrawing someone and blasting him before he blasts you, but shooting the gun out of his hand."

"Think it can be done?"

"By most lawyers, certainly not. By us, possibly."

"Excellent."

"Who's the potential plaintiff-artist?" Thomas asked.

"Little creep named Arthur Cleveland. Not an artist. An illustrator. A picture-drawer. A glorified draftsman. A—"

"Yes," Sandy said. "I have heard the name. Someone wrote an article recently saying that he has great potential."

"Conrad Marek," Tyler said. "Fat, middle-aged fag who thinks literature began with Kerouac. Cleveland's his newest protégé."

"And he was the farthest thing from your mind when you began putting brush to canvas on *Badger Game*?" Thomas asked.

Tyler smiled and shrugged, the hook at the end of his left arm lending a special emphasis to the gesture.

"If you can't trust your client, who can you trust?"

"No one at all," Thomas said. His lips split into a narrow grin beneath his mustache. "No one at all."

Chapter 5

Monsieur Secher . . . set what I thought was a remarkable table. . . . Sleep was to him a fashion of passing time between meals and love an activity for people without imagination.

—A. J. Liebling

"**I**t looks like an interesting case," Thomas told me over a car phone as the limousine carried him and Sandy toward midtown.

"Does it look like a solvent client?" I asked.

"He gave me a hundred-dollar retainer without blinking."

"You know what that means, don't you?"

"I should have asked for five hundred?"

"You're learning, Thomas," I said. "What's the first thing you're going to do?"

Thomas put his hand over the mouthpiece and looked at Sandy.

"What's the first thing we're going to do?" he asked.

"Talk to Professor Fauré, I should think."

"We're going to talk to a professor somebody," Thomas said then into the telephone.

"That sounds very promising. Listen, Thomas, if you think of it every now and then, perhaps you could drop by and fill me in on this little matter you've just taken in for me."

"Quite right. I'll be sure to keep you up to speed."

He hung up and looked again at Sandy.

"How do we get in touch with the good professor?"

She opened her briefcase and took out a packet of index cards.

She flipped through the cards for a moment, then pulled one out and handed it to Thomas.

"You can reach him at the number on top," she said. She glanced at her watch. "Call in fifteen minutes."

"Why wait fifteen minutes?"

Sandy pointed to a series of telegraphic notes and numbers she had written on the bottom third of the card.

"He meets with his History of the Romantic Movement class from four-thirty to five-twenty on Thursday afternoons. It will take him five minutes or so to get back to his office, so you ought to be able to reach him if you call between five twenty-five and five-thirty."

"Sandy, you're remarkable."

"System and method, Thomas. The hallmarks of French education."

"So I gather."

"You seem very buoyant, Thomas. I think you find this problem agreeable."

"I do, but it's not just the problem."

"Oh?"

"There's something intriguing about the profession that I practiced for a brief time," Thomas said. "Do you know who the real heroes are? In the eyes of the bar, I mean."

"I am certain that I do not."

"Not the lawyers who can conduct devastating cross-examinations, draft airtight contracts, negotiate like tigers, make appellate arguments that sing with eloquence, or interpret their way effortlessly through labyrinths of complex regulations. They get a measure of respect, but they're not the real heroes."

"I will oblige you, Thomas. Who are the real heroes?"

"The rain-makers. The lawyers who bring in clients, who produce new business."

"Ah, I understand. And today you brought one in."

"Well, you did, actually."

"But it was you he asked for."

"I congratulate you on your discernment."

"So," Sandy said, pressing herself a little farther into the ample plush of the seat, "you're smiling because you think there may be a place for limericks after all."

"Professor Fauré," Sandy said when they reached him at 5:27 P.M., "this is Sandrine Cadette."

"Sandy! How marvelous to hear from you." His French accent was just as pronounced as hers.

"Thank you. You also. I have some questions about a painter who is called Arthur Cleveland."

"Budding young realist. Superrealist, actually, if you will excuse the neologism. I have seen very little of his work, but of course it is hard for a pure realist to get himself taken seriously these days. The orthodox reaction so far is that his work is technique for its own sake, texture in search of theme, that kind of thing."

"Oh dear," Sandy murmured.

"It is not necessarily as tragic as that sounds. He is still fairly new to the upper reaches of the serious art world and he has not been allowed to show much yet. He seems to have sold a bit, but in privately brokered transactions rather than through galleries. In two or three or five years, if Louis Meisel or someone invents a chic phrase for what he is doing, he could ring the bell and the critics will look like idiots, as they usually do when some young rebel makes a breakthrough."

"Where could we see some of his work?"

"A good question," Fauré said. "I do not know that there is much available in any galleries. But if you know someone who has a hundred dollars, you could probably see as much at the Ackley Museum tomorrow night as you are likely to see anyplace."

"The Ackley?"

"Yes. They are having a symposium called Beyond Abstraction or something equally silly and they have tried to stuff everything they could plausibly associate with that rather broad category into it. Tomorrow night people donating a hundred dollars a couple to the acquisition fund can come and eat fattening food and view art and perhaps even meet artists and that type of thrilling activity."

"When does it begin?"

"Seven-thirty. You know someone with a hundred dollars?" Sandy glanced at Thomas.

"*Peut-être*," she said.

Forty-five minutes later Thomas and Sandy were in Thomas's kitchen.

"What do you call the sauce?" Sandy asked.

"I don't know. I suppose I could call it Curry sauce. But that's apt to be misleading, isn't it? Sauce Thomas, perhaps."

"It has what ingredients?"

"Flour, butter, salt, pepper, red wine, beef stock, and garlic. All good stuff."

"Depending on the proportions."

"Carefully measured proportions are the cookbook lobby's way of stifling creativity," Thomas said. "I prefer brilliant improvisation."

"Improvisation is a technique. Brilliance is a characteristic of results, not techniques. In recipes, whether a result is brilliant or tragic depends on the proportions, no?"

"System and method," Thomas muttered to himself, "encounters creativity." He whirled and thrust a spoonful of the brown-colored sauce aggressively at her lips. Sandy jerked her head back but couldn't avoid tasting the concoction.

"Quite good," she acknowledged, when she could speak again.

"Creativity prevails."

"This time," she conceded.

Thomas opened the oven and took the broiling pan out. With tongs he peeled four strips of bacon from the top of the slab of beef tenderloin sizzling on the rack. He used the tongs and a fork to finesse the tenderloin onto a large, oval platter. He ladled the sauce over the beef and covered the platter.

"Let's give it a few minutes while we go have our salad," he suggested.

Thomas and Sandy went into the dining room of his apartment. On tape, Billie Holliday was singing quietly. He held Sandy's chair out for her and she thanked him. Her eyes closed, she bowed her head slightly. He looked away. He always felt embarrassed when she prayed, and he felt ridiculous for feeling embarrassed.

He sat down. The salad was three leaves of Boston lettuce apiece with a dressing made of mayonnaise and tomato paste. Thomas would have bet that the amount of each ingredient had been calibrated with laboratory precision. Sandy was responsible for the salad.

"You really aren't a big fan of vegetables, are you?" Thomas asked. "They're an important source of vitamins or something or other, you know."

"They are all right in their place," Sandy allowed. "But we Normans believe that God in His wisdom created animals to eat vegetables so that human beings could get the benefit of vegetables efficiently by eating the animals."

"The argument from design."

The salads were gone. While Sandy cleared away the plates, Thomas got two dishes of raspberry sherbet from the refrigerator.

With considerable pleasure, Thomas watched Sandy take her first, delicate nibble at the sherbet.

"The more I think about this case that we took on today, the more I think that it might turn out to be tricky," he said.

"If it were easy, anyone could do it," Sandy commented, half-smiling.

"You sound like our landlord."

"You mean your father."

"Same fella."

"I know that, Thomas."

"Now don't be stern with me, Sandy. You know how badly I react to that."

She dabbed a pink smudge away from the corner of her lips

and offered him her full smile: mouth slightly open, head tilted back, teeth dazzling. Thomas decided that she could be stern with him all night long if she wanted to.

"If I ever have children," she said, shaking her head, "I must have only girls. If I have boys, I will never be strict enough with them, and they will end up spoiled."

They finished the sherbet. Thomas sliced the tenderloin into long, thin, sauce-covered strips and put three strips on each of two plates. Sandy broke a small loaf of dark bread into two chunks and put one of the chunks on each plate.

"How did you know about Professor Fauré?" he asked her as they started on the meat. "I thought geography was your field."

"It is," Sandy said. "But in the French social sciences we are not absolutely forbidden to know about other things. Besides, when you expatriate, you get to know a lot of the people in your adopted city who are in the same vessel you are."

Billie Holliday finished singing. Charlie Parker began playing.

"Do you think the Ackley will be worth a hundred dollars?" she asked.

"We have to start somewhere," Thomas said. "If it were cheap, anybody could do it."

They talked very little while they finished the tenderloin. They ate and listened to Charlie Parker's saxophone, sharing each other's pleasure in the savory meat and the smoky music.

Thomas cleared away the main course and came back into the room carrying two plates with wedges of white cheese on them.

"For dessert," he said.

"I am not sure if it is the most charming thing about you, Thomas," Sandy said, "but you do know how to dine."

"As long as you're not sure."

When they had finished the unostentatious dessert, Sandy took the sticky plates to the kitchen. Thomas put a snifter at each place and a decanter of Courvoisier in the middle of the table. Next to the brandy he put a humidor holding two Up-

mann cigars and a leather box filled with Caporal cigarettes.
He poured Courvoisier into each of the snifters.

"I do find it refreshing to deal with guests who consume
alcohol in an uncomplicated way," he said as she sat down
again. "No elaborate formulas, no mumbo-jumbo about cock-
tails shaken and not stirred, no esoteric mixture of liquids in
a glass that has had lime rubbed around its rim. One simply
finds very old brandy and pours it into an appropriate container."

"One should never stray too far from first principles," she
agreed, raising the container in question.

As Thomas returned to his seat, he glanced at Sandy,
her face glowing in the candlelight. He remembered the first
time he had ever really looked at her, almost the first time
he had ever seen her: seven years ago, in a very different
place.

"How do you feel about breakfast?" Sandy asked.

"It sounds like a perfectly splendid idea," Thomas said, raising
his head slightly from his pillow.

"Cheese omelet?"

"Ideal."

"I will be up in ten minutes."

"Some day, Thomas," he said to himself, "you're going to
lie in bed and have precisely that conversation with that formidable young woman—and it's *not* going to be over the
phone."

He hung up the receiver.

She was up in nine minutes and he had managed to dress
by the time she knocked. He buttered toast while she made the
omelet.

It was just after eight o'clock. Through the kitchen doorway,
they could see bright April sun streaming through the dining
room window. The butter smelled good. The cheese smelled
good. The eggs smelled good. The coffee smelled good. Even
the *New York Herald Tribune* smelled good. Everything was
perfect.

Then the phone rang.

Thomas stifled an obscenity while he answered it.

"Mr. Curry?" He recognized the voice of the day doorman.

"Yes, Tony."

"There's a guy here said he was a U.S. marshal and had a badge that said the same thing and he wants to see you."

"Send him up," Thomas said.

"He's on his way. He didn't wait for no say-so from me."

Thomas hung up the phone. He walked to the apartment entrance, stepped outside, and closed the door behind him. He had just finished doing this when he saw the elevator door open down the corridor. There was no mistaking the man Tony had been talking about when he stepped into the hallway. He was six-two, stocky, wearing an air force–blue suit and a white shirt and a navy blue tie. He was black.

The man walked without haste down the hallway, checking the numbers on the doors, seemingly oblivious to Thomas until he was standing directly in front of him. Directly in front of him and rather close to him.

"Are you Thomas Andrew Curry?"

"Yes."

"May we step inside for a moment?"

"Do you have a warrant?"

"No, Mr. Curry, I do not have a warrant."

"Then you may not step inside for a moment."

"Would you rather we did our business out here in the hall?"

"That's what I'd rather."

"Very well."

The man held out a white piece of 8½-by-14-inch paper, folded to business-envelope size. Stapled to the paper was a green, oblong check.

"This is a piece of paper with Latin and a judge's signature on it, and carfare from the taxpayers."

Thomas accepted the subpoena and the check.

"Grand jury?" he asked.

"It's not the House Un-American Activities Committee."

"When's it returnable?"

"Ten this morning."

"This morning? You mean less than two hours from now?"

"That's correct, Mr. Curry. Ten this morning."

"Anything else I can do for you, marshal?"

"Have a pleasant day, Mr. Curry. And don't forget to include those expenses on your income tax return next year."

Chapter 6

The greatest danger to liberty lurks in insidious encroachments by men of zeal, well-meaning but without understanding.

—Louis Brandeis

"Your name is Thomas Andrew Curry?"

"Yes."

"You are how old?"

"Thirty-two."

"What do you do for a living?"

"I'm self-employed."

"Self-employed as what?"

"I guess you might call it a legal assistant."

"You mean you work as a lawyer?"

"I don't practice law."

Grand jury. Almost as much fun as root-canal work.

"You did practice law at one time?"

"Yes."

"In fact you worked for this office, for the United States Attorney for the Southern District of New York?"

"Yes."

"But you resigned your position with this office several years ago, didn't you?"

"A little over two years ago."

"That was right after you came into some money, wasn't it, when your mother died?"

"My mother lost her life in Nanking in 1948. Money she had left to me in trust vested on my twenty-ninth birthday, in

March, 1959. I resigned from the U.S. Attorney's staff in April, 1960."

"And you haven't practiced law since?"

"No."

"While you were still in law school, you clerked for a major firm here in New York?"

"That's right."

"That would have been the summer of 1958?"

"Yes."

"That firm was what, please?"

"Caldwell and Ichabod."

The young lawyer going through the questions looked bored. The judge looked bored. The members of the grand jury looked bored.

"Does the name Casey O'Rourke mean anything to you?"

"Casey O'Rourke and I were classmates in law school."

"And you were both clerks at Caldwell and Ichabod in the summer of 1958?"

"Yes."

"In fact, you both worked on a project referred to as the Johnson Industries matter, didn't you?"

"I did. Casey may have. We didn't work together on it."

"What was the nature of that matter?"

"It was supposed to be a tender offer."

"Tender offer being what?"

"An attempt to take over a company by buying a controlling share of its stock."

"How does that kind of thing work, Mr. Curry?"

"Well, let's see. Whoever's doing it prepares everything very quietly and then puts an advertisement in all the financial papers on the same day, offering to buy shares of the target company's stock that are tendered to him by a certain deadline, at a certain price that's above the open-market price."

"You say prepares everything quietly. Why the secrecy?"

"Two reasons, I suppose. First, the incumbent management of the target company will try to block the tender offer as soon as they know about it, and the later they know about it the less mischief they'll have a chance to do in an effort to block it. Second, if word of the offer leaks out, it can raise the market price of the stock and frustrate the whole undertaking."

"Why will the incumbent management try to block the offer?"

"Because if there's a takeover most of the management in place can expect to be fired."

"And why would the price of the stock go up if word of the tender offer leaked out too soon?"

"Well, obviously—" Thomas saw the interrogating attorney and several grand jurors bristle at the adverb. "Well, anyway, say the tender offer price is twenty dollars per share. If you can buy that stock ahead of time for fifteen dollars, you can expect to sell it at an immediate profit as soon as the tender offer hits the street. If you know about the tender offer, that's a reason to buy the stock ahead of time. If a lot of people know about the tender offer ahead of time, then you have a lot of people bidding for the stock on the market, and that drives the price up."

"Did the Johnson Industries tender offer ever hit the street, as you put it?"

"Not in that case, no."

All of a sudden, the lawyer asking the questions wasn't bored anymore. The grand jurors weren't bored. Even the court reporter seemed to have perked up. Only the judge was still plunged in ennui.

"Why not? What happened?"

"Apparently, a rumor about the offer leaked out. The price started going up so fast that our client decided it had to raise its tender price before its first offer had even been made. Then word of that leaked out before it happened and the market price went up even more. Then the SEC started an investigation and our client got cold feet and backed out."

"To the benefit of the incumbent management?"

"Yes."

"And to the benefit of anyone who bought in before the price started going up?"

"Yes."

"At that time your trust fund hadn't, what'd you say, vested yet?"

"No."

"So you didn't have a lot of money that summer."

"No."

"What role if any did you play in the leak about the Johnson Industries tender offer?"

"None."

"What role did Casey O'Rourke play?"

"None that I know of."

"But you were both in a position to benefit from such a leak by buying stock before the leak took place?"

"I suppose so, yes."

The lawyer asking the questions paused. Everyone in the room seemed to have been holding their breath. Now they let it out. The lawyer opened a brown accordion folder and took out a dauntingly thick stack of paper. The page on top looked suspiciously like part of a tax return.

The grand jurors settled back in their seats. The interesting part of the morning was over.

I found Sandy sitting at her desk in the tiny clerk's office I'd finally been able to finagle for her after she started translating and summarizing telexes from my French and German clients. The job she held then isn't legal anymore. Her official title— Girl Friday—is now flatly against the law in the United States. In 1962, it wasn't. In the early sixties, if you had a dead-end office job requiring talent and initiative and not paying very much, you advertised for a Girl Friday and you hired a bright woman. Today, of course, things have changed. Today you advertise for an administrative assistant.

Sandy was writing with a fountain pen on wide-spaced, quadrille-lined lab-report paper. Above the pad of lab-report paper were three stacks of four-by-six index cards. The cards in one stack were canary yellow. The cards in the second stack were sky blue. The cards in the third stack were white.

"Yes, Mr. Furst?" Sandy said as soon as she noticed me.

"Is there something else you require? Are the summaries satisfactory?"

"No and yes, to answer your questions in order." I glanced at my watch. It was just after ten forty-five. "I have a meeting outside the office, but I should be back shortly before noon. I was wondering if you'd like to have lunch."

"Thank you very much, but Thomas is supposed to call me to let me know when to meet him as soon as he's through with the, I mean at the—"

"With the grand jury. Yes, I know. His father mentioned it."

"Oh dear."

"Well, I can't blame you. Another time then." I looked more closely at the pad. She was writing in French. "What are you working on?"

"My treatise."

"Your treatise on what?"

"*Les Principes de Geographie.*"

"You're writing a geography book?"

"Not exactly. It is not a geographic study. It is a study of the subject of geography."

"Oh, principles. I see. Very French."

"If you like."

"Why do you have three different colors of cards?"

"Yellow for material from primary sources, blue for material from secondary sources, and white for bibliographic data."

"*Formidable.* How long do you expect it to be?"

"My estimate right now is two hundred fifty thousand words."

"It sounds like a long-term project."

"Well, I have only been actually writing for about a year and I have done about twenty-five thousand words, so it should only be ten years or so."

"Ten years? My word. Aren't you afraid it'll be rather dated by that time?"

"One of two things must be true, I think. Either I am in the process of developing the correct principles of geography, or I am not. If I am, then they will still be valid ten years from now or twenty years from now or fifty years from now. If I am not, then it is better that my work never be published."

"Of course. Because the principles won't change."

"No. Principles never do, they say."

"So I've heard. Well. Give my best to young Thomas."

After I left, she kept at *Les Principes de Geographie* until shortly before noon, when Thomas called. He suggested that they meet at the Russian Tea Room at two-thirty.

"Two-thirty? Aren't they finished with you yet?"

"Well, yes they are, actually. At least for the moment. But they brought up a name from my past, Casey O'Rourke. I thought I might track my former classmate down and see if I can find out a little bit more about this mess I seem to have landed in the middle of."

"Yes, that seems like a good thought. Two-thirty then."

It was an offhand comment. It didn't occur to Thomas to say anything more, and Sandy didn't think to ask. She hung up and went back to her treatise. She stayed with it for less than a minute before she gave up.

She tore the top page of lab-report paper off of the pad and put it in a manila folder. She wound rubber bands around the three sets of index cards and put them in the folder. Into her briefcase she put three unopened packages of index cards: one yellow, one blue, one white.

Casey O'Rourke. To start with, she decided, she would put information from public records on yellow cards, unpublished information on blue cards, and leads on white cards.

"You got something against Negroes now?" Deputy United States Attorney Shapiro directed this question to Thomas in the hallway outside the maple-and-frosted-glass door of Shapiro's office, about three seconds after Thomas had finished his phone call to Sandy.

"Certainly not. What a remarkable question."

"What's the idea of pulling this jailhouse-lawyer routine? What's wrong with the man coming into your high-priced luxury apartment? He's just doing his job."

"Yes indeed. And if while he's in there he sees something that he takes to be Cuban cigars, he keeps on doing his job, and I find you wondering whether an indictment under the Trading With the Enemy Act might make me more forthcoming when that oily little minion of yours asks me questions downstairs."

"You really think we operate that way here, Tom?"

"Oh, I don't know. Why don't we dig up Telly Formolo and ask him?"

"Oh boy, Telly Formolo again. What were they supposed to do, stand there and let him drill you?"

"David, the first shot was fired with a handgun from ninety feet away and it hit Formolo in the center of his forehead. When that happens, you know and I know that the provoking act didn't come as a complete surprise to the marksman."

"Great. Next time I'll ask them to send out a buncha rookies."

"If you send a rookie to serve me with a subpoena next time, I might let him past my front door. But probably not."

"Is that it? You're ticked off about the subpoena?"

"It wasn't the highlight of my morning."

"What'd you expect? An engraved invitation?"

"There's an original line."

"I went to Fordham. I do the best I can."

"What I expected, actually," Thomas said, "was a phone call. 'Say, Tom, we wonder if you could stop down sometime soon and talk with twenty-three citizens who are helping the government with its work.' Something along those lines."

"No special treatment, Tom. Not for alumni, not for big shots, not for rich guys. We're not doing this because somebody wants to run for senator in two years. This is a genuine, legitimate criminal investigation. I'd appreciate a little cooperation from you."

"All right. Fine. What's it an investigation of?"

"Stock manipulation."

"You don't say. I mean what's the case all about? What are the facts that set you on to me and Casey?"

"No comment."

"Oh, I see. That kind of cooperation."

"Tom—"

"David, I have surmised the following from the events of this morning and our impromptu conference this young afternoon. One: A serious crime has been committed. Two: You believe that I have knowledge that could contribute to solving that crime. Three: I don't have the first idea what that knowledge might be. From this it follows that there is a criminal in New York City with a reason to do unpleasant things to me, and therefore I would like to be cooperated with as well as cooperate."

"No dice."

"All of you intellectual cops sound just like Lieutenant Jacoby on *Peter Gunn*. You ought to look around for a different role model."

"No dice."

"Very well, then. Am—"

"Tom, will you please listen to me?"

"Am I a subject of the investigation?" Thomas asked.

"Tom, I—"

"Am I a subject of the investigation?"

"Not at this time."

"Have a pleasant afternoon."

Chapter 7

Half the wrong conclusions at which mankind arrive are
reached by the abuse of metaphors.

—Palmerston

"**S**andy, you'll be quite proud of me," Thomas said when
he greeted her at the Russian Tea Room at 2:38 P.M. "My efforts
to locate Casey O'Rourke have been perfectly methodical."

"Thomas—"

"The name doesn't show up on the current bar list. So, first,
I went to the Columbia Law School alumni directory. That led
me to Marquardt, Squires and Jacobs downtown, where Casey
worked before moving on in early 1960 or so."

"Thomas—"

"Moved on to where? Good question. So the next step was
to check Marquardt, Squires in Martindale Hubbell and find
another classmate of mine who was still there and could tell
me. I did that without any problem."

"Thomas—"

"Unfortunately, he wasn't back from lunch yet when I called
him. But I'll call him again later this afternoon and I'll bet you
a thousand dollars that I'm talking to Casey O'Rourke before
we have to start getting ready for the Ackley reception tonight."

"Promise me one thing, Thomas."

"Anything. What?"

"If you do find yourself having such a conversation, you will
instantly get in touch either with the Vatican or a first-rate
psychiatrist."

"What do you mean?"

"Casey O'Rourke is dead," Sandy said.

She offered him a print of a microfilmed page from an edition of *The New York Times* published on March 3, 1962:

ATTORNEY KILLED IN FALL FROM HOTEL

Katherine Colleen Ferguson, a 28-year-old Manhattan attorney, fell to her death yesterday evening between 10:00 and 11:00 from a room in the Broadway District Hotel near Broadway and Seventh Avenue. Police at the scene declined to speculate as to whether Mrs. Ferguson's death was accidental or the result of suicide or foul play. They did say that no suicide note was found with the body.

Mrs. Ferguson was not a resident of the hotel and was not the guest to whom the room was registered that evening.

A 1959 graduate of Columbia Law School, Mrs. Ferguson was associated for a little over a year with a Wall Street law firm before joining the legal staff of Frampton Electronics, whose headquarters is in Manhattan. She is survived by her husband, Drew Ferguson, and her mother and father, Patrick and Bridget O'Rourke of Framingham, Massachusetts.

When Thomas had finished reading the brief story on page eight, Sandy handed him a second page. This page wasn't a print of a microfilm, but a photocopy of an actual page of newsprint. It was taken from the *New York Daily News*, and the headline effectively captured the tone of the story that followed it:

LADY LAWYER'S TIMES SQUARE DEATH PLUNGE

"Well," Thomas murmured, "this puts rather a new complexion on things, doesn't it?"

"It took me longer to find it than I thought it would," Sandy said. "That is why I was late. Once I realized that the Casey O'Rourke you knew in law school might have been a woman, it was easy for me to surmise that she could have married and would have a different last name now. From that point, it was simple to find her married name."

"Simplicity itself," Thomas said dryly.

"What threw me into four loops was the first name."

"Well, it was a nickname, you see."

"I have figured that out, I think. But I thought that the nickname for Katherine would be Kathy or Kate or maybe Kitty, no? How in the world did you and her other classmates come up with Casey?"

"Because of Casey Stengel, actually."

"Was he a lawyer?"

"No, he was the manager of the New York Yankees."

"I fail to grasp the connection."

"Yes. Well, Casey O'Rourke's first and middle initials were KC. Katherine Colleen. You see?"

"UC or KC?"

"UC? What—oh, I see."

"Whose initials were IC?"

"Nobody's. The relevant initials are KC."

"Well, make up your mind." Sandy looked away for a moment. Suddenly her eyes lit up with understanding. "But of course. KC equals Casey. So the initials of Mr. Stengel's first and middle names must likewise have been KC, no?"

"Well, no, actually. They were CD. Charles Dillon."

"Thomas, if you are deliberately making fun of my mediocre command of English, I can only say that my English is better than your manners."

"How am I going to get out of this?" Thomas wondered aloud. "Sandy, listen. I'm not making fun of you. Your English is better than Stengel's. You see—"

"Now it's UC again. I thought it was KC."

"No. I mean yes. Stengel was called Casey because he came from Kansas City. Kansas City is this little town out in Nebraska or Iowa or someplace."

"It is a city of over half a million people located in Missouri. There is a smaller city of the same name located next to it in Kansas."

"No doubt you're correct."

"Of course I am correct."

"Sandy, please. The point is, Kansas City is called KC for short. So because Stengel was from KC, they called him Casey. And Katherine Colleen O'Rourke was K.C. O'Rourke, so we called her Casey, sort of in honor of Stengel."

Thomas slumped visibly in his chair.

"Thomas."

"What?"

"I have decided to believe you."

"Thank God."

"The only thing I cannot comprehend is how you and your classmates ever found time to learn anything about law."

Chapter 8

We struggle not against nude art, nor against free art, but against ugly art.

—Friedrich Jodl, discussing
Gustav Klimt's paintings

"**N**obody said that this was black tie." The man who made this comment looked like William F. Buckley, Jr., doing an impression of a crocodile.

"They never do bother to tell you," Thomas said sympathetically to the tweedy, bespectacled protopatrician in front of the entrance to the Ackley Museum reception. "Pity."

Of the dozen or so men milling around the entrance at this moment, Thomas was the only one wearing a tux, white shirt with French cuffs and ruffled front, and black bow tie. Nevertheless, the man's ironic smile fluttered, like a television picture about to fail. When he entered the central gallery two minutes later, he was visibly relieved to see nothing more formal than a three-piece suit in the entire room.

"I think I understand what role you're playing, Thomas," Sandy said as they entered in their turn and headed immediately for the ample buffet. "But I am not altogether sure how to accompany it."

"I'd ask you to pass yourself off as a bubble head down from Wellesley for a weekend in the big city, but I think that that particular impersonation may be beyond even your considerable thespian abilities."

"Look, Thomas," Sandy squealed by way of rebuttal, "lobster!" They had reached the buffet. "Do you suppose it's fresh?

Oh, please let it be fresh." She tasted a forkful. "Fresh! Oh, Thomas, there is a God, after all."

"On the other hand," Thomas admitted, "you might be able to bring it off."

Thomas moved toward the right side of the room. A man and two women were admiring a canvas mounted near the center of the far wall. The canvas was blank except for a cobalt blue blob splattered near its left edge, from which paler blue dribblings ran incongruously upward. Arthur Cleveland hadn't painted it, unless he had started signing his paintings Stefan Meyers.

Thomas stood with his hands clasped behind his back and pretended to examine the work. He counted silently to thirty.

"Theme in search of texture," he said then.

The man who had been admiring the painting when Thomas came up turned his head very slightly at the comment.

"You really think so?" he asked diffidently.

"Absolutely. One thing you've got to say for it, though: It's not technique for its own sake."

"That's the marvelous thing about these gatherings," the man said. "Just when you think they've achieved perfect predictability, you hear something new."

"I sense irony in that comment."

"Well, you're not quite as dim as I thought you were, are you?"

"That depends on how dim you thought I was," Thomas answered, smiling blandly.

"You don't by any wild chance do this sort of thing for a living, do you?" the man asked.

"What, exchange witty repartee over lobster and champagne? No. It's the kind of thing I've found it hard to get paid for."

"What exactly do you get paid for?"

"I'm a literary interior design consultant," Thomas said.

"That's an occupational specialty I'm not familiar with."

"It's quite new, but it's really catching on. Suppose you're an interior decorator. You have a commission to do a pricey cooperative apartment on the Upper East Side. Naturally, it has to have a library. Naturally, the library has to have bookshelves. Naturally, there have to be books on the shelves."

"I'm beginning to see," the man said. He had by now turned and was actually facing Thomas. "The awkward question becomes, which books?"

"Quite. What books have covers that will complement the decor and at the same time have titles that will impress the client's guests? Leave it to the client and he'll come up with a pathetic mélange that'll make a hash out of the entire color scheme. Leave it to the decorator and you're liable to end up with eight shelves of *Readers Digest* condensed books. Come to me and for five percent of the price of the books I'll guarantee an aggregation of not less than two hundred and fifty books that'll satisfy every criterion of symmetry, spatial integrity, and chromatic complementarity and whose titles'll knock the socks off your old English lit. professor."

"I see. This takes up a good deal of your time, does it?"

"Oh, it keeps me busy."

"And you're quite sure you don't write an art column for some Long Island periodical or anything cultural like that?"

"Nothing like that."

"And you don't work for or with any gallery in this or any other city?"

"No."

"In that case—"

"In that case," Thomas said, "you'd appreciate it very much if I'd go right straight to hell, because you're Stefan Meyers and this work that I've been casually, ignorantly, and thoughtlessly disparaging is yours."

"You took the words right out of my mouth," Meyers said.

"It's a gift."

"I realize that you're in no position to appreciate it, but it does take blood, sweat, and tears to produce art at this level and you really shouldn't comment on it if you don't have the slightest idea of what you're talking about."

"Well, you used the blood to good effect, but I think you should have tried a little bit thicker base on the tears."

"And if that's your idea of snappy patter, I can tell you that you don't know much about that either."

"True, but I know what I like."

Stefan Meyers stalked off, and two other admirers of his painting followed in his wake.

Thomas took three steps toward the knot of people crowded around the next canvas. He turned in the direction of Meyers's retreating back.

"Dismiss him if you will," he said, calmly but a little loudly, "but five years from now Arthur Cleveland will be regarded as one of the foremost voices of postmodern art."

"Do you really think so?"

The question came from behind Thomas. He turned and smiled at the woman who had asked it.

"Absolutely. There's nothing more uplifting than theme in search of technique, unless it's the other way around. And there's one thing you've got to say about Cleveland's work: It's not texture for its own sake. My name is Thomas Andrew Curry."

"Sylvia Peece." She took the first two fingers of his extended right hand, held them for almost a second, and then let go of them.

"And what do you think of Mr. Cleveland?" he asked Sylvia.

"I'm afraid I can't agree with you," she said, and it was clear that this was in fact a source of real distress to her. "There simply is no sound philosophical foundation for his approach."

"What in the world has he been painting, undistributed middle terms?"

"You know what I mean."

Thomas didn't have the first idea of what she meant.

"He sells, though, I understand," Thomas said.

"So does Norman Rockwell." Sylvia Peece smiled to show that she could be gracious in rhetorical triumph.

"It's not the same market, though, is it?" Thomas asked.

"I wonder. And he doesn't really sell, you know. Not in galleries, I mean. He has these odd sales to buyers in Europe and Latin America, and his paintings show up in resale catalogues, but almost none of his work is handled through reputable galleries. It's all brokered through private contacts of some kind."

"The checks still clear, I take it."

"Oh, I'm sure, but that's not really the point. All the off-market sales in the world can't get him around the fundamental problem with hyperrealism as an artistic philosophy."

"Which is what, precisely?"

Sylvia Peece smiled in mellow delight. She had been praying that he'd ask that question.

"How can someone pass himself off as an artist for doing something that a machine can do just as well, and in only five-hundredths of a second?"

"You know," Thomas said, "at one of the colleges I went to there was a machine that could shoot tennis balls at you faster than any human being could return them, but I still get a bit of a charge out of watching Pancho Gonzales get three service aces in a row."

"But we're not talking about the same thing at all. You can't seriously believe that it's as important to be an athlete as it is to be an artist."

"Perhaps not, but after less than fifteen minutes in this room I'm convinced that it's a lot easier to pretend to be an artist than to pretend to be an athlete."

"My point about Arthur Cleveland precisely. If you'll excuse me, I see someone over there that I must talk to."

Sylvia Peece walked rather stiffly away.

"That line sounds familiar, Mr. Curry."

"Yes, I stole it from Chesterton."

Thomas turned to look at the new speaker. He was a white-haired, pink-faced man who except for his corduroy sport coat might have stepped out of the background of the Bayeux tapestry.

"I'm afraid I must've forgotten your name," Thomas said. "I'm terribly sorry."

"Actually, we've never met. I knew your name because Mademoiselle Cadette told me who you are. I am Gilbert Fauré."

"Professor! I'm very pleased to meet you."

"I have been watching you for the past few minutes. I must say I am not entirely sure what it is you are doing."

"I'm trying to be a flaming asshole," Thomas told him.

"Ah. If I understand the idiom correctly, you are succeeding."

"Thank you so much."

"The point of your effort being what?"

"To attract attention to myself, both in general and as someone who's interested in Arthur Cleveland's work. If as a result whoever is actually selling his paintings decides to contact me, I'll know more about him than anyone I've talked to so far seems to."

"You Americans are too subtle for me," Fauré commented.

"It's genetic," Thomas agreed. "Where was Sandy when you spoke with her, by the way?"

"The same place she is now," Fauré said, nodding his head toward the opposite side of the room. "Over there. Talking with Arthur Cleveland."

Sandy was not a great believer in the virtues of indirection. As soon as Fauré pointed Arthur Cleveland out to her, she had gone straight over to him, introduced herself, and told him that she was interested in his work but knew it by reputation rather than by sight, inasmuch as thus far she hadn't been able to find very much of it.

"Just wait," the intense young man said.

Arthur Cleveland was about the same height as Sandy was. He was thin, angular, and wound tight. His skin had a vaguely yellow tint, like the flesh tones on pictures shot indoors with daylight film. It seemed so dry she thought it might crack if she touched it. He was wearing a brown corduroy sport coat over a blue denim work shirt, black jeans, and black, high-top Converse basketball shoes. His dark eyes glanced constantly around him. Sandy would have guessed his age at twenty-two or twenty-

three. A taller, stockier man in late middle age stood near
Cleveland, and his solidity seemed to emphasize the artist's
fragility.

"I suppose," Sandy said wistfully, "that we have no choice
but to wait."

"Who is we?" the taller man asked in a voice suggesting polite
interest. He introduced himself as Conrad Marek.

"Thomas and I. Thomas Andrew Curry." Sandy nodded
vaguely toward the other side of the room.

"Not the chap in the James Bond costume?" Cleveland demanded.

"The very one."

"My lord. Where in the world did you meet him?"

"We met in Algeria, actually, in 1955. He was quite an
interesting young man, even then. Then a few years later he
turned twenty-nine and became an interesting young man with
four million dollars."

"You know," Cleveland said, "I believe I could be persuaded
that this friend of yours is every bit as fascinating as you say he
is. What kind of art is he interested in?"

"The kind that appreciates reliably and has long-term potential."

"Ah," Marek said, "ars gratia artis."

"Don't be a snob, Conrad," Cleveland instructed him. "At
least the man's not a hypocrite."

Cleveland took a wide, flat box of cigarettes from the outside
pocket of his jacket. He flourished it in Sandy's general direction. The cigarettes inside were pink and had filters wrapped in
gold foil.

"No, thank you very much," Sandy said.

"Are there any nonmarketing criteria that inform your friend's
artistic judgments?" Marek asked.

"Our preference is for representational art. But people keep
touting Harrison Tyler and painters like that to him, unfortunately."

"Whom you should consider only if your preferences were

for unintentional comedy," Cleveland said. "Trust your instincts."

"But that is a rather harsh thing to say about a fellow artist, no?"

"About six weeks ago," Marek explained, "Tyler was reported to have said about Mr. Cleveland here that he wasn't even an artist, he was an illustrator, and a mediocre one at that. Arthur is merely responding in kind. But Miss Cadette is quite right, you know, Arthur. It doesn't become you at all."

"Well," Sandy said. "You have been most encouraging. Thank you very much. I will continue to search for an opportunity actually to see some of your work, Mr. Cleveland."

"Would you like to see some tonight?"

"Certainly."

"Arthur," Marek said in a dubious voice, "I really don't think—"

"Right this way."

Cleveland began to lead the small group toward Thomas and Fauré. Or so it appeared to Thomas. What Cleveland was actually leading the group toward was a painting hanging immediately behind Thomas and Fauré. It was the painting that Sylvia Peece had been examining when Thomas's parting shot at Stefan Meyers had drawn her attention. It was Arthur Cleveland's contribution to the Ackley exposition—and Thomas had been standing within thirty inches of it for several minutes without bothering to turn around and look at it.

"There you are," Cleveland said when he had brought Sandy within effective viewing distance of the canvas.

Thomas turned around and, his bicep brushing Sandy's shoulder, looked at the painting with her.

"My word," he said.

"Quite," she agreed.

The title of the painting was *Justice Chastising Fame*. This was a literal description of what the canvas depicted. The allegorical figure of Justice, her blindfold raised and her scales cast aside, sat on a marble bench. Fame lay across Justice's allegorical lap. The hem of Fame's allegorical gown was pulled above her allegorical hips, and Justice's right hand was raised in unambiguous preparation for striking Fame's allegorical bottom.

The painting at least purported to be something more than a work of pure imagination. Looking at it—seeing the shadows cast by the objects in the picture, the unevenness of the marble bench as contrasted with the smoothness of the marble figures, the play of sunlight across Justice's left shoulder—you couldn't help wondering for a second whether some sculptor hadn't actually chipped this simultaneously vulgar and arresting vignette out of stone and deposited it in the law school yard of one of the lesser California universities, and whether you were actually seeing an enlarged photograph of that sculpture. That instant of wonder, Thomas surmised, that moment when imagination wrestled with objective reality for supremacy and the outcome was really in doubt—that was the painting's point.

It's hard to appreciate today how audacious—or reckless—a painting like this seemed in such a setting in 1962. What was daring about it wasn't the mild nudity or the oblique erotic allusion, but the fact that it depicted recognizable creatures doing identifiable things in a way that connected more or less directly to everyday experience—in other words, that it was pure depiction, without any genuflection toward some currently fashionable abstractionist theory. Putting a painting like that up at a serious exhibition in 1962 was like throwing a couple of scenes from *Gypsy* into the middle of *The Ring Cycle*: It not only broke all the rules, but did so in the most provocative way imaginable.

"You devil, you," Thomas said. "Look what he's done."

Thomas issued this instruction rather loudly, and a dozen people glared over their shoulders in apparent obedience to it.

"I'll take it," Thomas said, still rather loudly.

Cleveland raised his eyebrows.

A substantial crowd gathered around the canvas. Murmurs swept around the semicircle.

"Mr. Curry," Marek said, "this—"

"I mean it." Thomas took out a money clip. "I've got to have it. I've been hearing nothing but Harrison Tyler and Stefan Meyers for three weeks, and look what he's done."

Thomas freed a sheaf of bills from the clip. The bills on the top and bottom, at least, were hundreds. They got Cleveland's attention.

"By God he's right," a voice from the semicircle said.

"I'd like to buy the painting," Thomas insisted.

"Mr. Curry," Marek said again, "this is an exposition, not an auction."

"Wait a minute, Conrad," Cleveland said.

"I hate to be philistine about the whole thing," Thomas said, "but—"

"Please," Marek said, smiling tolerantly at the other two. "It's really very simple. This is a temple of art. Don't turn it into a rug merchants' bazaar. Don't give him money. Just give him your card."

"Are you pleased with yourself?" Sandy asked Thomas while he dialed Harrison Tyler's number less than an hour later.

"Immensely. . . . Nuts, the answering machine. The price, I suppose, of even modest fame. I always get tongue-tied with these things. Let's see now. Tyler, Curry here. We should talk. Cleveland's painted a picture that solves half of our problem, and I'm afraid I've drawn a considerable amount of attention to it, but the problem is he's given your face a rather uncomplimentary role in the thing."

The
Weekend

Chapter 9

The directors of the Union Pacific Railroad don't pay me
one hundred thousand dollars per year to tell them what
they can and can't do; they pay me to tell them how to do
what they want to do.

—Elihu Root

Thomas Graham Curry was sixty-four years old. He was in
the office, as he was practically every Saturday morning. Of
course, he wasn't wearing the charcoal gray, three-piece wool
suit that he wore on weekdays. Since it was Saturday morning,
he was wearing evening clothes. As long as I'd known him,
Thomas Graham Curry had put his tuxedo on around seven-
thirty Friday night and generally still had it on at nine the
following morning. In the interval, he might find time to eat,
drink, go to a play, gamble, entertain one or more women less
than half his age, even sleep a little bit—but if he found time
to change clothes he felt the weekend was off to a tame and
disappointing start.

Thomas Graham Curry was a criminal lawyer. Before him,
criminal law hadn't exactly been a Curry family tradition. But
the once substantial Curry wealth had greatly diminished by
the time he came of age, and he'd decided that he couldn't
practice law as a gentlemen's profession. He had to make money
at it.

To make money as a young lawyer without helpful connections, T. Graham decided, he needed the right clients. The
right client, in his mind, was two things: rich and desperate.
Starting in the mid-1920s, he found an ample supply of these

clients—rumrunners, drug pushers, bootleggers, white slavers, pornographers, pimps, bank robbers, cop killers, murderers for hire, bribe-takers, truck hijackers, rapists, and every other species of the scum of the earth.

Thomas Graham Curry was a crusty, flinty, hard-boiled throwback to a tough and demanding school. He didn't suffer fools gladly. He thought that his son was a fool.

On the other hand, I happen to know that he thought Sandrine Cadette was perfectly delightful. When Sandrine at ten minutes after nine o'clock on Saturday morning knocked on his door and, with the becoming shyness of a subordinate who knows her place, asked if he would possibly care to accompany her to lunch that day, he said after a moment's surprise that nothing would please him more.

I didn't wear a tux on Saturday mornings. In 1962 I wore a two-piece suit that, without being exactly casual, looked like something an English squire might wear to knock around his estates in early spring.

I am not a criminal lawyer. Never have been. I'm a commercial lawyer, specializing in international transactions. Some people occasionally express surprise that this area of practice fits in well enough with criminal law to make Curry & Furst a sensible arrangement. These people lack imagination.

"This appears to be a rather delicate matter that you've accepted on my behalf, Thomas," I said to Thomas Andrew Curry.

Thomas wasn't wearing a suit. He was wearing a camel-colored mohair sport coat, dark slacks, and a yellow button-down, oxford-cloth dress shirt with a dark brown tie.

"It certainly has its trickier aspects," Thomas admitted, "but after all, if they were easy, anyone could do them."

"I've heard that somewhere before. You're quite sure that one of the faces in this obscene painting you saw was Harrison Tyler's? That is to say, our client's?"

"Entirely. Not that it's a perfect portrait or anything, but the resemblance is unmistakable if you look for it, and it could only have been intentional."

"And so your thinking is what?"

"To see to it that the broadest possible publicity is given to what Cleveland has done. That much accomplished, our client should make *Badger Game* public in such a way as to maximize the provocation to Cleveland. When Cleveland responds by bringing suit, we'll spring the trap."

"How can you be sure Cleveland will sue?"

"He seems to have blustered his intention to do so around so much that it would be very hard for him to back down if Tyler proceeds in as provocative a way as I have in mind."

"Provocative or offensive?" I demanded.

"Take your pick."

"And what precisely is the trap we'll spring if things go as you expect?"

"Even if *Justice Chastising Fame* isn't libelous, it's an appropriation of Tyler's face for commercial purposes—the same thing, really, as if someone used a photograph of you without your permission to sell briefcases or—"

"I understand the concept," I said, a little testily. "Get to the part about the trap."

"Cleveland's only possible defense is that his painting is fair comment on Tyler's artistic philosophy, which is a subject of substantial popular interest and public importance. If he doesn't raise that defense, Tyler's claim against him dwarfs his claim against Tyler. If he does raise that defense, then he can hardly deny that the same defense applies with even more force to defeat his own claim."

"I expect on the contrary that he will deny it vigorously," I remarked. "But your basic point is valid. If things work out the way you expect them to, it's hard to believe that Cleveland wouldn't fold his case before trial. However, I see some areas of concern."

"What are they?"

"First, it might be best if Cleveland's painting were sold, preferably to someone not associated with this firm. A sale seems much more like a commercial use than display in a museum does."

"I did think of that, actually," Thomas said. "My rather ostentatious display last night was intended more to pique the interest of other potential buyers than to procure the thing myself."

"My second concern is that our client should clearly understand that this elegant little maneuver you've worked out entails exposing him to public ridicule. He has to be wholeheartedly behind it or we can't do it, no matter how clever it is."

"I put another call in to him this morning. I'm waiting to hear from him now."

"Third," I said in my best it's-a-good-thing-we've-got-some-gray-hairs-in-this-case manner, "I do hope you realize that you're playing a potentially dangerous game."

"What do you mean, exactly?"

"In the early nineteenth century, if one aristocrat felt he'd been publicly insulted by another, he didn't file a defamation action against him. He challenged him to a duel and did his level best to kill him. If he felt that a newspaper editor or some other nonaristocratic lowlife had insulted him, he likewise didn't resort to the courts. He dragged the miscreant to the edge of town and horsewhipped him. The tort of defamation was basically invented as an alternative to those forms of antisocial behavior."

"You're suggesting that, with the artistic temperaments involved here, if I push things too far, one of the principals might decide to dispense with our untidy system of justice and do something Byronic instead."

"Yes," I said, "that's what I'm suggesting."

"Well"—Thomas shrugged—"I take the point. I'll just have to do my best to see to it that it doesn't happen."

Thomas Andrew Curry didn't have an office at Curry & Furst, since his work there was much less regular than Sandy's was. He was sitting in Sandy's office, waiting for Tyler to call him back, when Sandy asked him about Casey O'Rourke Ferguson.

"Do you mind if I bring her up?" Sandy asked after she had introduced the name. "I had the feeling yesterday that you are a bit more concerned about the grand jury and that whole problem than you are willing to have people believe."

"I certainly don't mind," Thomas said. "You really were very helpful, and you have every right to know. But there's very little to tell. Casey was a rather attractive young woman, quite reserved, and dauntingly single-minded."

"You say she was attractive. How would you describe her?"

"Black Irish. Jet-black hair, fair skin, brown eyes. Medium height, very thin, must have had an incredible metabolism because she enjoyed eating as much as anyone I've ever known except you."

"You sound as if you knew her quite well."

"I was just very observant. Casey and I were in the same law school class, but there were a lot of people in that class and we didn't get to know each other well at all. We never dated. I took a stab at it once but she turned me down cold. In fact, I don't think she entirely approved of me. I believe she felt I wasn't serious enough about Law—that's Law with a capital L, the way she thought of it. We happened to clerk at the same law firm, but there must have been twenty-five clerks there that summer and we never worked together on anything."

"And yet," Sandy prompted.

"Yes. There is one thing. That summer when we were both clerking, she called me out of the blue one weekend."

"What did she say?"

"It was rather odd. She suggested strongly that I keep for my personal files a copy of anything I'd done on the Johnson Industries matter. She told the same thing to all of the Columbia students who were clerking at Caldwell and Ichabod that summer."

"Why would she tell you to do that?"

"The inference I drew was that it was for my own protection—so that I could prove later on what I had worked on and when and at what times I had had certain knowledge."

"That would be important if she thought something was wrong with that project?" Sandy asked.

"Yes. If the thing blew up in one way or another, the law

firm's first reflex would be to start looking around for scapegoats, and summer clerks are prime scapegoat material."

"And of course it did blow up."

"Indeed it did," Thomas said, "as I explained to the grand jury yesterday morning."

"That was a very—how would you say it?—comradely thing for her to do, no? I mean, not just for you but for all her classmates there?"

"Yes it was." Thomas looked reflectively for a moment at the walls of the tiny, windowless office. "She was a bit of a stiff, but she was a class act."

The phone rang. Thomas reached for it but checked himself as Sandy picked the receiver up. It was, after all, her office.

"Mr. Curry?" she said. "Thomas Andrew Curry or Thomas Graham Curry? A moment please."

She handed the phone to Thomas. He mouthed the word "Tyler" with his lips and arched his eyebrows to make it a question. She shook her head.

"Hello, Mr. Curry?" a male voice said.

"Yes."

"My name is Olivier Giraud. I understand that you have an interest in the painting of the very talented Mr. Arthur Cleveland."

Thomas sat up straight in his chair.

"I certainly have."

"Well, I may be able to help you." The voice was accented, German or Northern Italian, Thomas thought. "I have to leave to pick my daughter up at Idlewild, but if you drop by around two-thirty this afternoon we could possibly discuss the matter."

"I'd be happy to."

"Excellent." The man gave Thomas an Upper East Side address.

I walked by the open door of Sandy's office as Thomas hung the phone up.

"The bait's been taken," Thomas called to me.

"No doubt," I muttered. "But by whom?"

*   *   *

The dining room of the Association of the Bar of the City of New York is one of the very few things associated with the practice of law that is all it's cracked up to be. In 1962, its polished cherry wainscotting, linen tablecloths, and heavy plate bespoke perfect confidence in the elite apartness that the men and the handful of women who ate there regularly shared. It was here that T. Graham took Sandy to lunch.

He ordered steak and whiskey. She ordered veal and white wine.

She began by asking him about himself. There are very few people who can resist the charm of this kind of question, and T. Graham wasn't one of them.

"New York really had a death penalty back then and really meant it," he said when he had proceeded well into the topic and was talking about practicing criminal law before World War II. "Not like today, when an execution is a once-in-two-years phenomenon with protesters picketing the prison and candlelight vigils outside the governor's mansion and so forth. Back then it was routine. Nothing special about having a client executed if you were a serious criminal lawyer. It might show up in the paper on page sixteen, one column by three inches: 'Murderer Put to Death.' "

"You make it sound very grim, but it does not seem to have made you morose."

"On the contrary, it made me delighted to be alive," T. Graham assured her, then abruptly switched subjects. "Your father fight with de Gaulle?" he asked.

"No," Sandy said. "My father obeyed the order that de Gaulle disobeyed. He surrendered when the Third Republic surrendered. He resumed his rank after liberation."

"An irony I'd never really thought about. De Gaulle was disobeying orders when he hightailed it to Britain, wasn't he? And now he's a hero."

"A hero is usually a traitor to a cause that history has jilted."

"You follow your father around when he was stationed different places?" he asked after a long silence.

"Yes. Our whole family did, except when he went to Indochina. We were in Germany with him, and at all his posts in France, and then of course in Algeria in the mid-fifties."

"Algeria. Yes. That's where you met Thomas, isn't it?"

"Yes."

"I never learned exactly what he was doing there. Only that it was something reprehensible."

"He was running guns to the nationalists," Sandy said matter-of-factly.

"I beg your pardon."

"That is how we met. My father's men captured him in the *bled*—the Algerian countryside. He was in a helicopter loaded with rifles and ammunition for which he had no plausible explanation. When he was brought in for interrogation—this was in Tiaret, a little fortified village where my father was the resident officer and almost all the other soldiers were Algerian loyalists—anyway, my father said, 'Monsieur Curry, if that is your name, you are a gunrunner, a drug smuggler, and a spy.' "

"And what did my son say?"

Sandy smiled. "Thomas said, 'That's absolutely false. I am not a spy.' "

"Did he indeed? How did he manage to get out with his head still on his shoulders? Some Princeton classmate in the U.S. Embassy, I suppose."

"Not exactly. He got out because my father asked him to save my life and my mother's life and my sister's life. He agreed to do it and he did it."

"Save your lives how?"

"By flying us out before the village was overrun by the nationalists."

T. Graham closed his eyes. A few inches from his steak, the tines of his fork shook slightly as he concentrated. He had a friend or two in the foreign service, and this sounded like a story worth checking.

"You'll have to forgive me," he said when he opened his eyes. "I'm terrible about anyplace outside the United States and Europe. I had an acquaintance who was in a city over there about ten years ago, and I can't think of the name of it. Oran? Constantine? What was the capital of Algeria in 1955?"

Sandy looked at him steadily until their eyes met.

"Paris," she said then.

T. Graham's mouth opened slightly in an expression of surprise that gave way to an eye-lighting half-smile.

"I apologize, Miss Cadette," he said quite slowly. "I have underestimated you. That is something I don't usually do."

"There is no need for—"

"Now, let's get down to it." His voice was suddenly quick and decisive. "I have the feeling that the purpose of this luncheon wasn't for you to hear my memoirs or even for me to hear romantic stories about my scapegrace offspring. I have the feeling that you want something from me, Miss Cadette, and I think we should get down to finding out what it is."

"You are correct. There is something I want from you." She told him about the grand jury subpoena, Caldwell and Ichabod, and Katherine Colleen Ferguson, a/k/a Casey O'Rourke.

"So he's gotten himself in a bit of a fix. What can I do about it?"

"You probably know better than I. He wants to investigate this matter himself. But I don't think he really knows what to do next, and neither do I."

"Hmpf." T. Graham used his last piece of steak to mop juice from the platter and threw back the last quarter-inch of whiskey. "Excuse me for a moment," he said then. He wiped the corners of his mouth with his napkin and left the table.

He was gone for nearly half an hour. When he came back he apologized for the delay.

"It wouldn't have taken so long fifteen years ago," he explained. "If you called three lawyers at twelve forty-five on Saturday afternoon back then, you'd find two of them at their desks and the third one at his club."

"O tempora, o mores," Sandy said consolingly.

"Indeed. Anyway, it occurred to me that Thomas probably isn't the only alumnus of Caldwell and Ichabod to be invited before the grand jury looking into this business. It also occurred to me that that firm has no doubt been busily lining up experienced members of the criminal bar to provide independent counsel to those of its people and former people who, unlike Thomas, had enough sense to ask for it."

"It was rather short notice," Sandy offered.

"It could have been two months' notice and it wouldn't have made any difference. Fortunately, I know most of the experienced members of the criminal bar and by creating the impression that I was also representing someone in connection with this matter I tracked down one of them who's involved and who agrees that we should share information. In the nature of things, he has thus far shared more with me than I have with him."

Sandy smiled, lowered her eyes, and pretended to blush. T. Graham was a quick study and he wasn't fooled.

"The lawyer I talked to won't have anyone available to review our file on this matter until next week. A piece of good luck, inasmuch as we don't yet have a file on the matter for them to review. Fortunately, subordinates at Curry and Furst—"

"Meaning me?"

"—meaning you, are more dedicated, and have made themselves available to review my colleague's file this afternoon. I hope I'm not presuming too far on your interest in this matter?"

"Indeed not."

"Good. I thought not." He handed her one of his own cards, with a name and office address scribbled on the back. "If you can manage to get to this office within the next hour or so, you should get a head start on most of what there is to be known about this grand jury business to date."

"Thank you very much."

"You're welcome. I suggest that you review the material in light of two pieces of information that I picked up between my chat with a chap I know at Caldwell and Ichabod and my little talk with the criminal lawyer."

"What are they?"

"First, one of the witnesses that our zealous civil servants have been trying to subpoena is a woman named Gloria Monday. They can't seem to locate her."

"Is that very odd?" Sandy asked.

"Yes. If the United States Marshals Service in this district can't find someone, it means at a bare minimum that that person very much doesn't want to be found. That takes on a certain significance in this connection, wouldn't you agree?"

"I am afraid I would."

"The second thing I learned is that on the morning after Mrs. Ferguson made her final contribution to American jurisprudence on the pavement at Broadway and Seventh, the authorities found on the desk in her office a yellow legal pad. On the top page she had written two things: 'Badger Game' and 'T. A. Curry.' "

And so Sandy postponed her fencing lesson and spent the prime of that sunny Saturday afternoon in a lawyer's office, examining a thin but engrossing file. She did this, as she did everything, systematically and methodically. When she was through, she had notes on two canary yellow index cards. On the first she listed the items the police had found in the room from which Mrs. Ferguson had plunged. She put quick, three-stroke asterisks next to the things found in her purse.

On the second card she noted that, on the day before she died, Katherine Colleen Ferguson had called her office in New York from a pay phone in the Milwaukee County Courthouse in Milwaukee, Wisconsin. She had asked her office's switchboard to patch her through to one other local number, which Sandy dutifully noted—and which she recognized as the number of the phone in Thomas Andrew Curry's apartment.

Chapter 10

To sell a pearl that you have to someone who wants one
—that's not doing business; but to sell a pearl you don't
have to someone who doesn't want one—that's what's called
"doing business."

—Oppenheim the Goldsmith

"**Y**ou've done your usual thorough job. Very good."

"Thank you."

The man speaking first was short and slender. The smooth
sheen of his fair cheeks and neck suggested a straight-edge razor,
frequently and painstakingly applied. His thinning blond hair
was so fine that the individual strands seemed almost transparent. I know this because I saw him later on. I didn't overhear
this particular conversation, and neither did any other witness
I had access to, so I've had to reconstruct it. As any lawyer can
tell you, though, circumstantial evidence is more reliable than
eyewitness testimony anyway, and I'm pretty sure I've got it
substantially right.

As the first man spoke, he examined an eight-by-ten picture,
grainy because of the telephoto lens used to take it, showing
Sandy and Thomas approaching the entrance to the building
where Curry & Furst had its offices.

The man who thanked the first speaker looked tall standing
next to him. He was spare and taut, his chestnut hair short and
wiry, his muscles supple but tense.

"He fought in Korea?" the first man asked.

"Yes."

"Did he get a security clearance?"

"Good God no. He wasn't even an officer."

"Not ROTC, then?"

"Nothing like that," the second man said. "He dropped out of Princeton at the beginning of his senior year, enlisted in the ranks, declined an invitation to attend officer candidate school. He was trained as a helicopter pilot."

"Honorable discharge? Yes, I see you've got that here." The first man looked at a typewritten page that he had put on top of the picture.

"Right," the second man said.

"Eventually got his law degree but seems to have lost interest in using it shortly after coming into four million dollars. Can't say I blame him for that. What about the girl?"

"Just as you see there. She came to New York as a probationary intern with the French mission to the United Nations in September, 1959. She resigned January 20, 1960, and eventually got a job as some kind of functionary with an international lawyer here."

"Resigned or was fired?"

"Resigned," the second man said.

"She escaped from Algeria in 1955, where her father was killed defending the French colonial presence against the nationalists. We move to 1960. She resigns from a French government position on January twentieth—just about the time, if I'm not mistaken, that the barricades went up in Algiers and the French Algerian colonists essentially tried to overthrow the government to keep it from caving in to the nationalists. That is suggestive, isn't it?"

"The Algiers putsch started on January twenty-fourth. She resigned four days before the French government knew anything about the planned uprising."

"You're assuming the government was as surprised as it pretended to be. Have you considered the possibility that it had some inkling of what was about to happen and began getting rid of unreliable elements in anticipation of the event?"

"Bosh." The second man snorted. "I was in Paris when the barricades went up in Algiers. I can tell you that the government wasn't *pretending* to be surprised."

"Mmm," the first man said.

The door to the room opened. A girl about fourteen, light brown hair swinging insouciantly behind her, burst in. Both men looked up at the interruption. The first man beamed when he saw the girl.

"Dad," she said, "someone's here to see you."

"Thank you, pet." The first man walked past the girl into the front hallway of the aging brownstone. "Mr. Curry," he called jovially to the figure standing just inside the door at the other end of the hall. "Thank you so much for coming. I am Olivier Giraud."

He strode forward, shook Thomas's hand briskly, and led him back to the room where he had been talking.

"This is my daughter, Alison. Alison, this is Mr. Curry, an admirer of the work of Mr. Cleveland."

"I'm pleased to meet you," Alison said, suddenly trying to be a bit more than fourteen.

Thomas shook the adolescent's damp hand and returned her greeting.

"And this," Giraud said, sweeping his left arm outward to indicate the other man in the room, "is François Rocard, an international civil servant. He is with the U.N. Secretariat, selflessly devoting his talents to the cause of understanding among peoples and so forth. In the interests of world peace and one percent of the gross selling price he will facilitate cultural exchanges, principally in the form of exchanging art for money."

"It is a great honor and a distinct privilege to meet you," Rocard said, nodding in Thomas's direction.

"And meeting you is the highlight of my life to this moment," Thomas replied gravely, "excepting only my encounter a moment ago with Miss Alison Giraud."

"I'm disappointed that your companion of last night was unable to accompany you," Giraud said. "She made almost as great an impression on Mr. Cleveland as you did."

"Perhaps next time. She has a fencing lesson on Saturday afternoons and she never misses it."

"Well then, let's get down to business, shall we?" Giraud clapped his hands and glanced around the room. "Alison, you're perfectly free to stay if you wish, but you may find it rather dull when we start negotiating. . . ."

"I'm on my way out." Alison sighed.

"Before you leave, though," Giraud said cheerfully, "I'd appreciate it if you'd return the cigarette you took from the box on the table when I went out to greet Mr. Curry. When you're sixteen it's something I suppose I'll have to put up with, but smoking at fourteen is an obnoxiously continental affectation that I refuse to tolerate during the four months annually that I have the exquisite pleasure of your company."

Alison offered her father a luminous, good-sport kind of smile, almost as if she would have been disappointed had she not been caught, and returned a Gaullois to the cigarette box.

"Mother says it's obnoxiously American," she said.

"That's just what your mother would say. Not a patriotic bone in her body." He gave "patriotic" a British pronunciation, with the "a" short and flat.

"Now, then, Mr. Curry," he said, "I think you're right to start off by deciding what pleases you and concentrating on that. If what you buy appreciates dramatically over the next few years, so much the better. Since there's no guarantee of that, regardless of what type of painting you buy, you might as well gamble on something you like for its own sake."

"And even if that's kittens playing with balls of yarn or sunsets over the ocean, I'll be able to find someone willing to supply it to me at a respectable price."

"Someone, perhaps," Giraud said. "Not necessarily me."

"Because you insist on dealing with something a bit more serious, a few rungs farther up on the scale of cultural values."

"I think so, naturally. My clients think so, and they pay me for being right. But judge for yourself."

Giraud led Thomas over to the far corner of the room. Perhaps half a dozen paintings, mounted on mats but not framed, and separated by three-by-four-foot cardboard dividers, stood in an offset row along the front wall. Giraud lifted one of them and held it up at a slight angle, so that sunlight streaming in through an eastern exposure hit the canvas obliquely.

The painting showed an old woman, dressed shabbily, walking in front of a billboard. On the billboard, a six-pack of beer floated above a co-ed crew of college students playing volleyball on a sun-washed beach with a sparkling ocean in the background. You could tell that the real day—the day outside the billboard, the day the old woman was walking through—was overcast and bitterly cold. You could tell this even though there were no oversized snowflakes in the picture, no papers being blown by the wind, no clues except the interplay of real and artificial light and something about the way the woman was walking.

"I think that this is extraordinarily powerful," Giraud said. "It has layer after layer of comprehension. One looks at it and thinks he's picked it up in a glance, and then one looks at it again with different eyes and sees something totally new. This is the kind of work I like to deal with."

Thomas examined the canvas. He stepped back and changed his angle, as if to examine it again with different eyes. He concluded that his eyes were the same on both looks. For an instant, he felt instinctively that this must indicate some deficiency in his own aesthetic appreciation.

"You're good at this, do you know that?" he asked Giraud.

Giraud smiled complacently. "The difference between rape and rapture, I once heard an American in the life insurance field say, is salesmanship."

"I suppose a spoilsport might wonder," Thomas said then, "why Mr. Cleveland doesn't market his work through more conventional channels if it's that good."

"I can give you the answer in one word," Giraud said. "Accessibility. An Arthur Cleveland painting has impact on anyone who looks at it. You don't need to learn a code. You don't need to take a course three evenings a week for four months at

MOMA. You don't need a cultural mediator to tell you why it's good or bad. You just look at it, and it hits you."

"I see your point," Thomas said. "If the critics let people believe that this kind of work was good, then before long we wouldn't need critics anymore."

"Precisely. The galleries and museums depend upon a relative handful of quite wealthy people, most of whom have all their taste in their mouths. Properly distrustful of their own cultural impulses, those people rely uncritically on whatever the accepted wisdom of the moment is. And those who decide what the accepted wisdom should be are threatened by great painting that has a coherent representational foundation."

Giraud laid the canvas on a table underneath the window and pulled another painting up: high school prom, sky blue tuxedoes and wilted carnations. He produced a magnifying glass and held it over a pubescent face.

"The technique is extraordinary and the integrity of the artistic vision is never compromised. Look. One must examine it very closely even to see the brushstrokes."

"Quite impressive. I appreciate your showing me these. But the one I'm really interested in knowing the price of is that piece he had on display at the Ackley last night."

"I don't know that that one's for sale," Giraud said. "If it were, I don't see how the price could start much below fifty thousand dollars."

"So much for the frame. Now how much for the canvas itself?"

"I beg your pardon?"

"Old law school joke. Sorry about that. Tell me something before I start writing checks with lots of zeroes in them. How did you get into this intriguing little line of endeavor? How does one get started in this business of selling paintings outside the normal channels to people who are both rich enough to buy them and confident enough not to be shackled by the accepted wisdom?"

"I don't know that it's possible to generalize from my own

case," Giraud said. "I'm an entrepreneur. I don't pretend to be anything else. I happen to be a brilliant entrepreneur with superb aesthetic judgment and delicately refined artistic sensibilities, but I'm still an entrepreneur."

"You found the entrepreneurial grass greener over here than in northern Italy?"

"Switzerland, actually," Giraud said. "I suppose I should be flattered. Most people guess that I'm German."

"And one day you just popped in from Geneva and started entrepreneuring."

"Approximately. I came over here with a little capital and a desire to get into publishing. I succeeded. I got into the publishing of naughty books and magazines. Fascinating business. Except for the occasional encounter with the vice squad, a placid and regular return on capital. I just moved on from there."

"Yes. I can see where representational art would be a natural progression."

"You're having fun with me," Giraud said. "I guarantee you I'll laugh if you buy one of Mr. Cleveland's paintings."

"You said fifty thousand for *Justice Chastising Fame*?"

"I said at least that, if the work is for sale, which it very well might not be."

"It would be foolish of me to make an offer until you knew, wouldn't it?"

"Perhaps," Giraud acknowledged. "But it might be futile of you in any event."

"How so?" Thomas asked.

"You said you wanted to know a bit about me before we did business," Giraud said. "I can understand that. You have a right to know whether the middleman you're dealing with has been selling forgeries or fencing stolen paintings. Now I'd like to know a little about you."

"I pay my bills on time and there's a special account officer at Manufacturer's Hanover who'll say anything about me that I tell him to. Anything else you need to know?"

"You were disbarred, approximately two years ago?"

"No, I was not disbarred."

Giraud glanced over at Rocard.

"Oh?"

"No. I voluntarily surrendered my license to practice law."

"Ah. One of those Anglo-Saxon nuances that baffles those of us from civil law countries. Do you mind if I ask why you voluntarily surrendered your license to practice law?"

"No, not at all."

"Why?"

"I'd prefer not to discuss it."

Giraud looked at Thomas for perhaps half a second, smiling slightly. Then with surprising quickness he leaped forward and clapped Thomas enthusiastically on the arm.

"By God!" Giraud said. "I like this fellow, Rocard."

"I'm overwhelmed."

"And if I ask what in blazes you were doing in Algeria in 1955, do I get the same treatment?"

"It's sort of a long story," Thomas said, after a moment's hesitation. "My father once told me that the army might teach me a useful trade. As it turned out, the army taught me two useful trades: flying helicopters and killing people. When I got out, I thought I'd better go someplace where those were salable skills. I ended up in Algeria."

"Yes," Giraud said. "I understand perfectly. Well. I have your number. I will see if I can sell *Justice Chastising Fame* to you for fifty thousand dollars, and I'll give you a call."

"Why don't you see if you can sell it to me for fifteen?" Thomas asked, and smiled a chilly, strictly-for-the-record smile.

Giraud chuckled dryly.

"You'll be hearing from me, Mr. Curry," he said.

Giraud showed Thomas to the door of the comfortable home. When he came back, Rocard had already replaced the high school prom painting and was briefly examining the billboard painting before replacing it as well.

Giraud closed the door behind him.

"I'm not worried about him," he told Rocard. "He's smarter

than he pretends to be and tougher than he looks at first glance, but I have the feeling that there's not that much below the surface."

"You may be right."

"The girl's another story. The girl bothers me. What do we really know about her?"

"After escaping from Algeria—" Rocard shrugged—"she completed her secondary education and received a *bac* with distinction in geography. She applied to l'Ecole Nationale d'Administration and was rejected."

"Why was she rejected?"

"Hard to be certain. The school is extremely selective. The admissions committee mentions that her English is weak—'journalistic and nonrigorous.' "

"All right. She was frustrated in her quest for the ENA and took a job as an intern with the French UN mission?"

"Yes."

"Lowered her sights in a hurry, didn't she?" Giraud asked.

"I don't think so. A certain number of ENA slots are open each year to serving members of the French civil service. I think she had one of those in mind."

"But instead of pursuing that opportunity, she resigned on January 20, 1960."

"Correct."

"We approach the critical question," Giraud said. "Was she—is she—part of the Organisation Armée Secrète?"

"No. The OAS approached her in early January of 1960, but she turned them down cold."

"And then she resigned—and four days later they tried the putsch in Algeria. The daughter of a French officer refuses to have any part of a plot in favor of the position her father gave his life for, yet she also refuses to continue serving a government that's about to abandon that position."

"It's hard to understand," Rocard commented.

"It's depressingly simple to understand. She couldn't join the OAS without betraying her country. She couldn't expose the OAS without betraying men who had fought with her father.

And she couldn't keep silent and continue as an employee of the French government without violating the oath she took when she entered government service. So she did the only 'honorable' thing: She resigned."

"You're telling me that a girl in her early twenties, next to penniless and three thousand miles from home, abandoned the ambition of her life and left the only job she had for the sake of honor?"

"Exactly," Giraud said. "Appalling, isn't it?"

"You're worried about her, then?"

"Yes."

"So. What are you going to do?"

"I don't know." Giraud sighed. "I suppose I'll wait to see what happens Monday. The whole problem is supposed to go away on Monday."

Chapter 11

For likewise as it were utterly vain to lay natural reasons of comfort to him that hath no wit, so were it undoubtedly frustrate to lay spiritual causes of comfort to him that hath no faith.

—Thomas More

"**S**o you think that Cleveland has played into our hands?"

"Yes, assuming that you're willing to put up with the inconveniences necessary to exploit the opportunity."

"A delicate way of saying that anyone who didn't know that he was ridiculing me before will know it afterward."

"Right," Thomas acknowledged. "The more thoroughly they know it, the better off we are."

Harrison Tyler hefted an old-fashioned glass to eye level. He wrapped his index and second fingers around the lower part of the tumbler and marked carefully with his eyes the place on the glass where the top of his index finger came. He set the glass back down. He poured Old Grand-dad bourbon whiskey into the glass until the level of the whiskey reached the point he had noted. Then he splashed Coca-Cola into the drink until the level in the tumbler was just about one finger-width short of the top. He stirred the mixture with a wooden brush handle.

"One for you?" he asked Thomas.

"I could go for some scotch, actually," Thomas said.

"Not possible, counselor. Sorry."

"Well, bourbon would be splendid then." The customer was always right. "Straight."

Tyler smiled as he searched with the hand he still had for

another tumbler and measured a generous portion of undiluted bourbon into it.

"I guess not everybody likes it southern style," he said, handing the drink to Thomas.

"You're not from the South, are you?"

"South Lynn, Massachusetts." Tyler laughed briefly. "You think you can find someone to buy that creation of Cleveland's?"

"I'm rather sure of it. The only real doubt I have is whether he'll be willing to sell the thing at all."

"He'll sell," Tyler said. "Tell me something. How did you get in touch with Giraud? Did you find him or did he call you?"

"He called me, actually."

"That's what I thought."

Tyler took a long swallow from his tumbler. Two-thirds of the drink was gone.

"Did Giraud tell you about his adventures in the world of dirty books?" Tyler asked.

"He did mention that he started out in pornography when he first came to this country, actually."

"He stayed in it. After all, he's representing Cleveland."

"Now now."

Tyler put the drink down and turned the mounted .45 so that he could read the plate on the base of the stand.

"I've been trying to place the date," Thomas said, nodding toward the weapon-trophy. He sipped sparingly from his own drink. "I can't remember—"

"You won't find it in any of the history books," Tyler said. "I think the technical term is 'small unit action.' One company of ours against one company of theirs. It was at Hill zero-seven-three. We had no artillery, no armor, no air support. So we just fixed bayonets and charged and when it was all over we were at the top and the other guys weren't."

"That's where you lost your left hand?"

Tyler looked at the prosthesis. He killed his drink and began mixing another, bringing a little less precision to the process this time.

"That's where it happened. One of those neat little ironies that help you connect up with the genetic memory and the collective unconscious and all that crap. Seven years after Truman ended the war against Japan with the most technologically advanced device ever employed in combat, my company took Hill zero-seven-three with a sharp piece of metal on the end of a stick."

"An experience Arthur Cleveland probably hasn't had."

"That's a good one." Tyler offered another laugh, this one harsh and grating. "That little shit's idea of existential angst is his shrink not answering by the third ring."

"And he speaks so well of you."

"Fair enough."

Tyler accompanied this comment by heaving out of his chair and lumbering over to the footlocker. He knelt in front of it, set his drink on its lid, and began fishing in his pants pocket for a key.

"I wanna show you something," he said.

"Okay."

"Am I the first artist you've ever represented?"

"That depends on how broadly you define the term. My father had a client awhile back who was quite good on engravings of presidents, but the Department of the Treasury felt that his work was excessively derivative."

"Counterfeiter?"

"That was Treasury's theory. My father maintained that his client simply had a particular weakness for President Jackson and liked working in green ink."

Tyler had come up with a key and he put it in the padlock that tightly pinned the footlocker's hasp closed. He paused and glanced over his shoulder at Thomas.

"Do you ever take anything seriously?" he asked, grinning.

"Not counterfeiting, certainly."

"You're absolutely right." Tyler pulled the key out of the lock and stood up. "I'll show you what's in here later. After we talk a little bit more."

Tyler walked over to the back corner of his study and pulled a ceiling panel down. The bottom of a ladder-stairway peeked through the opening. Tyler yanked that to the floor.

"You bring the bourbon and the Coke," he said over his shoulder. "I've got all I can handle, so to speak."

Tyler began climbing up the pull-down ladder and disappeared through the ceiling opening. Thomas obediently gathered up the bottle of bourbon, the Coca-Cola, and his own glass and followed.

The ladder led to a small enclosure on the roof of the building. As Thomas finished his climb, Tyler opened a door onto the roof itself. A dazzling rectangle of late afternoon light breaking the enclosure's darkness marked the doorway.

Thomas stepped onto the roof tar, still tacky from the day's sun. He saw Tyler squatting, his back braced against a wall of the enclosure, gazing uptown.

"It's an incredible place, isn't it? New York, I mean."

" 'Incredible' is exactly the word I would have chosen." Thomas squatted beside Tyler and set the bourbon bottle where Tyler could reach it.

"I mean it's so goddamn American. You know? We're not good at surgical strikes, we're not good at refined miniatures. But give us something big to do—dig a canal between two oceans, throw a railroad across a continent, dump eight million people who can barely stand each other into one place and make it the most exciting city in the world—boy, can we handle something like that."

"It's important to know your limitations."

"You know," Tyler said, "I had two spiritual crises last year. Is it correct to call something spiritual if it had nothing to do with religion?"

"Oh, I think so," Thomas said judiciously.

"Maybe not. Maybe we should just call them crises of morale."

"Well, I suppose we could do that too." Thomas took another swallow of his drink. It was a bigger swallow than last time, and he was surprised when he noticed that the bourbon in his glass was half gone.

"Anyway," Tyler said, "the first one was Thomistic. You know Thomas Aquinas?"

"Only by reputation."

"I didn't think you played squash with him every Thursday. How else would you know him except by reputation?"

"I meant I haven't actually read him. Just got a sort of thumbnail sketch, overview kind of thing, you know. I remember distinctly that he was in there between Aristotle and Kant."

"Tell me something," Tyler said. "Exactly what did you study at whatever overrated Ivy League institution you undoubtedly attended? A cursory survey of art and culture, once over lightly on Western philosophy—was there anything you actually learned there?"

"How to make a mint julep, how to throw a decent left jab, how a bill becomes a law, never to lie unless it was in my interest to do so, and the six basic principles of British diplomacy. I think it's six. Let's see: Maintain the balance of power in Europe; never let a major power control the English Channel; maintain the neutrality of Belgium; preserve naval supremacy. That's only four, isn't it? Well, I'm quite certain there are two others I could think of if I were drinking scotch instead of bourbon."

"Thomas Aquinas wrote the work that defined Roman Catholic orthodoxy for about seven hundred years, right down to last week," Tyler said. He was mixing his third drink. His voice became more earnest as the bourbon took effect. "One fine day he said something like, 'All I've written is dross,' and went to bed, and the next important thing he did was die."

"I suppose you could call that a spiritual crisis or a crisis of morale either one," Thomas said.

"I don't think he meant that anything he'd written was wrong," Tyler continued. "I think he meant that it wasn't important, that he'd gotten some glimpse into a larger scheme of things that made all this poring over essences and accidents seem incredibly trivial."

"And your first crisis was like that?"

"Yeah. But I got over it. I mean, I went through a spell there where I thought, art, painting, who cares? What difference does it all make? Abstractionism, minimalism, realism, cubism, surrealism, impressionism—is anyone really going to give a flying fart in two hundred years about these labels that people are vilifying each other over now? I mean, in two hundred years, do you realize that what people will study as the culture of our age is Bob Barker and Rod Serling and Sid Caesar, and all of us fine-arts types will be a bunch of footnotes that they make high school students memorize during detention to punish them for talking in class?"

"A sobering thought," said Thomas, thinking that one might well be in order.

"I mean, no offense, counselor, but you're the future. Not me."

"A very sobering thought."

"So I thought, sure, I can do the same thing for the next seven years that I've been doing for the last seven years, and maybe it'll sell and maybe it won't, and maybe the critics'll like it and maybe they won't, but when all is said and done I could probably have more influence on human history by being the principal of a junior high school in Indiana."

"Let's not get carried away," Thomas said soothingly.

"But then, you know what happened?"

"No," Thomas said.

Tyler put his drink down. He rested his forearms on his knees and turned his head to look directly at Thomas. His eyes were shining and intense.

"I got an idea. I got an idea for a painting. And do you know what it made me feel like?"

"Better, I hope."

"It made me feel exactly like I felt when we charged up Hill zero-seven-three. Scared. Excited. Pumped up. Alive. Part of something bigger than myself, something that'd been going on before I was born and would keep going on after I was dead."

"My word."

"I mean, I didn't charge up that hill for Harry Truman. I didn't charge up that hill for the United States of America. I didn't charge up that hill to stop world communism or save democracy. I didn't charge up that hill because I thought anyone anywhere in the world would be one scintilla better off if we were at the top instead of the Reds. I charged up that hill because I was one of two hundred and seventy-three men and we were all going to do it and we were each going to do it because all the rest were going to do it, and when it was over those of us who were still alive would have had a shared experience that no one who hasn't had it can imagine and that no one could ever take away from us."

Thomas looked at Tyler. Giraud might have said that Thomas was looking at him with different eyes.

"You're stone cold sober, aren't you?" he said.

"I certainly am, counselor. And I swear to you, that's what I felt when I got the idea for that painting."

"*Badger Game.*"

"Right. And that was the end of my first spiritual crisis."

"Dare I ask what your second was?"

"It was much more mundane," Tyler said. He smiled and turned his head to look back over the rooftops. "The question was, could I live on four thousand dollars a year?"

"An elemental if somewhat puzzling question."

"See, I had eighty thousand dollars. I'd managed to put that much away. Grasping agents, crooked galleries, stupid critics, stupider buyers, and all the rest, even with all of that, I'd managed to save eighty thousand dollars."

"No small achievement."

"Now, eighty thousand dollars prudently invested will produce an after-tax annual income of around four thousand dollars. So you see, if I could live on four thousand a year, I was free. I could do whatever I wanted to. I could paint whatever I wanted to. I was independent. I was—"

"I grasp the notion," Thomas said.

"But I couldn't do it." Tyler shook his head weakly and went back to his drink. "It was pathetic. I tried. I really tried. I labored over budgets like a newlywed housewife. I scrimped and ate yogurt for lunch and drank cheap whiskey. And I just couldn't do it. I kept cheating, dipping into other income. It only took three months for me to realize that I just couldn't do it. I was trapped."

"But I suppose most people are trapped in that way, if you want to call it trapped," Thomas pointed out. "Very few of us can shrug off material conveniences that we've gotten used to."

"You aren't."

"Well, it's not quite the same thing, is it?"

"No. I mean, you aren't hurting but I've got a feeling you weren't trapped like that even before you came into money."

"I guess that's a matter of opinion."

"You knew exactly what I was talking about when I went into that Hill zero-seven-three routine, didn't you?"

"I think so, yes," Thomas said. "I was in Korea too. And then—but that's another story. I know what you mean about Korea and combat."

"And then—what? Where were you after Korea?"

"Algeria. But as I said, that's another story."

"I'd like to hear it."

"No war stories before I'm forty-five," Thomas insisted.

"I like war stories. I told you mine. I told you mine over drinks. You tell me yours. Tell me how you met that fabulous young lady you had with you the first time you came by, and tell me what happened that makes you get that look in your eyes when you talk about her or hear someone else refer to her."

"There's not much to tell. I was in a helicopter. She was in the same one. There were some people who didn't want the helicopter to make it out safely. It did. End of story."

"You're not playing fair with me, counselor. I've got some important decisions to make and you're a critical part of my calculations. Now, I opened up to you and you sat there and let me do it. So I really think you owe it to me to do the same."

"Very well." Thomas sighed and looked away. "Sandrine Cadette's father was a major in the French Army. The men in her family have been French soldiers of one kind or another going back to the Hundred Years War when some landless Viking made his way into Normandy and signed on to hack and slash for the highest bidder."

"Being a soldier, in 1955 he led a contingent assigned to Algeria," Tyler prompted.

"Not exactly. He was the resident in a fairly remote village. During the grimmest part of a very unpleasant night, Major Cadette's men came upon me a few miles from the village. I was in a helicopter, and in the helicopter was a little hot cargo."

"Very inconvenient."

"That's easy for you to say. At any rate, they took me back to the village in irons to be sent on to wherever they send people to chop their heads off without too much noise."

"Something that for some reason didn't take place."

"No. It seems that the nationalists who missed my rendezvous were getting together for an attack on the village. Major Cadette told me that if I would fly his wife and his two daughters to the nearest secure French position, a colleague of his would see to it that I was given clean papers and a plane ticket home. If I didn't and lived to tell about it, this same colleague would see to it that I got a bullet in the back of the head. It was not a difficult choice."

"Obviously."

"By the time I got the copter off the ground, the first perimeter had fallen. Debris from an explosion hit the copter and one splinter punctured the fuel line. I knew we'd never make it to the next French position unless we got the puncture fixed. Unfortunately, the nationalists knew that the helicopter must be carrying someone important and sent two jeeps after us."

"Sounds dicey."

"I got as much of a lead as I could and set the copter down long enough to make an improvised and highly inefficient patch. When I tried to take off, the engine didn't catch the first time. Sandy looked back to see how close the nationalists were. Then she took out this revolver her father had given her. She asked me if my sidearm was loaded. I said it was but opined that a forty-five wasn't going to make much difference against a dozen carbines and a machine gun."

"Did that put her in her place?"

"She just nodded. The engine caught. I got the copter off the ground again. Within four minutes, we were losing fuel again. Then Sandy looked off to our right and six miles or so away she saw the thing that saved us."

"What?"

"A plateau. Sheer sides, maybe a thousand square yards of flat surface. There was no way anyone on the ground was going to get to the top anytime soon. I swung the copter over to the plateau and put it down. The nationalists might as well have been eighty miles away. I repaired the fuel line while Sandy crouched near the edge of the plateau and kept an eye out for the nationalists."

"She was what, then, about seventeen? I can see why you thought she was a remarkable girl."

"You don't know the half of it. I didn't know anything about her family background then, about this history going back to mercenaries in the Hundred Years War. She told me all that later. Anyway, when I was through with the fuel line I walked over near the edge, where she was crouching, looking into the distance. I took out a pack of Camels and lit one. I wasn't quite sure what to do. So I held the cigarette out to her. She smiled at me in a tough kid kind of way, took a puff on the Camel, smiled again, and handed it back. Then do you know what she did?"

"I can't imagine."

"She broke the cylinder out of the revolver and dropped the cartridges out of it. There were three. Exactly three."

"I think I see."

"Yes," Thomas said. "You see, that was what she was talking about when she asked me if my own sidearm was loaded. When I said it was, that meant I could take care of myself. I could make my own decisions. She didn't need to worry about me. So she only put three cartridges in her revolver: one for her mother, one for her sister, and one for herself."

"All right, counselor," Tyler said with an air of finality, "you've done your part. It means a lot to me that you shared this with me. I want you to know that. But now I've got some things to do. Tonight, I'm going to get good and drunk. Tomorrow, I'm going to dry out. Monday, I'd like you and the charming Mademoiselle Cadette to come by about three in the afternoon and I'll give you my decision on this little maneuver you'd like to continue doing on Mr. Cleveland."

Thomas glanced at his watch. It was almost five o'clock.

"We'll see you in forty-six hours," he said. He figured he'd see whatever Tyler had in the footlocker then.

Monday

Chapter 12

Unintended consequences are inevitable. . . .

—*1984 Report of the President's Council
of Economic Advisers*

"**I** thought you would be apprehensive about this meeting," Sandy said. "But you seem to be almost looking forward to it."

"I most certainly am," Thomas acknowledged. "I don't like being the only one in the room who isn't in on the joke. Mr. Tyler either has a plausible explanation for the *Badger Game* coincidence or he hasn't. If he has, we'll learn something we don't know now. If he hasn't, we'll invite him to find himself another lawyer."

"Mr. Furst could not have said it any better."

"I suppose that's progress of a sort."

They walked into the coffeehouse and were surprised to find a substantial throng of people there. The "1812 Overture" boomed from the second floor, competing successfully with the incessant tattoo of a bongo in the coffeehouse itself.

"Is it just my imagination," Thomas asked Sandy, "or is part of the crowd here a bit tonier than one would ordinarily associate with this establishment?"

"You would be even more conspicuous in your dinner jacket here than you were at the Ackley," Sandy said, "but I believe there are more ties and collars per capita in this room than I would have predicted."

Thomas glanced at his watch.

"We have about five minutes before we're supposed to meet

with Tyler. Maybe we can find out whether this is happenstance or another coincidence."

He walked over to the nearest table. The young man sitting at the table wore blue jeans, a gray turtleneck sweater, and a maroon beret. The beard on the end of his chin stopped well short of his cheeks. He was nursing a cup of espresso and reading a volume of Emily Dickinson. He was, in short, a television caricature of a beatnik, which wasn't surprising—there were a lot of people in the Village in 1962 who had learned how to be beatniks by watching television.

"Excuse me," Thomas said. "Do you know what the occasion for this large and unwontedly elegant gathering is?"

"Like, man, are you talking to me, man?"

"As nearly as I can tell, yes."

"And like, what is it you'd like to know?"

"Why are all these people here? Are you scheduled to do a reading, or is there an even more important reason?"

"Surreal."

"No doubt."

"I mean, like, man, you have got to be kidding me, you know what I mean, man?"

"In a manner of speaking. What—"

"You mean you, like, really don't know, man?"

"I kid you not."

"It's like the unveiling, man."

"A striptease? This place has more imagination than I thought."

"Man, like, you are nowhere, you know that, man?"

"Strictly speaking, of course, I am in very nearly the same place you are. But perhaps we could dispense with the code and do the rest of this conversation in standard English. What's the unveiling?"

A familiar voice from behind Thomas answered this question.

"The first public display of Harrison Tyler's newest, you should excuse the expression, painting," Arthur Cleveland said. "Today's the day. This is the place. Less than half an hour from now. I wouldn't have butted in, but I thought if I heard any more of this borscht-belt excuse for hipster jive I'd vomit."

"Mr. Cleveland," Thomas said. "A pleasure to see you again. I had a conversation about you recently with a Mr. Giraud. He speaks very highly of you."

"Perhaps you'll have another one someday," Cleveland said, and shuffled away, his loafers softly scuffing the floor. Thomas turned back to the beatnik.

"Does Mr. Tyler always play music at an eardrum-splitting decibel level before he shows one of his paintings?"

"Like, who knows, man, y'know? This noise has been goin' on for, like, close to an hour. It started with that loud German thing and it hasn't stopped."

"Loud German thing," Thomas mused, thinking inevitably of Wagner. He searched his memory and hummed a few bars from "The Ride of the Valkyries."

The beatnik shook his head.

"No, man, that's not it. You must be Dutch."

"Not even close," Thomas said.

"It goes like this." He closed his eyes, pursed his lips, and whistled a measure and a half.

"Ah," Sandy said. "The 'Ode to Joy' from Beethoven's Ninth Symphony."

"Crazy," the beatnik said. "You don't even look German."

"Thank you so much for your invaluable assistance," Thomas interjected hurriedly, suspecting that Sandy might not react constructively to this observation. "Give my best to Maynard G. Krebs."

He and Sandy threaded their way through the crowd to the stairway and climbed toward the small landing outside Tyler's door. Church bells and cannon blared through the door, and Thomas surmised that things must be looking bleak for Napoleon. Thomas stepped onto the landing and abruptly stopped.

"Mr. Giraud. How unexpected. Comparison shopping?"

Olivier Giraud turned away from Harrison Tyler's door and gave Thomas and Sandy a sharply surprised glance.

"I had an appointment, actually," Giraud said. "But I seem to have been stood up."

"Curious," Thomas said. He walked over to the door. "You mean there's no one home, despite the music?"

"I mean there's no one answering the door."

Thomas rapped loudly on the door. Nothing but a dull resonance and a crescendo of Russian artillery responded. He tried again, with the same result.

"Harrison?" he called through the door. "It's Curry. We had a meeting, remember?"

Thomas tried the knob. The door was locked. He crouched to look through the keyhole. He saw nothing, but his nose twitched and his eyes widened.

"Well," Giraud said, raising his black homburg perfunctorily, "a pleasure to see you again and to meet you, Mademoiselle Cadette, as I presume you are—"

"Forgive me," Thomas said distractedly. "Olivier Giraud, Sandrine Cadette. Sandrine Cadette, Olivier Giraud."

"—but I believe I have nothing more to accomplish here under the circumstances, so until we meet again, farewell."

"It might be prudent for you to stay for a few more minutes, Giraud," Thomas said without turning around.

"Why is that?"

"Because unless I'm very much mistaken, I smell cordite."

"You're not serious."

"Entirely."

Thomas stood up, took a step back, lowered his right shoulder and slammed his body into the door.

"Ouch!" He scowled at the unyielding portal. He rubbed his shoulder and upper arm.

"Commendable enthusiasm," Giraud remarked, "but on the whole it doesn't look like a promising approach."

"Perhaps finesse will accomplish what brute strength won't."

He took out his Diners Club card. He worked it in between the door and the jamb just above the lock. He insinuated the front edge and felt for the bar of the lock. He found it. He pressed decisively.

Nothing happened.

"What can I say?" Thomas demanded of no one in particular. "It invariably works for Efrem Zimbalist, Jr. Where did Sandy go?"

"I can't say," Giraud answered. "I didn't notice her leave. I was too intent on your efforts at breaking and entering."

"I have to confess that I'm running out of ideas, but I'm also increasingly convinced that it's a matter of some urgency to get inside that room."

Thomas stood up again, stepped back again, and snap-kicked the door, so that the heel of his right shoe landed solidly just above the knob.

"Well done," Giraud said. "At this rate we should get in there just about the time your foot is out of the cast."

"I'm open to suggestions," Thomas said. He stepped back in preparation for another kick.

"Relax, Muscles," a gravelly male voice commanded him. "That only works on television."

Thomas and Giraud looked around at the speaker. He was somewhere between forty-five and sixty-five. He was wearing a white, shoulder-strap type undershirt, a pair of what had once been charcoal-gray dress slacks, and black, high-top basketball shoes. The leather belt he wore was very thin and the waistband of the slacks curled over it, exposing the waistband's yellowed inside. The man clinched the stub of a cigar in the right corner of his mouth. He was completely bald but had prominent, bushy eyebrows the color and texture of steel wool. Sandy in his wake, he advanced toward the door with a passkey.

"Here's the deal," he said. "I open the door, I take a quick look inside and see if the girl here's right about an emergency. Nunna you t'ree comes inside, 'cause I don't care how fancy you dress, as far as I'm concerned I never heard of ya."

He put the key in the lock above the doorknob. "Nice job you did on the finish there, Ace," he said over his shoulder to Thomas. He turned the key. The bolt snapped back. He opened the door.

He froze. The cigar dropped from his mouth.

"Don't try to nonchalant it," Thomas said from directly behind him. "That only works on television."

The man with the key didn't say anything. Thomas didn't blame him. About twelve feet inside the door and just off to the right, mounted on its easel, was the smeared and tattered remnant of what might once have been a painting called *Badger Game*. And sitting on the opposite side of a table near the ravaged canvas, in a direct line with the open door, was the painter who had once been Harrison Tyler.

Chapter 13

O zein, angeilon Dakadaimoniois, oti taede
keimetha tois keinon raemasi peithomenoi.
(Go tell the Spartans, thou who passest by,
That here, obedient to their laws, we lie.)

—Simonides at Thermopylae

Harrison Tyler's body slumped in a chair on the far side of the table. His head lay far back and lolled to one side. A dark stain, deep purple near the center of his chest and lightening by degrees to brownish red, discolored the sodden front of his white Ban-Lon shirt.

All four of them stood motionless for two seconds or so. Thomas felt his body temperature drop. Sandy's lips moved silently for a moment, then pressed together in a tight line. Giraud rocked three times from the balls of his feet to his heels. The thud of the rubber heels on the hardwood floor sounded like thunderclaps in the still room. For several moments, the shock continued to grip them, and all they could do was look stupidly at the head lolling crazily and the eyes staring sightlessly and the stunning quantities of blood.

Thomas walked slowly over to the body. He laid the backs of his index and second fingers on the left side of the body's neck. The skin wasn't room temperature yet but it had made considerable progress in that direction. Thomas couldn't feel anything that gave much promise of being a pulse.

"He's dead," Thomas said.

The assessment was superfluous. Thomas recognized for that matter that his cursory examination itself had been a gesture, without any real utility. It had just been something to do, a modest improvement over standing there with his mouth slightly open. Everyone had known the moment they'd seen the body that Harrison Tyler was dead.

Sandy gently gripped the right shoulder of the superintendent who had let them in.

"Perhaps you should call the police," she said.

"Yeah."

The man continued to stand there. Sandy pushed him slightly and began turning him toward the door. That did it.

"Yeah," the man said again. He left the room.

The .45, still on its display stand, rested directly across the table from Tyler's body. A C-clamp pinned the stand to the tabletop. Through the trigger guard lay a gray metal rod about eight inches long with an ovoid handle of black plastic at one end. To the left of the gun rested an oblong tin box with rounded ends, its bright red enamel chipped off in a few places. The words "Outers Gun Cleaning Kit .45 Auto" appeared in yellow letters near the lower right-hand corner of the lid.

Thomas came around the table and leaned over the pistol. He smelled the muzzle and the breach. The acrid odor of burnt powder stung his nostrils.

To the right of the gun a thick book lay open. The top of the page on the left-hand side said "Gray's Anatomy." The facing page was a color plate showing the location of the heart in the human chest.

"So he pulled a Vronsky," Giraud said.

"Vronsky survived and left it up to Anna Karenina to do the right thing," Thomas muttered. "A good thing she did too. One of them had to go or the book would've gone on forever."

Miscellaneous detritus littered the floor immediately in front of the table, as if someone had swept everything indiscriminately from the tabletop. Thomas glanced at the clutter without consciously inventorying it. He noticed one or two brushes, a couple of broken rubber bands, some half-used tubes of paint, paint-stained rags, several pencils, and some pieces of oversized paper.

Giraud came up to the desk and bent slightly to peer at the body on the other side.

"I wonder what his problem was," Giraud said.

"Sometime in the last hour, I'd say his problem was a massive cardiac arrest incident to the penetration of his thoracic cavity by a piece of lead."

Thomas walked over to examine the canvas mounted on the easel a few feet from Tyler's body. Only if you had seen the painting before could you form much idea of what Tyler had intended *Badger Game* to be. Gaping slashes and jagged rips disfigured the canvas. Wide smears of paint covered most of the surface that wasn't torn. Less than two square feet of canvas at the very top of the easel remained undefiled.

Halfway between the easel and Tyler's chair a tumbler lay on its side. Thomas went to his hands and knees and sniffed the glass's rim and the residue of its contents on the floor.

"What was our brave artist's last drink?" Giraud asked.

"Bourbon and Coke and something that reminds me of a doctor's office," Thomas said. "I'm not sure what chloral hydrate smells like, but it wouldn't surprise me to learn that that's it."

"What's chloral hydrate?"

"Go to the Pier Bar on Front Street in Brooklyn and ask for Mickey Finn. He'll tell you all about it."

"Oh. That."

Across the room, the reel-to-reel tape on Tyler's deck continued to turn, now playing the "Radetsky March." Giraud went over and turned the intrusive music off. He glanced around, as if searching for a place to sit.

"It's up to you," Thomas said, "but my suggestion is that you not touch anything else until the police arrive."

"If you ever wish to get anywhere in the circles of high culture to which you apparently aspire, Mr. Curry, you're going to have to drop the clichés. You sound exactly like a mildly dotty professor of classical languages who's just stumbled over the lord of the manor's body in a second-rate English mystery."

Having said this, Giraud nevertheless didn't sit down.

"Clichés don't get to be clichés unless there's something to them," Thomas rejoined.

"I see that you come honestly by your taste for representational art. Do you seriously expect the constabulary to come in here with its array of intimidating paraphernalia and discover the latent fingerprints of an intruder?"

"On the contrary," Thomas said, "I fully expect them to come in here and find that the pages of that book and the top of the table and this glass and the doorknob show no fingerprints at all—something that will be highly suggestive to me and, I expect, to them."

"I assure you I sympathize with your preference for dramatic and nonobvious explanations of apparently sordid realities. But reality being the way it is, appearances in my experience are seldom deceiving. The evidence of our senses suggests that Harrison Tyler experienced a failure of moral courage and took his own life with a self-inflicted gunshot wound. That is rather disappointing and tawdry, I'll admit, but I'm confident that that's the way it is. Harrison Tyler shot himself with his service revolver."

Thomas looked through the window on the east side of the room. There was a fire escape directly outside but it was hard to see how you could get to it through the window. An air conditioner blocked the bottom half and the top half looked as if it was painted shut.

"That weapon on the table isn't a revolver, Giraud," he said, turning back toward the other two people in the room. "It's a pistol. Specifically, a United States government-issue Colt forty-five semiautomatic self-loading pistol—a standard U.S. armed forces sidearm for at least the last two wars."

"Fascinating, if a trifle pedantic."

"The distinction is a matter of some significance. You see, one of the respects in which semiautomatic pistols differ from revolvers is that automatics, as they're called, generally have safeties, whereas revolvers don't. You see that little tab there just below the breech? That's a safety. Click it on and the gun can't be fired."

"Apparently, however, this gun could be."

"Obviously. The safety I've just pointed out to you is off. But the military-model Colt forty-five differs from most automatics, in that it has not one but two safeties. In addition to the one just below the breech there, it has a secondary safety in back of the grip. Do you see how that plate in back of the handle sticks out a little bit?"

"I suppose so, yes," Giraud acknowledged.

"That's a squeeze safety. When that plate is pressed in, the safety is off and the gun can be fired. When the plate isn't pressed in, the safety's on and the gun can't be fired. When you're holding the gun in the normal firing position, of course, that safety is off because your hand is pressing the plate in. When the gun is just sitting there, though, that safety is on. It makes it a lot harder for the gun to go off accidentally."

"I'm beginning to see your point."

"My point is that you can't fire a United States Army model Colt forty-five automatic by sitting in front of it, running a gun-cleaning rod through the trigger guard, and pressing that rod against the front of the trigger. If that's all you do, the gun won't fire."

"Then you're saying that—"

"I'm saying that Harrison Tyler didn't commit suicide. He was murdered."

"Did someone say murder?" a voice with a no-nonsense, parade-ground timbre asked from the doorway.

Thomas looked up and Giraud glanced around. A uniformed policeman and a thickset man in a dark suit, white shirt, and dark tie stood there.

"Well," Thomas said, "it looks like the professionals have arrived. Amateur hour is over."

The police kept them there for another hour and forty-five minutes. Thomas was the last one the detective, who introduced himself as Lieutenant McShea, talked to.

"Do you know any reason he'd have wanted to kill himself?" McShea asked, after they'd gone over Thomas's basic story.

"I don't know of anything in his life that'd cause me to kill myself if it were part of mine," Thomas said.

"From the way you described your session with him Saturday afternoon, I'd say he sounded depressed."

"I'd've said maudlin, self-pitying, in the mood for preintoxication wallowing in self-absorption. I wouldn't say depressed, and certainly not despondent."

"Do you know anyone who'd want to kill him?"

"I'd be speculating," Thomas said.

"Speculate for me."

"No."

McShea looked surprised.

"I thought this guy was your friend."

"He was a client. In time he might've become a friend. I liked him, if that's what you're getting at."

"If he was murdered, don't you want us to catch the murderer?"

"Yes."

"Then why won't you help us?"

"I've been helping you," Thomas said. "I've told you what I know. I told you about the powder smell and the chloral hydrate smell and everything I saw."

"You didn't tell us about the turpentine smell on the pistol grip. We had to get that for ourselves."

Thomas looked sharply at the detective.

"I didn't pick up any turpentine smell."

"Of course you didn't. You overwhelmed your sense of smell for a good minute with the overpowering odor of burnt gunpowder. But that's okay. We got it, all by ourselves."

"My tax dollars at work." Thomas nodded. "I'm impressed."

"So, you can help us more by naming anyone you think might've had a reason to put a bullet through Tyler's heart, and telling me what that reason is."

"If I knew anything more, Lieutenant, I'd tell you. But I'm not going to stand here and name names on the basis of conjecture and imagination."

McShea glanced over his shoulder.

"I'm going to let you in on something," he said in a con-spiratorial whisper.

"Whatever you think best."

"There's a real Village type downstairs who seems to have been a fixture here most of the afternoon."

"You mean the young man who looks like he's waiting for *The Many Loves of Dobie Gillis* to make a casting call?"

"That's the one. He told my sergeant that he was keeping a close eye on the stairway leading up to this apartment for what looks like it may have been a fairly critical thirty minutes."

"Was he now? Why was he doing that?"

"Because he happened to notice someone go up who looked like he had blood in his eye, and he wanted to be in on the dramatic developments that he figured were in prospect."

"I see."

"Mr. Curry, I would very much like to talk to the person this gentleman saw going up. Because, Mr. Curry, this gentleman didn't see that person come back down."

"I don't blame you. Did you get a description from your nosy beatnik?"

"Right. We have a very good description of the back of the head of a white male."

"I wish I could help you."

"You can."

"On that we differ."

"All right," McShea said, "we'll just have to see if we can clear this case without your help. If a sudden sense of civic obligation should come over you, give me a call, wouldya?"

"Certainly. By the way. I'm certain you've thought of it, but if Tyler did keep anything bearing on whatever led to this, there's a chance it'll be stored in that GI footlocker in his office. I got the idea that he kept things that were personal and important to him in there."

McShea, who had turned disgustedly away, spun back and looked up into Thomas's face.

"What footlocker?" he demanded.

"It's in his office, against the wall to the side of his desk,"

Thomas said. "A standard, olive-drab barracks footlocker like you get in the army."

"I've been over the office very carefully," McShea said. "I've been over this entire place very carefully. There isn't any footlocker here."

Chapter 14

Almost all philosophers, in their ethical systems, first lay down a false doctrine, and then argue that wickedness consists in acting in a manner that proves it false, which would be impossible if it were true.

—Bertrand Russell

Sandy raised her glass and sipped the scotch cautiously. There was still only one Thomas Andrew Curry across the table from her. He wasn't even particularly blurry yet. Just a little soft around the edges, like a photograph shot with Vaseline smeared on the camera lens.

"Sandy," Thomas said over the rim of his own glass, "tell me something. Do you think Arthur Cleveland is homosexual?"

The question simultaneously surprised and reassured her. It was a question that Thomas wouldn't have asked her that bluntly if he were completely sober.

"No," she said. "He is effete but not effeminate. And I cannot be sure how he feels about men, but if he does not care for women then he is a better actor than most people with Equity cards."

"Why do you say that?"

"The question you just asked crossed my mind the evening I met him at the Ackley. And so I observed him discreetly for a minute or two, and gave him something to look at, just to be certain. He has that knack that well-brought-up men develop of ogling women only with the pupils of their eyes, without turning their heads and staring overtly. He followed every bounce of my breast and every sway of my bottom."

Veritas in vino est said Catullus, or somebody, she thought. That was an answer she certainly wouldn't have given that bluntly if she were completely sober.

It was just after nine o'clock at night. They were in the Rainbow Room on top of the RCA Building. Harrison Tyler was wherever people like him go when they die, and his body was in the morgue. Sandy and Thomas were drinking, and they weren't drinking after-dinner digestifs. Thomas was getting drunk and he wasn't making any bones about it. Sandy was getting drunk along with him.

"I'm scared," Thomas said after a short interval of silence.

"I know. I do not blame you for being scared."

"It couldn't possibly be coincidence. Tyler didn't just happen to seek me out about the same time a grand jury got interested in me. There has to be a connection. That connection was probably what got Tyler killed, and it could get me killed as well. But that isn't what frightens me."

"Then you are quite remarkable. It certainly frightens me."

"What scares me is that I can't even begin to imagine what the connection could possibly be. I feel like I'm sitting here waiting for something to happen to me."

"At least you are not sitting alone."

He raised his eyes and then his glass. They drank.

Thomas refilled his own glass. He looked at hers, saw that it was still half-full, and put the bottle of Pinch back down. They sat in silence for the time it took Sandy to finish what was in her glass.

"Isn't it a serious sin to get drunk?" Thomas asked.

"Yes. It is a species of gluttony, which is one of the seven deadly sins, so it is just about as serious as a sin can be."

"Then I must apologize for leading you toward perdition."

"You are not leading me anyplace that I do not choose to go. Sometime when I am more clearheaded, we can discuss the principle of double effect."

"I think I must have snuck out of Sunday school the week they covered that," Thomas said.

"Perhaps that is just as well. It is potentially a rather mischievous notion."

"I'll take that much on faith."

Sandy started to put her glass down on a cocktail napkin near her elbow. She realized that her chances of hitting it on the first try weren't much better than even.

"Faith," Thomas said reflectively, "is an enchanting concept."

"It has advantages and disadvantages."

"Sandy," he said suddenly, his face brightening as if he were about to propose a picnic in the country or some other impulsive romp, "do you think I should become a Catholic?"

"No, Thomas, I do not think you should become a Catholic. You are a very good agnostic and I should think that you would be a rather poor Catholic."

"You are a distressingly levelheaded, cold-bloodedly analytical young lady." He looked into his glass, swirled the scotch around, and gazed contemplatively at the eddies and whirlpool. "He was trying to tell me something Saturday afternoon, Sandy," he said then.

"What do you think he was trying to tell you?"

"I can't put my finger on it. That's the worst part of it. He expected something from me, something that I wasn't coming up with, but I couldn't figure out what it was."

"I suppose he could have asked for it."

Thomas looked back up at her.

"Obviously," he said, "he couldn't."

"Perhaps not."

A clock struck the half-hour.

"Thomas," Sandy said then in a carefully controlled voice, holding her head and her upper body quite still, "I have something very important to ask you."

"What's that?"

"Where does one go in this establishment if one expects to be ill?"

Thomas succeeded in giving Sandy passable directions to the

ladies' room. She got there in time. She enclosed herself in a stall, sank to her knees in front of the toilet, took a deep breath, and vomited. She sagged back weakly on her heels and waited to see if another heave was going to grab her torso. None did.

She caught her breath. She found her way to a sink and leaned over it. She dampened a piece of brown paper toweling with cold water and washed the area around her mouth.

She took a tiny paper cup from a gray metal dispenser on the wall. She filled it with cold water, rinsed the inside of her mouth, poured the rest of the water out, and threw the cup away.

She looked at herself in the mirror. She patted her forehead and cheeks with the damp towel.

The principle of double effect, as all good Catholics were taught back then, holds that an action that would be morally blameworthy if done for its own sake is morally permissible if its evil effect is merely the known but unwanted consequence of an action taken to accomplish a different, morally desirable end, so long as the morally desirable end is not accomplished by means of the evil effect, and so long as there is a due proportion between the good sought to be accomplished by the action and the evil to be acquiesced in as a result of it. This principle, for example, holds that it is morally permissible for a secret service agent to throw himself on a hand grenade tossed by an assassin toward the president, and smother the blast with his body.

Tonight was the third time in her life Sandy had deliberately gotten drunk, but as she explained to me much later, she was confident that her action this time was morally blameless. Thomas Andrew Curry was a friend of hers. Tonight, he needed to get drunk. If Thomas needed to get drunk, then he had a moral right to have a friend who understood get drunk with him.

Because she was his friend and did understand, it followed ineluctably that she had to drink with him as long as he wished to drink, or at least until she passed out. The due proportion between the transcendent value of comradeship and the transient evil of getting so soused that one couldn't hit the floor with one's hat, if one wore a hat, which in this case one did not, was clear to her, even if nothing else at this moment was.

She threw the paper towel away and looked again in the mirror. The vomiting had worked wonders. She felt much better.

Tuesday

Tuesday

Chapter 15

American morality was . . . high when compared with the morality of many older societies but, like American intelligence, it discouraged excess.

—Henry Adams

"**A** client of the firm is dead," T. Graham said. "In and of itself, that is not a matter of particular moment: The firm doesn't do probate work, and I understand that the decedent's retainer was large enough to cover the billable time booked on his behalf prior to his demise."

He paused. Thomas, Sandy, and I sat there and waited. We were sitting in T. Graham's office. It was one-thirty Tuesday afternoon. I could tell that Sandy and Thomas had the kind of throbbing heads that result from a night of alcoholic excess. Particularly in Sandy's case, I was rather relieved. I'd never completely trust anyone who hadn't had at least one terrible hangover before they were twenty-five.

"Given the circumstances of our late client's death, however," T. Graham continued, "there is reason to believe that it may be in the firm's interest to look into the matter further. Do I understand the situation correctly?"

"You do," I said.

It had taken me the better part of an hour to convince Thomas that it was absolutely indispensable to bring his father formally into the case. Before the shooting, I'd pointed out, it might have been essentially Thomas's problem and, peripherally, mine. Now that there was a stiff in the picture, as I delicately

111

put it, the matter had become Curry & Furst's problem, and T. Graham was after all the Curry of Curry & Furst.

T. Graham waited a moment before speaking again. He glanced deliberately at us, a half-smile playing at his lips.

He had an important advantage over us. Unlike any of us he had on more than a hundred occasions tried cases to juries. He could read faces and body language. He had a well-honed instinct for knowing when what everyone expected you to say would be exactly the wrong comment to make.

"Well," he said mildly. "I'll be happy to help in any way that you would find useful."

We looked at him in varying degrees of surprise. I recovered more quickly than my two younger and less experienced colleagues.

"Very well," I said, swiveling to face Thomas, "where do you think we should start?"

"I suppose there are two areas," he replied. "First, the voluminous but routine detail: the stories of everyone who was present, a thorough search of Tyler's belongings, vagrant and unexplained keys found on the premises, residues on the windowsill and fire escape of clay found only in particular sections of Central Park near which one or more suspects were seen lurking shortly before the shooting, fingerprints, that kind of thing. The police will be working on that, and it will be useful for us to find out what they've learned. Second, there is the bothersome matter of the footlocker. It seems probable that it would not only be useful but critical to find it."

"That assessment seems sound enough," T. Graham said. "Sound enough" was the second-highest accolade he ever conferred on subordinates, the highest being "sound," period. "There is one other moderately interesting point, and that is the whereabouts of Miss Gloria Monday."

"She's one of the people who've been subpoenaed to testify before the grand jury investigating the Johnson Industries matter?" I asked.

"Yes. At least, she's on the the list of those who are supposed to be subpoenaed, but apparently hasn't been served yet because the marshals can't locate her."

"Why do you attach particular significance to her?"

"Oh, I don't know," T. Graham said carelessly. "She caught my attention. As I told Miss Cadette, it's rather unusual for the United States Marshals Service not to be able to find someone. If she is that reclusive, one naturally wonders why."

"Do you remember her from your clerkship, Thomas?" Sandy asked.

"Fairly well. She was a tall blonde—"

"No wonder you remember her," T. Graham muttered.

"—rather plain, who kept pretty much to herself. She was older than most of the other women on the staff, and I always thought she wore too much makeup. She was soft-spoken and had a rather low, quiet voice."

"She was a secretary?" Sandy asked.

"Not really. She was a typist."

"The distinction is what, please?"

"A secretary was what you got if you'd been there at least four years and looked like you might hang around. Typing for clerks and junior associates went to a typing pool: twenty-five women sitting shoulder to shoulder in some interior rabbit warren, pounding keyboards all day long under the supervision of the sharpest-tongued battle-ax in the firm. Gloria Monday was in the pool."

"Well." T. Graham sighed. "No doubt you are all right. We should defer any conjecture about Miss Monday until we have completed our look into areas of more pressing concern. Can I be of any assistance?"

"Actually," Thomas said, "it occurred to me that you might have the best chance of extracting information from New York's Finest, due to the contacts that you've built up over the years and so forth. And I thought that Theodore might check with some of his European colleagues to see if there was anything more to be learned about Olivier Giraud and his buddy Rocard."

"There's something to that," T. Graham commented. "You

and Miss Cadette would then go searching for the missing footlocker?"

"Right."

"Have you given any thought to where you might begin?"
the white-haired man inquired innocently.

"Actually," Sandy said, "we have. We thought that if someone got something that size out of Tyler's apartment surreptitiously and had it taken away from the area, the most likely
means would be by taxicab. On the assumption that cabs frequent the same general area day after day, we considered starting
by going back to the vicinity of Tyler's apartment, flagging cabs
in the area, and asking questions."

"Very creative," T. Graham murmured, nodding sagely.
"May I offer two bits of advice—strictly for what they're worth,
of course?"

"By all means," Sandy said.

"First, you may find it more effective to wait for the cabbies
to speak first, and I think you may trust them to do so. The
typical New York cabdriver is incapable of refraining from conversation. Second, I think you will find that New York cabbies
are all highly principled—and the thing they're principally high
on is money."

For a moment we all looked at each other with the slightly
forced pleasantness of participants in a transaction in which one
party has sold a fake Renoir to the other and received counterfeit
money in exchange.

"Well," T. Graham said then, slapping his palms on his
desk, "you've given me my marching orders, so I'd better get
right to work."

A hustler is someone who can induce you to get him drunk
on your whiskey so that you can talk him into letting you do
what he wanted you to do in the first place. It was a real pleasure
to watch a master at work.

"Thomas," Sandy said when they were out on the street and
looking for a cab to take them back to the Village, "I agree that
the sudden disappearance of the footlocker is an arresting phe-

nomenon. But you are acting as if you think that it is more than that—that it might be the key to this entire problem."

"Right. He may not think so. That's why he doesn't mind us looking for it."

"You are being rather hard on your father, Thomas. He could not have been more perfectly charming during that conference."

"Nevertheless, that's what he thinks. He believes that looking for that piece of luggage will keep us harmlessly busy while he steps in and finds the answer."

"He believes we will be chasing a wild goose in a haystack?"

"Something like that."

"Whereas you are convinced that we are in fact looking for the solution?"

"Maybe ensure," Thomas said, in an unsuccessful stab at *mais bien sûr*.

"Is that an idiom?"

"Sort of," Thomas answered, distractedly and without thinking.

"It has what meaning, please?"

"You betcha."

"Why do you think the footlocker is so important?"

"I'm more and more convinced that Tyler must have known something was up, and may well have made some record of whatever it was that had him worried. If he did, and the police haven't found it yet, it's probably in that footlocker."

"But why do you think that?" Sandy pressed. "Masculine intuition?"

"Not just intuition. You see, whoever carved up that painting that was mounted near Tyler's body didn't quite get all of it. There's a section near the top that's almost unscathed. Not much. Just five or six inches from one side to the other. But it's enough."

"Enough for what?"

"Enough to show that that painting wasn't the one he had on the easel Saturday afternoon when I was with him. It was either an alternative study or the result of a significant revision that must've taken him most of Sunday."

"You mean that the real *Badger Game*—"

"I mean there's a chance that an important version of the real *Badger Game* hasn't been destroyed. At least not yet. It may still exist. And if it does I'll bet anything that it's in that footlocker."

T. Graham settled back in his swivel chair. The tips of his fingers were cold. Crossing his arms, he thrust the chilly digits underneath his coat, over his vest and into his armpits to warm them up.

He frowned. At sixty-four, he didn't consider himself old. Eighty was his idea of old. At the same time, he had every intention of being old someday. Cold fingertips and other reminders of what awaited him when he reached that condition didn't please him.

The frown gradually gave way to a rather patronizing smile as the incubating fingers warmed up. Police contacts. That was a good one. Just call up some detective you'd met during cross-examination while you were in the process of getting a hijacker back out on the street and ask him if he wouldn't like to share a little information with you for old time's sake.

He'd get information from the police all right. But he'd get it the only way you can ever get information from the police: He'd get some of his own to trade for it.

He thought about what information he could possibly gather that the police might be interested in. His thoughts returned inexorably to Olivier Giraud, far and away the murkiest character in the story his son had told him.

Decisively, he stood up and reached for his hat. He always wore a hat when he went outdoors, regardless of the season. He told his secretary to call his driver and have him bring the car to the front of the building immediately. After some forty years of practicing criminal law, he had useful contacts, all right, but most of them weren't with the police. He was going to see Bad Rug.

Chapter 16

. . . the resulting beliefs will be private, since the heart says different things to different people. Some savages are persuaded by the "natural light" that it is their duty to eat people, and even Voltaire's savages, who are led by the voice of reason to hold that one should only eat Jesuits, are not wholly satisfactory.

—Bertrand Russell

Roughly 90 percent of the time, Sammy Ralston lived and worked in a dreary, dilapidated building in the South Bronx. While doing so he had, by general agreement, the worst toupee in the state of New York. This is a bit like being the worst actor in the Royal Shakespeare Company: It's worthy of note but it's not a mark of real distinction, and by itself it would never have been enough to earn him his sobriquet.

Periodically, however—specifically, at the approach of the first Tuesday after the first Monday in November in years divisible by two—Ralston found it advisable to decamp across the Hudson River for a couple of months. The prospect of a general election seemed to incite the vice squad's taste for photogenic gestures, such as raiding homosexual bars and smut shops. Ralston had no objection to raids on homosexual bars, but he thought it best to be elsewhere when New York's moral guardians turned their attention to smut shops, because that's what he ran.

During his biennial sojourns across the river in the Garden State, Sammy Ralston had the worst toupee in the state of New Jersey. This was a genuine phenomenon. This could make you stand out. It was as a result of this achievement that everyone in the New York demimonde knew Sammy as Bad Rug Ralston.

Bad Rug's building looked deserted and uninviting, the front door hanging off one hinge, the windows broken and boarded up by bolted and cross-braced four-by-fours. Behind the broken front door was a heavy metal grille welded into place.

T. Graham climbed out of his car and strode into the alley between Bad Rug's building and its neighbor, slopping his freshly polished black oxfords through the muck and the gray, standing water. He didn't flinch. You don't find alibi witnesses in felony murder cases if you're afraid to venture away from Park Avenue.

In the center of the rear of Bad Rug's building, T. Graham found a heavy metal door, freshly painted dark brown. He took out one of his cards, stood directly in front of the peephole in the door, and used the ferrule of his umbrella to press a white button near the doorknob.

Several seconds passed. The door opened a crack. T. Graham held his card out within reach of the crack.

"Please give this to Bad Rug and tell him that I'd like to see him for a few minutes."

After a moment's hesitation, long, crooked fingers snaked out and snatched the card through the crack. The door slammed.

In 1957, the state of New York had tried very hard to send Bad Rug Ralston to prison for five years for wholesaling dirty magazines. T. Graham had defended him. The fact that Bad Rug was just as guilty as he could be of the offense charged somewhat complicated the defense, but T. Graham overcame that obstacle. T. Graham had no doubt that Bad Rug would admit him. He was right. The door opened and a white-haired woman let him in. She led him quickly to Bad Rug.

Bad Rug was bent over a slanted draftsman's table, painting a white fluid with delicate strokes onto a transparent sheet with black type imprinted on it. His skin was nut brown and sagging. Sparse, gray-white whiskers were strewn apparently at random on his cheeks. His toupee was jet black and glossy. It looked like a dead mink.

"What can I do for you, counselor?"

"I'm trying to find out about some European money that I think came into this business just after the war."

"Into my business?"

"Not necessarily yours individually. Yours or one of your competitors'."

"I been at the game a long time, counselor. That doesn't ring a bell."

"The European I'm interested in calls himself Olivier Giraud these days. Of course he may have used a different name."

"I know almost everyone who's been anyone in this dodge for twenty-five years anyway. I don't remember that name and I don't remember anyone getting capital from over the water."

"Rather short, thin, fair-skinned man. Very la-de-da manner. Blond hair."

"And he's supposed to have bought into the skin trade?"

"Yes."

"What makes you think so, counselor?"

"He said so. Told my son he was an entrepreneur, implied that he came to the U.S. after the Second World War, and said explicitly that he started out in pornography."

"He could've been lying. About the last part, I mean."

"Yes, but I don't think he was. It's hardly the kind of thing you'd lie about."

"Begging your pardon all to hell, counselor, but it's hardly the kind of thing you'd tell the truth about."

"That was sort of my point."

"You had me fooled."

"What I meant was, it's a disparaging thing to say about yourself, and the only reason to say it would be if it were true and you were afraid it could be found out. In that case, you might bring it up preemptively, to forestall inquiry that could be even more damaging."

"You're over my head, counselor."

"It's like bringing out a felony conviction on direct examination so that you don't have to admit on cross-examination that the conviction was for child molesting."

"Oh. Now I getcha."

T. Graham glanced at a slick magazine cover to Ralston's
right, waiting to be cannibalized for the mock-up of next
month's cover. The cover depicted a woman, gagged and seated
uncomfortably on a floor. It might reasonably be surmised that
the woman had no clothes on, unless the gag counted as clothes,
but it was hard to be certain about this because thick yellow
rope coiled around the woman's shoulders and arms, down her
torso, over her hips and buttocks and down her legs to her ankles.

The title of the magazine was *Knotty Ladies No. 6*. According
to the cover, issue number six included such articles as "Bound
and Determined," "Suspended Animation," and that perennial
favorite, "Bound to Please."

"I take it you're working on *Knotty Ladies Number Seven*,"
T. Graham said.

"No, I'm not. I *would* be working on it if I weren't sitting
here trying to think of who this faggot European investor you're
talking about could possibly be."

The door to the office opened. A middle-aged man with wiry
brown hair poked his head in.

"We're all through in the studio. Three hours and forty-five
minutes."

"All right. Send 'em in."

Two models, amply if recently clad, came in. They glanced
uncomfortably at T. Graham and then turned their attention
studiously away from him.

"Tammy and Leslie, Counselor Curry," Bad Rug said.
"Counselor, Tammy and Leslie."

"Delighted," T. Graham said.

"Same thing to you," one of the models responded.

"You know what?" the other model said in a low, breathy
voice. "You look exactly like the little tycoon in Monopoly.
You know, the little round-headed old guy with the top hat
who's so happy when there's a bank error in his favor or when
he gets to advance to Go? You look just exactly like him."

"Please forgive Leslie, counselor," Bad Rug said as he swiv-
eled around. "Been tied up all day."

"Literally, I gather."

Bad Rug gave forty-eight dollars in cash to Tammy and thirty-seven dollars and fifty cents in cash to Leslie. They took the money and left the office without further conversation.

"I don't want to be presumptuous, Bad Rug, but it seemed to me that Leslie could've used a shave."

"Fact of life." Bad Rug shrugged apologetically. "I like high production values as much as anyone. But boys don't cost as much as girls. When you're doing something for specialty tastes, like *Knotty Ladies*, there're a lot of shots where you can achieve verisimilitude without anatomical authenticity."

"Verisimilitude without anatomical authenticity?"

"You know what I mean."

"I'm very much afraid that I do."

"Counselor, I'll tell you the truth. I'm drawing a blank on this and that's a fact. I'll ask around a little bit. Curiosity isn't something people take to real well in this business, but I'll do my best."

Chapter 17

It is very difficult to tell the truth, and young people are rarely capable of it.

—Tolstoy

"Columbia University."

"Long ride. Get in."

Thomas slammed the taxi door. For three blocks he tried to obey his father's admonition to wait for the driver to speak first. Then he couldn't stand the silence any longer.

"You usually work around here?" he asked.

"I don't get as far uptown as Columbia much. Usually Wall Street to midtown."

"Not that much in the Village, then?"

"Anh."

Thomas wasn't sure whether this was an affirmative or a negative response. He was beginning to get discouraged.

"You see some crazy things in the Village, though," the cabbie said.

Thomas's spirits rose.

"Do you now?"

"Honest to God. Like just recently, I saw something, I tell ya, you wouldn't believe it."

Thomas's spirits soared.

"What was it?"

"Okay. There's this guy, see? Just your regular businessman type, you know, mid-thirties, early forties, something like that, three-button suit, snap-brim hat, absolutely garden variety. Except you'll never guess what he had with him."

"A footlocker?"

"Footlocker? Who said anything about a footlocker?"

"Oh. Well, what did he have with him?"

"A lion. Honest to God. He was walking this regular lion along the street on a leash. Big mane and everything."

"I see. Yes, I can imagine that that would draw your attention."

"Turned out it was just an advertising gimmick."

"Really."

"Yeah. They were doin' a photo spread for some mutual fund. You got any mutual funds?"

"I beg your par—oh, I suppose I probably do, yes. Listen, I'll tell you why I was thinking about footlockers just now. In the last couple of days I happened to see a man get into a cab down near where you picked me up. And he had a footlocker with him. That was why I noticed him. But as he got in he dropped a brown envelope on the ground and the cab drove off before I could get his attention. I retrieved the envelope, but there's no identification on the outside and I've been trying to track the man down so I could give it back to him. It's become sort of a burden, actually. I was hoping I'd run into the cabdriver who picked him up so that he could at least tell me where the guy got off and I'd have someplace to start. It's gotten to be such an aggravation that I'd even be willing to throw in a little tip to whoever got me to the guy. A nice little tip."

"Why doncha just take the envelope to the cops?"

"Well, I—"

"Can't help ya myself. I think I'da noticed a guy cartin' a footlocker around inside my cab."

"That's okay. Thanks anyway."

"Sure t'ing. Wish I could help. Tuesday's sorta a slow day."

"Tuesday?" Thomas said, feigning surprise and badly overacting in the process. "Is today Tuesday?"

"Yeah, perfessor, comes between Monday and Wednesday every week."

"Bloody hell. My appointment at Columbia isn't until tomorrow. You might as well turn around and take me back to where you picked me up."

"You sure about that, perfessor?"

"Entirely."

"It's your nickel."

The cab did a U-turn on Broadway, across all four lanes of traffic. The cabbie waved cheerfully at the blaring horns, as if they were a form of applause.

Thomas found himself developing a whole new respect for actors. The first time he had used this story about the envelope, about eighty minutes ago, it had seemed fresh and plausible. The second time, it had sounded all right, a little too pat but still solid. The third time it had seemed stale and mechanical. This time, it was all he could do to say the words without throwing up. Anyone, he thought, can be good on opening night. How anyone could be good for their three-hundredth performance was more than he could understand.

The cab deposited him at the corner near Tyler's apartment where he had flagged it. He spotted Sandy half a block away, also getting out of a cab. He ambled toward her, mopping his glistening face with a handkerchief as he did so.

"Am I right that your luck has been as rotten as mine so far?" he asked.

"Maybe ensure," she said, happier with the new piece of American slang she'd picked up from Thomas than with the results of her inquiries.

"I'm sorry?"

"Maybe ensure," she said patiently. "You told me that it has the meaning 'you betcha.' "

"Oh. Quite right."

He put a dime in a Coke machine near the door of a small grocery. An eight-ounce bottle of Coca-Cola dropped down the chute.

"Would you like one?" he asked.

"No, thank you. I have not totally assimilated. Yet."

"Well, let me see if I can find a place around here where we can get you some Chablis or schnapps or something," Thomas said after chugging about a third of the Coke.

"Ice water will be fine."

A drugstore on the other side of the street seemed a likely source for that beverage and they started toward it. They had progressed about two yards in that direction when a yellow cab screeched to a stop in front of them. The cabbie rolled down the passenger side window and leaned across the seat to talk to them.

"You the two trying to buy information about the guy with the footlocker?" he asked.

"This sounds promising," Thomas observed.

"If you wouldn't mind terribly, Thomas," Sandy said, sensing that the promised ice water was receding into the indefinite future, "I think I would like a swallow of that drink you have after all."

He handed her the bottle. She took it first at a forty-five degree angle, then sixty, then seventy-five, and finally ninety, the arch in her back almost balletic as she held the bottle perfectly vertical. She handed it back to him. It was empty. Abruptly, she covered her mouth with one hand and, as genteelly as possible under the circumstances, belched.

"Okay," the cabbie said after he had pocketed an advance on the generous tip Thomas promised him. "There's not much to tell. Guy on the corner near where I picked you up flags me, I pull over, he climbs in with a footlocker, tells me to go to this address near the Battery."

"What was the color?" Thomas asked.

"White. Just between us, I don't like pickin' up spades in this kinda neighborhood, an' I don't go anywhere near Harlem. Forget it."

"I mean," Thomas said, his tone icily formal, "what was the color of the footlocker?"

"Oh. Green. You know, dark green, with black straps and hardware. Like in the army."

"What was at the address near the Battery where he asked you to take him?"

"I'm takin' you there now. There was nothin' there that I could see. A junkyard and some warehouses that weren't in exactly A-one condition."

"Hm," Thomas said.

"This is not what you expected?" Sandy asked.

"I guess not what I hoped for. I was sort of looking forward to Grand Central Station, La Guardia, someplace with a storage locker."

"Did this happen yesterday in the morning or yesterday in the afternoon?" Sandy asked.

"Didn't happen yesterday at all," the cabbie said. "It happened Sunday, mid-evening."

"Sunday?"

"That's what I said."

"This doesn't make a lot of sense," Thomas mused. "You're sure it was Sunday?"

"It was Sunday," the cabbie confirmed. "Comes between Saturday and Monday every week."

The cab stopped across a sidewalk from an eight-foot-high cyclone fence. Fender panels, tires, bumpers, axles, and miscellaneous metal lay in disordered piles on the other side of the fence.

"He got out here," the cabbie said. "He toted that footlocker over to the gate, had a chat or something with the guard, went inside for about ten minutes, and came back out without the footlocker."

"What do you mean he 'had a chat or something'? What's something?"

"I mean what you think I mean. I mean I think he slipped a bill to the guard so the guard'd let him in."

"Did you actually see that?"

"No. I mean they didn't exactly broadcast what they were doin'."

Thomas looked through the window at the junkyard.

"What do you think the chances are that the footlocker is still in there?" Sandy asked.

From the cab, Thomas could see only the junked cars and

other detritus piled just beyond the fence and, above them and in the distance, the top of a claw crane. He could see the top move as the claw picked up cars and the crane dumped them into a masher. And he could hear the masher pulverize the full-sized cars into two-foot cubes.

"I think the chances are not very good."

"Nobody asked me," the cabbie said, "but I'd say the chances are slim and none. If that footlocker wasn't nothin' more than a green grease spot by now, the police'd have it."

"The police?"

"Yeah. They found me yesterday night, lookin' for the same information you were. But they don't pay as good as you do."

The cabbie split his lips and showed them a set of yellowed dentures.

"How would you describe the man with the footlocker?"

"Your basic white guy, except he had a hook."

"Hook?"

"That's what I said, a hook. See, he was missin' a hand an' he had a hook down there instead."

Thomas sagged back in the seat and gave the cabbie the address of the building where he and Sandy lived.

"And then," Sandy said to the cabbie, "the man returned and you took him back to where you'd picked him up?"

"Yeah. No, wait. No. He wanted to stop three blocks away, where there was a mailbox. He got out there and paid me and said he'd walk the rest of the way."

"Did he post anything?"

"You mean did he put anything in the mailbox?"

"Yes," Sandy said.

"Matter of fact, he did. A small, yellow envelope."

"You're joking." Thomas groaned.

"Why would I joke about that? Nothin' funny about that."

"You mean one of those mustard-colored business envelopes?" Sandy asked.

"No. A small envelope. And not light brown or tan or anything like that. Yellow. Bright yellow."

Returned to their apartment building at last, Thomas and

Sandy got out and Thomas gave the cabbie the fare on the meter plus twenty dollars.

"By the way," he said, "for future reference. If I'm paying, it's Negroes, okay? Not spades."

"Up yours, college boy."

The cabbie pocketed the bill.

"I said if I'm paying. Have a nice evening."

"Hope not," the cabbie said. "Can't make any money that way."

Chapter 18

Always being right is a big mistake.

—Edgar Faure

The telex is a marvelous device. It permits you to send a message from New York to Paris in less time than it takes to get the first installment on an afternoon's worth of back talk from Gotham cabbies. While my three colleagues were exposing themselves to the New York City elements, climatic and otherwise, I sent a cable to a corresponding counsel I'd worked with in Paris, asking him to see what he could find out quickly about a supposed Swiss national now calling himself Olivier Giraud who had an American wife or ex-wife living in Europe and who appeared to have gotten out while the getting was good sometime not long after V-E Day. I also asked him to get me anything he could on a UN functionary named François Rocard.

I did this about three o'clock in the afternoon. When it's three o'clock in the afternoon in New York, it's nine o'clock at night in Paris.

Did I think my corresponding counsel was at his desk at nine o'clock at night? I did not. But I knew that he'd get my cable first thing the following morning when it was 9:00 A.M. in Paris and sensible New Yorkers were fast asleep, start the inquiries, and try to have a report for me by the end of his working day, which would be shortly before noon for me.

I like telephones even more than telexes. After cabling Europe, I called Geoffrey Singleton, a law school classmate of

129

mine who had chosen to go to work for a big firm in Milwaukee instead of a small firm in New York. He was jovial, competent, and memorable, and his manner was St. Paul's Boat Club all the way. I made a lot more money and attended more Broadway shows and New York Philharmonic concerts than he did. On the other hand, he was still married to his first wife. You pay your money and you take your choice.

It's hard to remember now, but long-distance was still kind of a big deal back in 1962. You didn't dial the call yourself, you placed it through an operator. And when you got a call like that—especially if you were in a place like Milwaukee and the call came from a place like New York—you made a special effort to take it. Singleton came on the line immediately.

"Greetings from America's Dairyland, Theodore," he said. To get an idea of his voice, try to imagine Elliot Richardson's nasal tone in flat Midwestern instead of New England twang. "What can I do for you?"

"I need to know if there has been anything of a legal nature in Milwaukee since the first of the year involving a company called Frampton Electronics, and if so what it was."

"Frampton Electronics. Any idea of what kind of thing it could be?"

"Not really. Maybe securities, maybe something else. The kind of thing that would cause someone from the general counsel's office to make a trip out there."

"Litigation?"

"Could have been. Not necessarily."

"Hm. Mrs. Pierce," he called, "would you please bring me our new matters file since the first of the year?"

We sat in what seemed like expensive silence while Mrs. Pierce compiled.

"Let's see," he said. Then he began humming. I could tell that he was humming while he paged through the file. The tune sounded familiar.

"What's that you're humming?" I asked.

" 'On Wisconsin.' Well, Theodore, coming up empty so far. But that doesn't mean it didn't happen. It just means that we didn't have a piece of it. I'll see what I can find out at the MAC."

"MAC?"

"Milwaukee Athletic Club. If no one there had a piece of it, then it didn't happen."

"Thank you."

I hung up, confident that I'd accomplished more in fifteen minutes than my three colleagues among them would the entire afternoon. In a way, I was right.

Chapter 19

Modern philosophy begins with Descartes, whose fundamental certainty is the existence of himself and his thoughts, from which the external world is to be inferred. This was only the first stage in a development, through Berkeley and Kant, to Fichte, for whom everything is only an emanation of the ego. This was insanity, and, from this extreme, philosophy has been attempting, ever since, to escape into the world of everyday common sense.

—Bertrand Russell

When Thomas called to say that he and Sandy wouldn't be back in the office until tomorrow morning, I arranged to meet him around six at the soda fountain in Greenwalds Drugstore, near where Thomas lived. I would've preferred to meet someplace where I could get a martini. All those movies you've seen about organization men who treated the daily predinner cocktail as a sacred ritual have a basis in reality, and I was part of that basis.

Thomas, however, had a firm rule about drinking nothing alcoholic within twenty-four hours after waking up with a hangover. I didn't see why that meant that I should have to refrain from my coveted gin-and-vermouth fix, but it would never have occurred to Thomas in his charming egotism to consider that aspect of the question. So we ended up at Greenwalds, him with a cup of black coffee and me with a Coca-Cola.

Greenwalds served my Coke in an inverted white conical paper cup stuck in a gleaming silver metal holder. I don't know why, but Coke served that way tastes different from Coke poured out of a can into a glass, which is about the only way you can get it most places today. It tastes better. But it still doesn't taste as good as a dry martini.

I wasn't really surprised to learn that it was Tyler himself who had gotten rid of the footlocker. I was prepared to believe that, in the middle of the day, on the floor above a coffeehouse full or soon to be full of people, someone had entered Tyler's flat and set up an elaborate murder and then made a clean getaway. It seemed to strain plausibility, though, to suggest that the murderer had humped a conspicuous piece of luggage out of the place and taken off with it in a taxicab. It was like winning the daily double five days in a row at Belmont.

I actually had something else I was more anxious to talk about with Thomas. I began by asking where Sandy was.

"She's on her way to Framingham, Massachusetts," he said, the way you'd say that someone had run to the corner for some soap and toothpaste.

"What's she doing in Framingham, Massachusetts?"

"She's meeting with Casey's mother around nine-thirty tonight. She'll stay overnight in Framingham and be back by noon tomorrow."

"Initiative," I muttered.

"Excuse me?"

"Nothing."

Sandy was the only one who had a strategic idea of the problem. The strategic problem wasn't to figure out who'd killed Harrison Tyler. That was a tactical issue. The problem was to find out why someone had done whatever they'd done to get Thomas and the firm roped into this mess in the first place. Sandy obviously had that in mind. I was glad one of us did.

"You know, Thomas," I said, "I don't want to be indelicate, and I know gentlemen don't discuss these things specifically—"

"Theodore, the concept of you being indelicate is positively mind-boggling."

"—but I've always had the impression that you weren't exactly shy as far as ladies are concerned."

"No. There's not a lot of point in being shy."

"That's what I'm finding a little hard to figure out. I mean, anyone can see that you're crazy about Sandy."

"How could I not be crazy about her, Theodore? She is absolutely without fault."

"Actually, that's not quite true." He looked up at me sharply. "The last time Marge and I had you two out to play tennis, I noticed that she sometimes uses a complicated passing volley when a simple drop shot would do just as well. Not a major fault, I'll grant you, but a definite imperfection."

"Where are you going with this, Theodore?"

"To be blunt—"

"For a change."

"—I was wondering when you were going to do something about it. About your being crazy about her, I mean."

"For God's sake."

"What's that supposed to mean?"

"Theodore, I was running guns to the people who killed her father. That's how we met, remember?"

"I do remember that, actually."

"I am at least indirectly responsible for her father's death."

"You're also directly responsible for saving her life and her mother's and her sister's."

"Really, Theodore—"

"She's a soldier's daughter, Thomas, with a military tradition going back for generations in her family. I think she understands that people can honorably be enemies in combat and something else when circumstances are different."

"Theodore, that's rather abstract. Come back down to earth for a moment. Every time she looks at me, she has to see me pulling the trigger of a gun aimed at her father."

"You're overdramatizing the situation, Thomas, and in a singularly self-absorbed way that does you no credit."

I paused and took a sip of Coke.

"Am I really?"

"Yes you are, really." I deliberately slowed down my rate of speech. "You're beginning to sound like your father."

"Theodore, you're losing what little credibility you had to start with."

"There was a war on. Someone on one side pulled a trigger and someone on the other side stopped the bullet. It happens. It happens in desert villages in Algeria and it happens in big cities in China."

Thomas's head snapped to full center.

"In concrete, real-world terms, Thomas," I continued, "you are about as responsible for the death of Sandrine Cadette's father as that silly Communist you were dating when you were at Princeton was for the death of your mother in Nanking."

His gaze held for one second of absolute silence. Then he favored me with the vilest epithet in his repertoire.

"Theodore, that was a cheap, goddamn insurance lawyer's trick."

"Thank you, Thomas. I haven't been accused of that in over fifteen years—since I was in fact an insurance lawyer, now that I come to think of it."

He looked disgustedly away from me.

"Your mother felt it was her duty to supervise the delivery of relief supplies by the International Red Cross to Nanking. Some peasant who was working for Mao Tse-tung instead of Chiang Kai-shek that week fired a howitzer and the shell destroyed a building and the roof of the building crushed your mother. You can trace the chain of causation all the way back to Princeton and say that Emma Schwartzman's dues paid for the shell. But what's the point?"

"What indeed?" Thomas muttered.

"Halfway around the world, a few years later, some Arab who thinks of himself as Algerian instead of French kills a symbol of French colonialism. It happens that that symbol was a human being with a wife and two daughters. If you'd never flown a round of ammunition into Algeria, Major Cadette would still be dead—and so would Sandy and her mother and her sister."

Thomas relaxed and I could see the anger flowing out of his face. All at once he was sheepish, apologetic about the insurance lawyer crack, although it was entirely accurate.

"You're right," he said then. "About my being crazy about her, I mean. She's the first woman I've ever even imagined the possibility of loving. But I just can't believe that she could allow herself to love me, after what happened. If I asked her and she said no, I suppose I could handle it. But if I asked her and she said yes and it was because she felt she owed her life to me, I don't know if—"

"Spare me." I sighed, shaking my head disgustedly.

He looked at me, hurt and surprised. He'd been expecting appreciation for the poignancy of his emotional dilemma, and sympathy for his anguish.

"That is the most pathetic, puling, maundering exercise in self-pity that I've been exposed to in a long time. You love her and you're not doing anything about it because you're afraid she'll either reject you or accept you. That's what you've just told me. Do you realize that?"

"Theodore—"

"Thomas, I'm going to exercise one of the rare privileges of senior middle age and tell you a didactic story from my youth. Are you ready?"

"I'm all ears," he assured me, speaking without the slightest tincture of enthusiasm into his coffee cup.

"When I was seven I had a dog. It was a beagle named Shep."

"Shep?"

"Shep. I apologise for the solecism but, as I said, I was only seven."

"Not much of an excuse, Theodore."

"One day, Shep was hit by a car and died. I was of course inconsolable. My parents were understanding. After a suitable period of grief, my father informed me that I was going to get a new dog."

"Another beagle?"

"We hadn't reached that issue. I told my father that I didn't want another dog, that I loved Shep and Shep was the only dog I'd ever want."

"Sentimental little cuss, weren't you?"

"Look who's talking. Anyway, my father informed me that I

was indeed going to get another dog, and that further exposition of my views on the question was not necessary. He then explained to me, somewhat less brusquely, that if I wished to experience the gratification of love, I had to accept the concomitant risk of loss. There is no love without risk. It was to teach me this important lesson that I was going to get a replacement for Shep whether I liked it or not."

" 'Thank you for listening to Sermonette.' "

"The application of this parable to your situation is obvious," I said.

He glanced up, cocking his eyebrows skeptically.

"You should take your chances with Sandy," I continued. "Then, if things don't work out between you, you should get yourself a puppy."

I think that it showed great presence of mind on his part that Thomas reached over and picked up my Coke and threw that in my face, instead of splattering me with his own coffee. As I sat there, my face and three-piece tweed suit dripping Coca-Cola, he looked at me for a moment, absolutely appalled by what he had done.

Then he burst out laughing. I felt that I'd done a fair afternoon's work.

Chapter 20

I had a distaste for asking direct questions, a practice that I considered ill-bred. This had handicapped me during my brief career as a reporter in Providence, Rhode Island, but not as much as you might think. Direct questions tighten a man up. . . . What you want is to get him to tell his story. After he has, you can ask clarifying questions, such as "How did you come to have the ax in your hand?"

—A. J. Liebling

The curtains weren't lace, but the doily underneath the bowl of fruit on the dining room table was. The table itself was maple, not varnished cherry. The fruit in the bowl was real, not wax. The bowl was Royal Doulton china, not polished clay.

They were drinking hot tea from cups that showed red sailing ships gliding across red oceans. Bridget O'Rourke had offered Sandy coffee, tea, or lemonade. No liquor, no wine, no beer.

"She never wanted to do anything but litigation. In law, I mean. She told me she refused to take trusts and estates in law school. She said that New York firms always tried to push women into their probate departments, so she deliberately made herself unqualified for that."

Bridget O'Rourke was in her mid-fifties. Her face was doughy, her hands plump and milk white. She wore a navy blue dress with white cuffs, plain but well made. She spoke in a dry, matter-of-fact voice, her eyes searching her visitor's face as she talked, as if to get a reading on how she was doing.

"She decided she wanted to be a lawyer well before she went to high school. She went to every courtroom movie that came to town. I know it sounds silly, but it's the kind of thing you remember."

"Yes," Sandy said, "I imagine it would be."

"What she really loved was the puzzle, taking pieces and putting them together. She thought that if she worked things just right, she'd get to a point where she could actually have that be what she did as a lawyer, figure out how things had happened."

Sandy sipped her tea. She took it with lemon but without sugar. Bridget O'Rourke's face fascinated her and for seconds at a time she couldn't take her eyes off of it. It was the face of a woman who hadn't known hardship or deprivation for many years, who had come to accept the comfortable home and plentiful food and elegant furniture as part of a natural and unchanging order. And yet, at the same time, a resignation in her brown eyes, a glimmer of quiet irony in her expression suggested a sense of tragedy that had lurked there long before she had answered her phone and learned that her only daughter was dead.

Bridget O'Rourke's great-grandfather had carried hods full of bricks. Her grandfather had worn a blue uniform and carried a billy club. Her father had worn a green eyeshade and sleeve-garters and had kept the books for a city of Boston public agency. Her husband sold paving materials and ready-mix concrete, figured out a way to make colored concrete blocks cheaply just in time for the housing boom after World War II, and bought linen tablecloths for Bridget instead of whiskey for himself. And through it all, Sandy sensed, as the money accumulated and the O'Rourkes settled into the upper-middle-class respectability that the hod carrier and the cop and the patronage worker had dreamed about, just as her ancestors had known that they would wake up one morning with the sweet stench of potato blight in their nostrils, Bridget O'Rourke had known with quiet, implacable infallibility that the world had heartbreak in store for her.

"The *idea* of the law was very important to her. She always studied very hard. Not just hard. Intensely. The first time she mentioned this Curry gentleman you spoke of was actually an example of that."

"Oh?"

"Yes. Over Christmas break of her first year, she told us a story about how one of her classmates had asked her out and she'd said no because she was too busy. Anyway, this young law student—it turned out to be this Curry—said that she had to take some time off from the books and have some fun. And she said, 'The law is a jealous mistress.' And so he said, 'What does that make you?' She thought it was very funny."

"I suppose it was. How did you find out it was Thomas she told that story about?"

"The second time she mentioned him, she used his name. And she commented that he'd been the one in that story."

"He must have made more of an impression than he appreciated."

"Perhaps that's true. The second time was just before her third year. She spent a long weekend with us after her summer job was over and just before the term began. She was upset—as upset as she ever got, which wasn't very, if you had known her—because something had gone wrong at the firm where she'd worked over the summer, and she was afraid she wouldn't get an offer to go back and work there permanently."

"And she mentioned Thomas in that connection?"

"She said there were three suspects. About the thing that had gone wrong, I mean. That's the way she referred to it. There was someone at the firm who was sort of looking out for her, and she'd talked to him about it. She meant three people that the firm thought might have given the information out that was leaked. She was one of them and this Mr. Curry was another."

"I see."

"I don't remember the third. A typist she said."

"Gloria Monday?"

"I don't remember. It could have been that."

Sandy dabbed brown specks of tea from the corners of her mouth. Bridget O'Rourke watched her placidly, a faint and faraway smile flickering now and again across her face. In the living room beyond the door, her husband sat in a recliner in the center of the room and numbly watched skittering blue images pass across the television set. Sandy occasionally heard snatches of sound from it, always of commercials: "Outstanding. *And* they are mild." "You expect more from Standard. And you get it." "It's what's up front that counts. If it hasn't got it there it hasn't got it."

"You're either extremely tactful or extremely patient," the older woman said.

"That is very kind, but why do you say this?"

"You're obviously interested in Katherine's death, but you haven't asked me whether I know of any reason that she might have been despondent just before she died. I've talked with several outsiders about this—the police from New York and a rather earnest young man from the FBI and someone from Frampton Electronics—and they all brought that matter up right away. Very delicately, but unmistakably."

The first suggestion of bitterness marred Mrs. O'Rourke's voice. Suicide, for a believing Roman Catholic, is the gravest of all possible sins. The drunk, the adulterer, the apostate, even the murderer offend God mortally, but they can still repent and be forgiven. The suicide commits the dreadful sin of Despair, of irrevocably giving up hope in God, and in the very act of sinning cuts himself off from any possibility of redemption.

"I don't believe your daughter killed herself," Sandy said.

Mrs. O'Rourke looked at the young woman across the table from her. She had had considerable experience of late with white lies told to spare her feelings, and she thought she knew how to tell the difference between those and the truth. A current of understanding passed between her and the young French-woman.

"Because of the rosary," Mrs. O'Rourke said.

"Yes."

"I tried to explain that to them, to the others, but they wouldn't understand. They sat there bobbing their heads like they were fooling someone, but I could read in their eyes what they really thought. They thought I was a naive old woman, a pious simpleton. I could almost hear the words going through their heads: 'Sure, sure Mrs. O'Rourke. The rosary. But we fish three dozen micks a year out of the East River, Mrs. O'Rourke, and they've all got a rosary in their pockets and a medal of the Blessed Virgin around their necks and they kill themselves just the same.' I knew all that. That wasn't what I was talking about."

"I think I understand."

"I think perhaps you do. You see, Patrick and I bought that rosary in Rome on what we called our second honeymoon. It was really our first honeymoon—our first real one. It wasn't until 1949 that we finally had a little money and we decided we could take the trip. It was the most wonderful time we ever spent together. We had an audience with Pope Pius the Twelfth—I don't mean a private audience, there were about three hundred people there, but it was special to us—and the rosary was one of the things we kept to remember the trip by. I gave it to Katherine when she graduated from St. Mary's Academy."

"Yes. I thought it must be something like that."

"I don't know if Katherine was still practicing her faith. I'm not saying she wouldn't have slept with someone she wasn't married to or that she went to Mass every Sunday. You can't be sure about that kind of thing when your only contact is three days over Christmas every year and a phone call after the eleven o'clock news on Sunday night."

"No."

"But she wasn't a thoughtless person, Miss Cadette. She wasn't hurtful. She wouldn't have killed herself with that rosary in her purse. She would have found a way to get it back to me and been sure I had it. She wouldn't have just left it there, knowing it was going to be pawed over by policemen and medical examiners."

"Yes. I have thought about it a good deal and I am quite certain that you are right."

"I think that you and I are the only ones who believe that."

"At least one other person believes it."

Mrs. O'Rourke looked up from her handkerchief.

"What do you mean?"

"Whoever killed her knows the truth, just as we do."

"Yes," Mrs. O'Rourke said softly. "That's what it means, isn't it? It's funny, Miss Cadette. That thought must always have been there but there's something about just saying it flat out, the way you just did, that's very chilling. I can almost appreciate why the others instinctively seized on suicide as the most, the most comforting explanation of—of what happened."

"Mrs. O'Rourke, do you have any idea of what Katherine was working on at Frampton Electronics just before she died?"

"No. I'm sorry. She only called us on Sunday nights and we never talked about work. It's funny. The man from Frampton Electronics asked the same thing."

"Did she mention the phrase 'badger game' at all?"

"No. I'm sure I would have remembered that."

"Did you get to know her husband very well?"

"Only in general." Bridget O'Rourke smiled briefly. "We weren't close. Katherine's husband is a WASP. You see—this is difficult—you see, I think one of the reasons Katherine married Drew Ferguson was that she wanted to, not escape, really, but get away from being Boston Irish. We did our best to like Drew, but I have to confess that our relations were what I would call formally polite."

"I see. The man from Frampton Electronics—did he for his part say anything that might suggest what your daughter was working on?"

"No. In fact, he was very guarded in the way he phrased his questions, as if he wanted to keep from giving me any hint about what Katherine was doing."

"You have been very helpful. Would it be possible, do you think, for me to look at her room before I go?"

"If you like. When she was last here, over Christmas, she stayed in the room she had when she was growing up, of course. I'm sure she left nothing, but it couldn't hurt to look."

"Thank you."

Mrs. O'Rourke led Sandy into the living room, up a flight of stairs and into the first bedroom at the top. As they passed through the living room the television blared what sounded to Sandy's unpracticed ears like random nonsense: "Double your pleasure, double your fun."

Katherine's room reminded Sandy of a noncommissioned officer's quarters, ready for inspection. Bed made. Rug vacuumed. Dresser top dusted and bare except for a handful of debate trophies and a small, framed portrait. Closet door closed. Ashtray without the slightest smudge of gray. Sandy knew even as Mrs. O'Rourke opened drawers and examined shelves that nothing relating to Katherine Colleen Ferguson's work was in the room.

"No, I'm sorry," Mrs. O'Rourke confirmed. "There's not a thing. If she ever had anything here, she took it back to New York with her."

"Do you have a photograph of your daughter?"

"Well, we do have photographs, but we prefer to keep them."

"Of course."

Mrs. O'Rourke picked the portrait up from the dresser.

"This may do as long as it's handy. Patrick and I really don't like it very much."

Sandy looked intently at the framed painting. It was sixteen by twenty inches, one edge pulled away from the frame. The young woman in the portrait was elegant and detached, her eyes laughing at you, her expression challenging you to figure out what she was laughing about. Her black hair was pulled straight back from her forehead and parted in the middle. Her dark eyes were cool and reserved. Her face was round, like her mother's, but she had opened her mouth slightly in an effort to elongate her cheeks and disguise the roundness. She was wearing a white blouse, buttoned to the throat and unadorned except for a black velvet band around the neck.

"She brought that portrait back the last time she visited before she brought Drew here to meet us," Mrs. O'Rourke said. "She asked us to keep it."

"Oh? You did not have it made?"

"Oh no. I'm not sure where it came from. It's only a fair likeness, it seems to me. It makes her look so calculating, so remote. I don't know who painted it."

"I do," Sandy breathed, for she had seen Harrison Tyler's work before.

Wednesday

Chapter 21

If I were to visit Italy my curiosity would be more attracted
by convents than by palaces; though I am afraid that I should
find . . . life in both places supported with impatience and
quitted with reluctance. That it must be so soon quitted is
a powerful remedy against impatience; but what shall free
us from reluctance? Those who have endeavoured to teach
us to die well, have taught few to die willingly. . . .

—Boswell's *Life of Johnson*

To meet Drew Ferguson I went to the New York Athletic
Club. Unlike most of the other standard-issue accoutrements
associated with New York's monied establishment in 1962—
the Stork Club, Georgian and Tudor architecture, the Metropolitan Opera, St. Bartholomew's Episcopal Church and so
forth—the NYAC wasn't essentially an imitation of a European
model. It was a real gym, in the American sense of the term:
a rather Spartan place for men to work up a sweat, with an area
for eating and drinking tacked on as an afterthought. It wasn't
the kind of place where you wore underwear with someone
else's initials on it.

I got there about fifteen minutes early and walked out onto
the gallery overlooking the squash courts to watch Ferguson
finish his match. You can learn a lot about a man—about a
woman too, I suppose, though it didn't occur to me back
then—by watching him play squash.

In squash at the New York Athletic Club, trying too hard to
win was a bit nouveau, because winning wasn't the main thing.
The main thing was to get some stimulating exercise. The sec-

ond thing was to do this without picking up a twelve-stitch gash across your forehead from your opponent's racquet, or giving him one with yours, or suffering a leg injury that might interfere with the winter's planned activities in Gstaad.

If without compromising these objectives you could score fifteen points before the other fellow, that was splendid—but that was a subsidiary goal. The notion that winning should take precedence was a plebian misconception, propagated by people who played sports for money rather than for, well, sport.

What you could learn by watching someone play squash was whether he knew this. If he did, that was significant, because there wasn't any course you could take or book you could read that would let you in on it. It was part of a life attitude that you assimilated effortlessly if you'd been correctly brought up by the right people. It was one of the things that distinguished Us from Them. We knew it and They didn't.

Drew Ferguson knew it.

I walked back to the club room to wait for him. He sauntered in right on schedule, wearing a sky blue blazer, light tan shirt with dark brown tie, and dark slacks. He was tanned, blond-haired and clear-eyed, pushing forty but not yet showing it around the midsection. He looked exactly like the guy in all those 1930s movies who periodically stuck his head into the drawing room, smiled cheerily, and asked, "Tennis anyone?"

Instantly, and without the slightest rational basis, I made a snap judgment: spoiled rich kid who'd deliberately dipped into the middle class for a wife just to get one back on pater and mummy.

I stood up to draw his attention. A waiter came over immediately.

"Scotch and soda," Ferguson told the waiter, without waiting to be asked.

"Thank you for seeing me," I said to Ferguson as we shook hands and sat down.

"Happy to do it. Cousin Artie spoke well of you and said that I might be able to be of help to you."

I had called Cousin Artie—Arthur Van Meyer—that morning to ask for an introduction to Ferguson. Sigmund Warburg had just invented Eurodollars, and I was in the process of helping one of Cousin Artie's partners make his first, tentative exploration of that exotic commodity. The world of New York money was a small one. If there was somebody in it that you wanted to talk to, you could almost always find somebody you already knew who could ease things along.

"I was very sorry to hear about Mrs. Ferguson."

"Yes. Quite a jolt." He had a tight, stiff-upper-lip expression on his face. IBM and General Motors suspending dividends on the same day would be "a bit of a jolt." When he said "quite a jolt," he meant it.

The waiter reappeared. He handed Ferguson a tumbler of slightly diluted scotch.

"Katherine and I met at the blood bank," Ferguson said, after the waiter had again drawn away. "We were both AB negative, which is fairly rare, and we ended up getting called to donate on the same day."

"That's a little out of the ordinary."

"Everything about her was extraordinary. I was lying there on the couch or bed or whatever you call those things that you lie on to give blood. She was lying on the one next to mine, and I noticed she was reading a Spanish-language newspaper. Do you know what the title was?"

I spread my hands to indicate ignorance.

"The Mexican Bond Buyer."

"Not exactly light reading."

"No. Then I noticed that she had a Spanish-English pocket dictionary sitting on her tummy, and every once in a while she'd pick it up to look up a word. You see the point?"

"I'm not sure I do."

"She was teaching herself to read Spanish, and she was doing it strictly to help her in her career. I mean, she was lying there with a needle in her arm and a pint of her blood flowing out through a tube, and her first instinct was to use this thirty minutes of enforced leisure to brush up a language skill that might or might not come in handy four or five years down the road."

"That was what attracted you?"

"Not at first. At first it repelled me. She was attractive enough, in a rather Celtic kind of way, but I thought she was one of those single-minded, asexual drones who can't think of anything but getting and spending."

"What changed your mind?"

"The first thing she said to me."

"What was that?"

"I can't remember. But she had the most beautiful voice I've ever heard. It was a rich, rolling contralto, and she had an instinct for modulation that just took my breath away. I sat there like a fifteen-year-old on his first date, trying to think of things to say just so I could keep hearing her speak."

"Remarkable," I said.

"There's something I should perhaps explain," Ferguson responded. "You see, I was blind from the age of two until I was twelve. Some kind of arterial abnormality that pinched my optic nerve. It finally took surgery to correct it. Anyway, I got in the habit of forming first impressions based on what I picked up aurally."

"I can imagine."

"I told her that I thought she had an extraordinary speaking voice, and then I just blurted out that she ought to come with me to read for Books for the Blind. It was a terribly rude thing to say, but it just came out."

"Did she do it?"

"Yes. She agreed instantly."

"Very generous of her."

"She wouldn't have thought of it in those terms," Ferguson explained. "Once I'd pointed out to her what a marvelous voice she had, reading for others became something she had to do. She couldn't just write out a check to pay for the cost of having someone else come in to read for a year. Actually reading herself was a moral debt, sort of a way of paying God off for giving her a lovely voice. She was very old-fashioned in a lot of ways like that, and I'm afraid I found it captivating."

"I can well understand why. She must have found something captivating about you as well."

"Me?" Ferguson said. "Yes, she did, of course, but in a very different kind of way. I remember once she put together something she called a sale-and-leaseback arrangement for a small college my mother's family has endowed in Pennsylvania. I'm sure it would've seemed routine to a commercial lawyer, but it impressed the blazes out of me. It seemed like inventing money out of thin air. So I told her she was a genius. Can you imagine what she said?"

"What?"

"She shook her head and said, 'You're the genius, Drew. I just work hard.' "

"Did you know what she meant by that?"

"No, so I asked her. What was I a genius at? She said, 'Living.' "

"Fairly cryptic."

"She meant that I was able to live in the way that, in her view, an intelligent and cultivated person would wish to live, virtually all of the time. She meant that I was able to have everything necessary to make me happy, and the things that made me happy were things that a person ought to want, instead of things that most people do want."

"Was she right?"

"She was indeed—until she died."

"I'm sorry. I—"

"Don't be. This is the first conversation I've truly enjoyed since she died. You can't imagine how much pleasure I experience just sitting here and talking about her."

"Do you have any idea what she was working on when she died?"

"No. She was very firm about that. She never discussed work with anyone away from work."

Ferguson finished his scotch and looked at me rather indulgently, like J.P. Morgan examining an office boy who showed some promise.

"I have the feeling that you're tiptoeing around the question you really want to ask," he said then.

"You're right," I admitted. "In the last year I've negotiated commercial contracts worth over ten million dollars in six countries on four continents in three different languages, but I feel tongue-tied sitting here talking to you about your—your recently deceased wife."

"*Figée.*" He nodded.

"Frozen?" I asked, trying to translate the French.

"I think in this context I'd translate it as 'constipated.' Not you. Our whole way of dealing with grief and death."

"You're exactly right. Precisely what I want to know is what I'm most reluctant to ask."

"I'll make it as easy for you as I can. Katherine drank gin and tonics, she didn't smoke marijuana. She read the *Atlantic Monthly* and *Saturday Review*, not Marxist poetry. Her idea of heaven was champagne brunch and the Sunday *New York Times*, not flying a kite in Central Park."

"You must have loved each other very much."

"I loved her. She admired me."

"Perhaps, for her, it was the same thing."

"Katherine was a complicated person. There were dimensions of her that I never knew. But I didn't care about knowing those kinds of things. I'm a worldly man, Mr. Furst. She was twenty-six when I married her. I accepted her on her own terms. Could she have been harboring some dark and terrible secret that related in some way to her death? Yes, I suppose so. Do I think she was? I don't know. I don't think so but in perfect honesty I can't say that I know for certain."

"I know exactly what you mean." I thought about my first wife.

"You see, before I met Katherine, I always thought of women as the one plausible argument for the existence of God. They're just so ideal in the way they fill in the gaps that men leave.

They're a perfect fit. There are only a few things worth having that you can't get from men, but those are exactly the things you can get from women. Women are complements par excellence."

"If they didn't exist, we'd have to invent them," I remarked, trying to suggest irony.

"Exactly," Ferguson agreed. "I suspect that that's what accounts for the prevalence of a particular variety of homosexuality in the performing arts."

"I take it you are fairly discreet in your expression of this view." What he was saying was rather outré, even for 1962.

"To be sure. But you're missing the point."

"Then by all means enlighten me."

"Katherine was a totally new experience for me as far as women are concerned. She was self-contained—fully sufficient just as Katherine. She was much more than I'd ever thought of a woman as possibly being. Finding her for me was like someone who'd been using books as paperweights for years suddenly discovering that he could read them. She was one of a kind."

I signed the check the waiter had left, and stood up.

"Thank you very much for talking to me."

"My pleasure. I've talked a very long time but I'm afraid you haven't learned much."

We shook hands and I left.

Ferguson was wrong. I had learned that he had loved Katherine Colleen O'Rourke Ferguson. I had learned that he had loved her more, or perhaps in a different way, than she had loved him. From Ferguson's twenty-six years old/worldly man remark I surmised confidently that she had had at least one lover before she married Ferguson, that he knew about it and didn't care. I had learned that Mrs. Ferguson was someone who was unlikely to be in a cheap Broadway hotel unless she had a good reason for being there. I had learned that I was very angry that she was needlessly dead. And I had learned to be skeptical of snap judgments. Not a bad piece of work, in my humble opinion.

Chapter 22

At the approach of a major decision in a difficult situation,
the colleagues whom he consulted always heard him begin
with a disastrous hypothesis. From that point, he proceeded
by apocalyptic amplification.

> —Anne and Pierre Rouanet,
> describing Charles de Gaulle

I like New York when it rains. It's an eccentric taste, but I
can't help it. The yellow cabs lined up bumper to bumper the
length of the block and six lanes wide on Lexington or Park
look sleek and glistening in a downpour. The pavement seems
washed and fresh. The lighted windows in the office buildings
make the afternoon streets seem like friendly, populated valleys
instead of empty canyons hidden from the sun. Even the traffic
cops in their cowled, bright yellow slickers brighten things up,
which is one thing they don't accomplish in regulation blue.

I don't even mind walking in the rain, as long as I don't have
to go more than five or six blocks. When it's a gentle, spring
rain, as it was this time, I actually enjoy it. Partly that's because
I always wear a hat. Always have. I realized full well in 1962
that this was stodgy and conservative and out of synch with the
spirit of "vigor" then in fashion—but it kept my head dry.

On this particular Wednesday—the second day after Harrison
Tyler's death—the rain was perfect for strolling in. I got myself
a decent lunch after my talk with Ferguson and I took my time
going back to the office.

I thought about what Marge and I might do over the weekend. We could see *The Night of the Iguana* at the Royale or

156

Come Blow Your Horn at the Brooks Atkinson. On the other hand, something called *A Thousand Clowns* had opened earlier that month at the Eugene O'Neill. Marge would lobby for off-Broadway, like *The Fantasticks* or *Oh Dad, Poor Dad*, and we'd end up compromising on a musical: We'd already seen *Camelot* and *My Fair Lady* and *How to Succeed in Business*, but we might try *I Can Get It For You Wholesale* at the Shubert, or perhaps *No Strings* at the 54th Street.

But not *Milk and Honey*. I would absolutely refuse to see *Milk and Honey*. Marge would say I shouldn't let *The New Yorker* make my mind up for me, and I'd say, fine, what with parking and dinner you can easily spend thirty dollars on a night that includes a Broadway musical, and I'm not going to spend that kind of money on a play where the sets are more imaginative than the score.

I'm not exaggerating. Those were the kinds of choices we had back then, and that's how casual we were about it. We thought it'd always be that way. None of us dreamed that we were living through the twilight of a golden age; that in a very few years having an array of first-run plays and musicals like that to pick among would seem like a mindless fantasy.

Anyway, I enjoyed my walk and it was close to two when I finally stepped back into the confines of Curry & Furst. I was barely through the front door and hadn't yet reached the reception desk when Thomas pounced on me as if he were the partner and I was the clerk.

"Do you know where Sandy is?" he demanded.

"No I don't."

"Is she back from Framingham?"

"Yes." I escaped from the reception area and began strolling down the hallway toward my office. "She was at her desk at ten-fifteen. She must have left Framingham around dawn. I told her that her efforts were above and beyond the call of duty and that she could easily have justified not coming in until midafternoon. She said she wanted to find out what response I'd received to my query to Europe about our friend Giraud."

"What response did you receive?"

"It came in just before eleven. Mr. Giraud has a checkered and interesting past, starting with some out-of-the-ordinary activities during the war."

"Collaborator or Resistance?"

"Neither one. I think he would say that he was an entrepreneur. Black market, ration-trafficking, and a fairly specialized kind of smuggling."

"What's that supposed to mean?"

"Smuggling human beings. Getting people whose names were on the wrong lists from occupied countries to neutral ones."

"Sounds like a tricky business."

"There were a lot of lists. A lot of people who were involved in it got killed. Giraud didn't. These opportunities naturally diminished with the end of hostilities, however, and Mr. Giraud had to seek other areas of endeavor. Do you know much about Marseilles in the years just after World War Two?"

"No."

"Imagine Chicago in the twenties without the Jazz Age charm."

I had managed, by my deft deflection of his attention from Sandy to Giraud, to get all the way into my own office and hang up my hat and raincoat. I now sat down at my desk. Thomas paced back and forth in front of it, providing a sharp contrast to the picture of serene composure that I presented.

"Are you saying he was mixed up with organized crime?"

"Almost all crime in France is organized. They don't believe in disorganized activities over there."

"Why did he come here?"

"A gang war got under way in Marseilles in 1947. It was a fairly major thing, and the French papers were sort of keeping score, letting their readers know each morning which side was ahead after the previous evening's body count. Giraud had managed to get crosswise of both sides and the *flics* as well. He sized things up, figured that his life insurance premiums were likely to skyrocket if he hung around, got himself some clean papers, and headed for the New World. He got here with only a modest amount of capital and then started doing whatever he did here, which we haven't found out yet."

"My father's inquiries haven't produced any results?"

"Only in a negative sense," I said. "He did get a call this morning from Bad Rug Ralston, who informed him that no one meeting Giraud's description has been involved as an owner, producer, or even a photographer or layout artist that anyone can remember in the field of exotic literature in the New York metropolitan area since the end of World War Two."

"But Giraud's a gangster."

"Or at least was."

"And for all we know Sandy is out by herself with designs on confronting him."

"I'm quite confident that she's doing no such thing."

"Why?"

"Because after she and I discussed this information, we arrived at an understanding that she wouldn't make any effort to contact Giraud until we'd all had a chance to sit down and talk things out and figure out together what we should do next."

"She's perfectly capable of pronounced insubordination."

"No doubt. But she's not capable of breaking her word."

"I'm still not comfortable about the fact that we don't know where she is."

I was about to answer when Mrs. Valbach came in. Mrs. Valbach was the senior secretary at Curry & Furst. She was pushing sixty and her hair was battleship gray, which was perfectly appropriate. She intimidated everyone at the firm, its senior partner included—and that was no mean feat. Reproachfully, she deposited on my desk a stack of pink telephone message slips that I should have picked up myself from the switchboard on my way in. Properly abashed, I rose and thanked her. She murmured a for-the-record acknowledgment and turned her censorious glare to Thomas, whom she correctly viewed as the immediate cause of my dereliction. She then stalked out, looking as if she fully intended to mark demerits against our names in some giant record book buried in the bowels of her desk.

I glanced automatically through the message slips. One of them said that Geoffrey Singleton had called.

While Thomas stood there doing an Actor's Workshop exercise on impatience, I went through the process of returning Geoffrey's call. The end result was the information that Mr. Singleton hadn't yet returned from lunch.

I looked at my watch. Two-ten P.M. That meant that it was 1:10 P.M. in Milwaukee. I wasn't surprised that Geoffrey Singleton hadn't yet returned from lunch. I was just irritated that the rest of America insisted on having its own time, instead of conforming to New York's. I left my compliments and expressed the hope that Mr. Singleton would find it convenient to try to reach me again later in the day.

"This isn't getting us anywhere," Thomas said.

"Thomas, you seem to be a good deal more agitated than the circumstances warrant. You weren't here all morning and it didn't occur to any of us to worry about finding your bullet-riddled body at the end of some dark alley. Have you learned something this morning that's contributing to your anxiety— something that it might be appropriate to share with me?"

"Well, yes, actually, now that you mention it."

"I'm listening attentively."

"I wasn't in this morning because Lieutenant McShea called me and asked me to come down to his precinct. He wanted me to see if I could identify some voices on the tape from Tyler's answering machine. One voice was mine—and the other was Giraud's."

"Hardly surprising, is it? You and Sandy met Giraud at the scene and he said he had an appointment with Tyler."

"Quite right. It was what he said that got my attention."

"What'd he say?"

" 'Harrison, I may have to ask you to lend me a hand.' "

It took a second for the full impact of that to reach me, but when it did I found myself a lot closer to Thomas's nervous attitude than I cared to be.

I sighed and lurched out of my chair. I gathered all the

courage I had. It formed a congealed and unpromising ball in the pit of my stomach. I went out to approach Mrs. Valbach.

"Excuse me," I said to her. "Did Miss Cadette say where she was going when she left the office?"

"She did not." The criticism in Mrs. Valbach's tone was unmistakable. This was a violation of procedure even graver than leaving your telephone messages at the switchboard.

"When did she go out?"

"Around eleven forty-five, about half an hour after you did, Mr. Furst. There were two telephone messages waiting for her. She came out and got them—" pointed glare, emphasizing the fact that at least some people in the office obeyed some of the rules some of the time—"and then left."

"Do you happen to know what the telephone messages were?" Thomas asked.

"Certainly not, Mr. Curry."

"Can you retrieve them?"

She could and did. They were wadded up but not torn. I smoothed the first one out.

" 'Michel Thierry called,' " I read. " 'Time confirmed, place confirmed.' Who's Michel Thierry?"

"He's the chap she fences with," Thomas said. "She missed her session with him last Saturday."

"Okay. I'm not sure that helps much. What does the second one say?" I asked Mrs. Valbach.

"Something about travel plans."

"Travel plans?"

"Yes. It's from a Professor Fauré. It says, 'Cleveland arrangements made.' "

"You coming?" Thomas demanded, already headed for the door.

"I suppose so," I said uncertainly, beginning to follow him.

"Where are you going?" Mrs. Valbach asked.

"You know, Mrs. Valbach, now that I think about it, I don't have the faintest idea. Thomas," I called out after him, "let's start with the telephone."

Chapter 23

Gesta Dei Per Francos
(God's Deeds Done by the French)

> —Title of the first history
> of the First Crusade

It was a good thing we used the telephone instead of rushing headlong down to NYU, because it turned out that Professor Fauré had last seen Sandy about one-fifteen, while I was lingering over my lunch and Thomas was stewing ineffectually in the office. From what we were able to learn about that encounter and what led up to it, however, it wasn't hard to figure out where Sandy had gone next.

Shortly after one o'clock, Fauré was wending his way back to his office from his Contemporary Voices in Art class. He was wending his way back with Arthur Cleveland.

It seems that Cleveland had just spent the last fifty minutes pontificating to Fauré's students. Cleveland enjoyed pontificating—he could've given lessons in it to the pope—and it had been no trouble at all to persuade him to take advantage of an opportunity to do it.

Heading back to Fauré's office, they had passed through the gymnasium—a route that Fauré claimed was a shortcut. Fauré believed that it was the sound of clashing metal that had attracted Cleveland's attention, but it was unquestionably the sight of the flashing swords that had held it.

Cleveland had never seen real fencing before, and from his first glimpse of it his trained eyes were riveted to the delicate, elegant spectacle. The two figures seemed to glide up and down the long canvas mat spread off to one side of the basketball court. Their cream-colored poplin fencing outfits contrasted with their gray wire-mesh masks and the rust-colored suede gauntlets they wore on their right hands. The interplay of color and shape instantly captured his imagination.

What really grabbed him, though, was the moving swords themselves. The tips swished through the air with incredible speed, much faster than he would have imagined. He couldn't actually see the swords touch. He'd see a blur in the shape of a figure eight and then he'd hear the clash of metal on metal, but he never truly saw the point of contact between the blades.

He found himself intrigued by the professional problem of how to go about catching that evanescent blur so that he could later put it on canvas. He couldn't film it without overwhelming the evocative admixture of natural and tungsten light that gave the scene half its impact. He might photograph it, but no camera could provide both the speed and the persistence of vision that his own eyesight did: If the shutter speed were high enough to catch the action the way his eye did, the camera would only stop the blades for a thousandth of a second and would lose the sense of motion; if the shutter speed were low enough to blur the blades, it would falsify the glaring, shadowy light that glinted for a heartbeat from the flashing blades and then winked away.

With ferocious intensity he sought to freeze the scene in his own memory so that he could reproduce it, exactly, shadow for shadow, photon for photon—reproduce it better and with more truth than any camera. His concentration was total. He was oblivious to Fauré, to his surroundings, to everything except the two sweating, masked figures fifteen feet or so away from him.

"Touché," one of the suddenly frozen fencers called.

Cleveland thought the voice sounded familiar.

The two fencers relaxed and took off their masks. Sweat glistened on their faces. Tucking the bulky masks under their left arms, they tugged off their gauntlets and shook hands.

"Miss Cadette!" Cleveland called suddenly. His voice was loud and astonished.

"Mr. Cleveland," she said, as if she were as surprised as he at this encounter. "Professor Fauré. Good afternoon."

Fauré and Cleveland walked over to Sandy and her companion. The other fencer was a man. He was much taller than Sandy, with light brown hair and elongated facial lines that Cleveland thought of disparagingly as aristocratic. Immediately he felt a sense of competition, a predatory rivalry with the strange male.

"I was transfixed by your swordplay," Cleveland said.

"If we had been fighting for really, I would have been the one transfixed," Sandy said. "Père Thierry, please allow me to present Professor Gilbert Fauré and Mr. Arthur Cleveland, a painter. Professor Fauré and Mr. Cleveland, Father Michel Thierry, Society of Jesus."

The thrill of predatory rivalry drained out of Cleveland, leaving a rather sheepish sense of anticlimax behind.

"I've never met a real Jesuit before," Cleveland said. "I was raised in circles where they were spoken of as shadowy characters, given to disguises and conspiracies."

"Then perhaps you have met one without knowing it," Thierry replied.

Cleveland gave no evidence of having gotten the joke. After a moment of awkward silence, Thierry bowed slightly and padded away.

"Interesting fellow, for a priest," Cleveland said, his instinct for verbal faux pas unerring.

"Yes. He was chaplain to my father's unit before my father was sent to Algeria."

"Oh. I see."

Cleveland turned and looked directly at Sandy. She stood there, only slightly shorter than he was, her hair matted with sweat, her face aglow from the recent exercise, her eyes mischievous, speculative, and questioning. To say that Sandy was flirtatious would capture such a tiny and unnuanced portion of the truth as to be seriously inaccurate. She had grown up surrounded by few women but by many men who couldn't help being fascinated by her but who couldn't even consider touching her. In certain moods, she found men genuinely interesting. When one of those moods was on her, all she had to do to incite the male sexual instinct was breathe.

At this moment, two equivalent and acute longings gripped Arthur Cleveland. One was to paint the picture he had seen just before the climax of the fencing practice. The other was to have sex with Sandrine Cadette.

"You must be very warm after that vigorous piece of exercise," he said. "Can I take you somewhere for something to drink?"

"That is very kind, but I must return to my apartment. You see, this lesson was a makeup and was somewhat improvised. Father Thierry and I do not usually fence here at the university, and I lack locker privileges here. I will have to return to my own apartment to take a shower."

"Of course." Cleveland's heart sank for an instant, but the explanation struck him as more elaborate than a simple brush-off would have been. He convinced himself that he was picking up intriguing vibrations. "Of course," he continued, "if you like, my own apartment isn't far from here. I don't want to seem forward, but you'd be most welcome to shower there, if you wish."

Fauré winced. He knew that there were very few suggestions Cleveland could have made that would have shown more con-clusively how ignorant he was of the background and worldview of the woman he was talking to. Fauré's eyes therefore widened in undisguised astonishment when he heard Sandy say, "That is most generous of you. I would be delighted."

As Thomas and I heard from Fauré what had happened, our consternation mounted by the syllable. I was the first one to manage an intelligent question. Well, maybe not an intelligent question. A question that wasn't totally stupid.

"I take it that this whole thing wasn't just happenstance, that it was prearranged in some way?"

"Oh, of course. The morning after Tyler was shot, Sandy called me and asked me as a special favor to invite Cleveland to speak to one of my classes as soon as possible. She explained that I was to make certain that Cleveland got into the gymnasium at some point, and that she would arrange to encounter him there as if by chance. Obviously, she made parallel arrangements with Father Thierry and the encounter took place."

"You moved very quickly."

"I was afraid it was too quickly. I called Cleveland immediately after I talked to Sandy, and he leaped at the opportunity. It was all I could do to convince him that my next class didn't meet until today at twelve-ten."

Thomas was on his feet before we hung up.

"Theodore, we've got to hurry. It's already after two-thirty."

At the moment he said that, I thought it was melodramatic nonsense. But I hurried anyway.

Chapter 24

Well cut, my son. Now we have to sew things back together.

> —Catherine de Medici to Henry III,
> on seeing what was left of the
> freshly assassinated Duc de Guise

Cleveland couldn't sit still. The sound of the water cascading into his bathtub a room and a hallway away increased his tension along with his desire. He prowled around the modest living area of his apartment, drumming his knuckles on the top of his blocks-and-boards bookshelf, clasping his hands behind his back and then abruptly folding his arms across his chest.

He was no stranger to seduction, of men or women. It had been some time, however, since he had seduced someone out of pure lust, as he intended to do in Sandy's case. Most often, at least in the last couple of years, he had seduced people because there was something he wanted from them. The completeness and single-mindedness of his motive for bedding Sandy heightened the excitement he experienced in pursuing her.

He looked with sudden dissatisfaction around the living room and the kitchen that, for all practical purposes, was part of it. He frowned at the foam rubber showing through the split vinyl on his couch. He grimaced at the dingy blanket draped over the armchair to cover the rips in its upholstery. He shook his head at the faded yellow woven-reed rug under his scarred coffee table. The only thing in the room that didn't seem wholly inadequate to the task at hand was the half-finished canvas turned now to face the wall near the door, and the sketchpad and case of brushes and paint lying next to it.

None of this had ever bothered him before. He figured that people who came to his apartment knew they were getting an artist whose life revolved around painting and not a junior account executive who read the *Playboy* Advisor for tips on furnishing his bachelor pad. He couldn't have said why it was bothering him now, and it would never have occurred to him that it was because he was stepping out of his class.

Snatching up the sketchpad and a long number-one pencil, he perched on the armchair and began making tentative strokes depicting the whirring, swishing passages of arms he had witnessed a few minutes before. The shower stopped and almost immediately Sandy's voice from the bathroom interrupted him.

"Excuse me," she called. "Do you mind if I go into your bedroom to look for some more comfortable clothes? I adore men's clothing."

"Not at all," he called cheerfully.

He attacked the sketch with a new zest. It absorbed his attention and he didn't realize how much time was passing. He had drawn both circling tips and the swords attached to those tips and the gauntleted hand and the arm moving one of the swords before Sandy stepped into the room. He looked up in delight.

The delight faded from his face. He had expected her to be wearing one of his pullover sweaters that she could have tugged down to about mid-thigh, or perhaps his pajama top. Instead she was wearing a no-nonsense beige dress. She looked like a young librarian or the assistant prefect of studies at a private girls' school.

"I found nothing that appealed to me," she explained briskly in reaction to his undisguised disappointment.

She was carrying a large canvas bag that he assumed was stuffed with her fencing outfit. She had her purse on a strap over her shoulder and she was holding her sword in her right hand, just below the hilt, a folded white handkerchief between her hand and the blade. Astonishing though it seemed to him, Cleveland saw no way to avoid the unwelcome conclusion that she was about to leave.

"Wait!" he said, rather suddenly. "Wouldn't you like something to drink? Beer or water or—" he thought about the sticky, sweet Ripple that was the only wine he had in the apartment and decided that offering her that would likely do more harm than good—"or, something," he concluded weakly.

"Thank you, but I really must get back to my office. I do have a job, you know."

She smiled and started to walk toward the door.

"Wait!" he enjoined her again. He leaped out of his chair and got between her and the door. Improvising madly, he looked around for some excuse to keep her there. His eyes fell on the sketch he'd been working on.

"Look!" he instructed her, raising the drawing and pointing to it. "Your fencing practice this afternoon."

"That seems a very impressive start. I hope you will show me the final work. Would you mind getting the door for me? My hands are full."

"One moment. Please. You can help me."

He dropped the sketchpad at his feet. He raised his hands, thumbs at right angles and pointing tip to tip a few inches apart, as if framing a movie shot.

"I need to see that flash of light on the tip of the foil, that blur when the tip has already moved but your eye continues to see it."

She smiled again, tolerantly this time.

"Very well."

She dropped the canvas bag and her purse, flipped the sword up and caught the hilt. He was waiting for her to duplicate the side-on view that he had gotten in the gymnasium. When, instead, she turned her right profile toward him and flicked the sword a quarter-inch or so from his nose, he leaped back and slammed his right shoulder painfully into the door behind him.

"Be careful," he said, pressing his back rather urgently against the wall. "That was almost assault."

"It *was* assault, actually," Sandy said. "It was *almost* battery."

The sword flicked again and sliced effortlessly through wheatstraw wallpaper a few centimeters from Cleveland's left ear. For the first time he realized that her sword wasn't a blunt-end fencing foil but a naked-edge sabre—a French Army light cavalry sabre, to be exact.

"That is assault," she explained. "This is battery." Her left hand streaked up and slapped his face. "You see the distinction?"

She waited for an instant. Cleveland tried to look at the lacerated wheatstraw without moving his head.

"Assault," she said then. Flick.

"Battery." Slap.

"Assault." Flick.

"Battery." Slap. "You see the distinction?"

"Don't do that again," he said.

She slapped him again.

He wanted to push himself off the wall and attack her, shove her away, knock her down. He told his muscles to do it, willed them to do it. But he couldn't take his eyes off the naked steel in her right hand, and his body disregarded the instructions.

"You are very foolish," she said. "You should have gotten rid of the shoes."

The whites of his eyes seemed to swallow the irises. His voice sounded strangled when it finally came out.

"What do you mean?"

"Stop talking like an idiot. While I was in your bedroom, I found the canvas shoes you were wearing the night I met you at the Ackley. They are obviously the shoes you usually wear. There was roof tar stuck to the soles of both shoes."

"And so?"

"The day Tyler was killed, when Thomas and I saw you in the coffeehouse beneath Tyler's flat, you were wearing loafers."

"That's why I have them. To wear them when sneakers wouldn't be appropriate."

"They were no less appropriate at the scheduled unveiling of Tyler's work than they had been at the Ackley. Hypothesis: You were wearing canvas shoes when you first went to Tyler's flat that day; you entered the flat, did something that made you want to leave without being seen, and exited through his attic, up to the roof and down the fire escape; in the process, on the unseasonably warm day, you got roof tar all over the soles of your canvas shoes; recognizing that this might be incriminating, you came back to your own apartment, changed shoes, and returned to be present at the hour scheduled for the unveiling. Owing to your own stupidity, however, you failed to dispose of the canvas shoes, but left them where I could find them by a ruse that should not have deceived a child. As I said, you are very foolish."

"Hypothesis, you called it, and that's all it is."

"No. The roof tar is a fact. And this is a fact."

From her dress pocket she drew a scrap of painting canvas no more than a few centimeters in area.

"What's that supposed to be?"

"A piece of canvas that I'm confident the police will be able to prove came from the painting *Badger Game* that was displayed in ruins near Tyler's body. It stuck to the sole of your shoes while you were destroying the painting, and was then glued into place by the roof tar while you were making your escape."

She put the scrap back into her pocket.

"*Quod erat demonstratum*," she said.

"You're making a mistake," Cleveland said. His voice now was dry and despairing, as if he no longer even hoped to be believed.

"Tell me the mistake I am making."

"You're right. I went to see Tyler. I saw that—that obscene atrocity of a painting that savaged me and savaged my work. And you're right: I went to work on that painting with a scraper and a jackknife and my bare hands and I ripped it and shredded it and did everything I could to destroy it. But I didn't kill Tyler."

"Of course not. He saw what you'd done and committed suicide in black despair over the destruction of his work."

"No."

"Americans have no sense of irony."

"No," Cleveland repeated. "I don't know how he died. But he was already dead when I walked into the room."

"And your reaction to coming upon a corpse was to turn *Badger Game* from representational satire into Dada."

"You have to understand. When I walked into the room, I must've been initially conscious of him there at the table, but almost instantly all I could see and all I could think of was that vile, hideous piece of trash. I'll grant you, if he'd been alive and standing there I probably would've killed him, or tried to. My blood was pounding, screaming. I couldn't think of anything else until I'd obliterated that. I locked the door behind me and I charged that painting like the Light Brigade charged up San Juan Hill."

"A remarkably engagé approach to art criticism, particularly since Balaclava is a third of the way around the world from San Juan Hill."

"Then, when I'd exhausted myself, I realized that there was a dead man within a few feet of me. I panicked. I knew that I had to get out and get out without being seen. I knew about the attic stairs and the roof and I went out that way. The rest of it was just the way you said."

"How did you know about the attic stairs?"

"I'd been there before," Cleveland said, shrugging and avoiding her eyes. "More than once."

"When did you come to his flat?"

"Around two o'clock Monday afternoon."

"Why?"

"He'd called me on Sunday and asked me to come by before this unveiling that he had set up all of a sudden."

"Why did he call you?"

"I don't know."

"Why did he say he wanted you to see him?"

"He didn't say. I assumed it was because he wanted to try to talk me out of taking legal action over *Badger Game*."

"You must be lying. I very much doubt that he was dead by two o'clock."

"That's when I got to his flat. I didn't go in right away. I wanted to be sure I could go in without being seen. I waited until the counterman at the coffeehouse was doing something in the storeroom and then I went up. It probably wasn't until two-twenty or even a few minutes later."

"You wanted to go in without being seen because you planned to kill him."

"No."

"Then why?"

"I thought—I suspected that he might be having me over there to humiliate me, to set me up, have someone from the fine art press see me leaving the flat just before he unveiled the painting, as if he'd made some last-minute change in response to my being there."

"For someone who lies as poorly as you do, you have a very active imagination."

"I know that it sounds extreme, but you have to understand. People in art circles had been whispering about this painting for weeks, and everyone was saying it was aimed at me. I sound paranoid because I was paranoid."

"What happened when you got to the flat?"

"I went up the stairs. The door was closed. I heard music playing very loudly through the door. You could hear it all the way downstairs. I knocked on the door. There wasn't any answer. I tried the knob. It was unlocked. I went in. The rest of it happened like I've told you."

"What music did you hear?"

" 'Ode to Joy' in the symphonic setting by Beethoven."

"If you were so worried about him humiliating you, why did you go to see him at all?"

"To try to talk him out of using the painting to attack me."

"How can you expect me to believe that? You are an artist. You must have known another artist wouldn't change his work simply because you asked him to."

"I had an argument I expected him to find very persuasive."

"What was that?"

Cleveland nodded minimally toward the canvas turned to the wall, a few feet away from them.

"Turn it around," Sandy commanded.

Cleveland scraped along the wall toward the canvas, keeping

as much distance as he could between Sandy and himself. As soon as he could reach the canvas with his left hand he tried clumsily to turn it over. It fell and landed face up on the floor.

Sandy glanced quickly at it, keeping an eye on Cleveland. It was an early sketch of *Justice Chastising Fame*. It was preliminary, done entirely in heavy pencil. There was no mistaking the fact, however, that in this sketch Justice was chastising Wisdom, not Fame. The likeness was uncanny. Cleveland had captured in gray pencil strokes every nuance of the same mural figure that Tyler had lampooned in *Badger Game*.

"You are saying that Tyler stole from you the concept of satirizing a particular figure from classical allegory," Sandy said. "But this sketch proves nothing of the sort. You could have drawn it yesterday."

"But I didn't draw it yesterday. I drew it months ago, before I could possibly have seen even the earliest study of *Badger Game*. There are half a dozen people who can swear that they saw this long before Tyler began work on his painting."

"Name one."

"Conrad Marek," Cleveland answered. "And believe me: I would have gotten a thousand times more satisfaction out of forcing Tyler to cancel his unveiling and hide his precious painting forever than out of killing him. He would've done it too. He called himself an artist, but he'd never have risked his stinking reputation for the sake of his art."

"You truly hated him, didn't you?" Sandy asked, her tone suddenly tinctured with wonder.

"Passionately. I hated him as much as I love painting."

"Why?"

Again Cleveland avoided her gaze.

"You don't need to know that," he said.

She flicked the sabre and his eyes snapped open.

"Perhaps not," she said, "but you need to tell me."

Cleveland sighed and in the sigh lay the suggestion of a sob.

"He—he *gave* me to Giraud."

"What do you mean?"

"He didn't want Giraud ever to handle any of his paintings again. So he turned me over to Giraud as a substitute."

"I had never heard of Giraud handling Harrison Tyler's paintings."

"You can bet he didn't advertise it," Cleveland spat bitterly. "Once he was established enough to make real money through a reputable dealer, he wanted to forget he'd ever let Giraud peddle anything for him. So he used me to get free of him."

"Why did you let him?"

"It happened at a time when—when I thought I could trust him. Besides, my work is so unorthodox I had to take anything I could get."

"*Bien.*" Sandy stepped back and flexed the sabre, drawing his eye back to the blade. "Now I need for you to tell me what connection all of this has to Thomas Andrew Curry."

"I have no idea. I'd never heard of him until the night we met at the Ackley."

"What connection does it have with Katherine Colleen Ferguson?"

"I don't know."

"You might know her as O'Rourke."

"I have no idea."

The sabre blade flicked again and the edge rested against Cleveland's throat. She pressed in slightly. The whisker-stubbled skin dimpled around the blade. A short high-pitched cry escaped from Cleveland.

"I don't believe you," she said. "You're lying."

"No! I swear to you I'm telling the truth."

"Save your oaths. They will do you no good."

"Please believe me." He had begun to weep and the plea came out in a strangled cry.

"I have no intention of believing you. You must understand something. I love Thomas. I love him enough to kill for him. He is in danger and you know why and I am going to kill you unless you tell me."

Cleveland's lips formed the word "no" but no sound came

out. He pressed his lips together and bubbles of saliva formed around his mouth. A stain darkened the crotch of his khaki slacks as he lost control of his bladder.

"Please," he whimpered. "I don't know."

Sandy stepped back and lowered the sabre. Cleveland sagged to the floor, keeping a wary eye on her.

She picked up her canvas bag and her purse.

"I am sorry," she said. "I had to be sure."

Cleveland sat nearly motionless. He had begun panting, taking his breath in shallow spurts.

"Please get the door for me," she said then. "My hands are full."

Chapter 25

Quarry the granite rocks with razors; moor the vessel with a thread of silk. Then may you hope with such keen and delicate instruments as human knowledge and human reason successfully to oppose those giants, the passion and the pride of man.

—Cardinal Newman

"Thomas, what meaning does the word *wasp* have?"

There was nothing intrinsically wrong with this question. In and of itself, it was a perfectly legitimate query. At the time Sandy asked it, however, it came against a background that made it something less than the ideal issue for her to raise. That background can be summarized basically as follows:

Once Thomas and I were out on the street after having learned from Fauré that Sandy was probably at Cleveland's apartment, Thomas muscled two elderly matineegoers out of the way to get us a cab. I got an umbrella across the shins for Thomas's trouble.

We offered the cabbie a huge bribe to get us to Cleveland's address near Washington Square in less than ten minutes, and the cabbie responded by finding every traffic jam, construction project, and pothole between midtown and the Village. After twenty-one bone-jolting, nerve-jangling minutes, we pulled up with heaving stomachs and bruised extremities to the West Broadway address we'd asked for.

Even though the cabbie hadn't come close to the ten-minute deadline, we gave him half the exorbitant tip we'd promised, climbed out, and asked him to wait for five minutes with the meter running. He cursed us roundly, proposed an improbable exercise in sexual gymnastics, and screeched away with more energy and driving skill than he'd shown at any point during the trip we'd engaged him for.

We turned toward Cleveland's building. We were rewarded by the sight of Cleveland hurtling away from it—and us—at a very respectable speed. He was already close to a block away, so there was no reason to believe that our arrival had provoked his flight. Thomas yelled after him, to no discernible effect, and then took off in pursuit. Having nothing to contribute to that effort, I stepped into the building's entryway and began filling a pipe.

I had barely succeeded in getting it lit when Thomas returned, quite breathless. Cleveland had bolted down the steps of the Bleecker Street IRT station and Thomas had reached the platform just in time to see a train pulling away.

We consulted gravely but urgently about what to do next. We decided that as long as we were in the building anyway we might as well go to Cleveland's apartment and see what we could find out. We did so, thinking it fortunate, initially, that the lock on the security door inside the entryway was broken. Arriving outside the apartment of a man we had just seen leaving the building, we knocked. Or, rather, Thomas knocked. There are depths of inanity to which I refuse to descend, even in the interest of social convention.

Not surprisingly, there was no answer to Thomas's knock. He tried the door. Not surprisingly, it was locked.

"Sandy!" he yelled. "Are you in there? Are you all right?"

These questions went unanswered, unless utter silence can be construed as an answer. It's an interesting philosophical question. I'll have to ponder it sometime.

He turned toward me.

"What do you think we should do?" he asked.

You can acquire a considerable reputation for sober wisdom if, instead of saying something obvious the moment you have the opportunity to do so, you make it a practice to hold your peace, puff on a pipe, and then say something obvious. I did this.

"I think we should call the police," I said through a cloud of King Edward smoke, after a suitable pause.

The moment after I had made this recommendation, the door to Cleveland's apartment opened. It opened in a hurry. I was conscious of a blue-gray blur before something hard and meaty hit me in the diaphragm and knocked me winded onto my backside.

To Thomas's credit, he got in one good punch. Unfortunately, it was a Princeton punch. It was forthright, solid, and technically proficient, but it wasn't anything like enough to stop the other half of the blur from stepping firmly onto Thomas's instep, raking the front sight of a snub-nose revolver across Thomas's left cheekbone, smacking his nose and mouth with the hand that held the revolver, and bouncing his head off the corridor wall.

The blur made it to the stairs and the landing below before Thomas could react. He shook his head to clear it and gamely dashed for the stairs, but I extended a leg and tripped him before he could get there. I saw John Wayne do that in *Sands of Iwo Jima* and I figured I'd never get another chance to try it.

"There are at least two of them," I explained as he looked furiously at me, "and they've got at least one gun. You're not going to do Sandy any good by getting your brain tissue smeared all over the ceiling of this fetid rat-trap."

I walked to the end of the hallway and looked through a grimy window to see if by some incredible stroke of luck the two men who had blurred past us might climb into a car with a license plate that I could read. That didn't happen. What did happen, however, surprised me even more.

"What's going on?" Thomas asked.

"Unless I'm very much mistaken," I said, "our assailants are being taken into custody."

Thomas rushed to the window and I pointed with my pipe-stem across the street. Four men in business suits who looked

like they knew what they were doing were bundling two hand-
cuffed men, one wearing a blue jacket and the other a gray
raincoat, into the backseat of a car that had a very long radio
antenna. It occurred to me to send Thomas out to try to flag
the custodians down, but the car was pulling away before I
could begin to act on this ambitious notion.

"Did you notice that extra little bit of technique the one who
hit me had?" Thomas asked. "Planting his foot on my instep
and then letting me have it?"

"A thoroughly unpleasant experience I'm sure," I said.

"It reminded me of the last time exactly the same thing
happened to me—in the Algerian desert."

"What are you suggesting?"

"That the chap in blue and the sergeant in charge of the
troops who arrested me in Algeria got their unarmed combat
training in the same outfit."

I thought that over for a moment.

"I still think we should call the police," I said then.

The police arrived two minutes later. Not because we called
them; we were still looking for a phone. The police arrived
because a tenant had called them quite some time ago, when
she noticed two sinister-looking men break through the security
door and then seek entry into Arthur Cleveland's apartment,
where they proceeded to behave in a sufficiently antisocial fashion to send Cleveland out the door and bolting up the street as
if the devil was after him when he came home and spotted signs
of their forced entry shortly before our own arrival.

So that's how it was that, having received a report about two
sinister-looking men up to no good in the building, the police
arrived and found Thomas and me.

It only took about fifteen minutes to straighten that out. It
was a tedious fifteen minutes, to be sure, but we finally got it
done. I was glad for the nasty and obviously recent cut on
Thomas's cheekbone and the swelling of his upper lip, because
it was that physical evidence that finally convinced the cops I
was telling the truth.

They even let us take a look around Cleveland's apartment.

It had been ransacked: drawers yanked out and their contents spilled onto the floor, furniture slashed open, books pulled off shelves and thumbed through, and so forth. I offered my professional opinion that the two gentlemen who'd manhandled us had been looking for something. One of the police officers gave me a funny look and said we were free to go. In fact, if I read his expression correctly, we didn't really have any choice.

We walked back outside.

There were no cabs in sight.

It was still raining.

We walked to the subway and shared a car back to midtown with a wino, a panhandler, and a Holy Roller preacher speaking in tongues. At least I think it was tongues. Either that or he had a cleft palate.

We got back up to the office. We were rather the worse for wear. We saw Sandy sitting at her desk, reading contentedly through her four-by-six index cards and enjoying a cup of hot tea.

That was when Sandy asked Thomas what *wasp* meant.

" 'Wasp,' " he said, rather tepidly but not without gallantry, "refers to a fairly large insect with a sharp and painful sting."

"That is odd," Sandy said. It wasn't odd that we were back in the office, tired, soaked, sore, and battle-scarred, after having chased her fruitlessly over half of Manhattan. It was odd that the word *wasp* referred to an insect.

"Odd?" Thomas asked. Frustration and annoyance sharpened his voice.

"Yes. Is the term ever used with reference to people? Especially in a disparaging way?"

"Oh. You mean WASP."

"Yes. That is what I said."

"WASP is an acronym."

"Excuse me?"

"*Un sigle*," I explained.

"Oh, I see. It stands for what, please?"

"White Anglo-Saxon Protestant," Thomas said.

"Ah, that fits then. It was the only thing Mrs. O'Rourke told me that I hadn't understood. Thomas, does that mean that you are a WASP?"

"I suppose it does. At least if *Protestant* is taken as describing an attitude rather than an affiliation."

"Yes, I think I am beginning to understand."

"Sandy," Thomas said, "may I ask you a question?"

"Of course," she snapped, still absorbed with the index cards.

"Where in the bloody—where exactly have you been?"

She glanced up, surprise written plainly across her face.

"I have been to an improvised fencing lesson at New York University, and then I stopped and had a discussion with Mr. Cleveland. I learned some interesting things that we should discuss without delay."

"I daresay," I interjected in an effort to lighten things up, for I could see that they needed lightening.

"Maybe ensure." She grinned at me.

"Come again?"

"Maybe ensure," she repeated. "It is an idiom I learned from Thomas. He told me that it means the same as 'you betcha.' " She glanced from the blank expression on my face to the exasperated one on Thomas's and she leaped to a conclusion. "Isn't that the meaning?" she demanded. "Thomas, have you been having fun with me again?"

"No, Sandy, it's—"

"It is aging, Thomas. *Ce n'est plus drôle.*"

"Sandy, this is a misunderstanding."

"Another misunderstanding?"

"Yes. You see—"

"Thomas, you are a very poor liar."

"That's not true," he said, quite calmly. "I am an excellent liar."

"Thomas," I said, "calm down."

"Please leave my office," Sandy said in a tone of icy dismissal.

"I will not calm down and I will not leave anyone's office. Theodore and I have spent the better part of two hours chasing all over this misbegotten island trying to protect you and—"

"Trying to protect me from what?"

"—you have the nerve to sit here drinking tea while—"

"Trying to protect me from what?"

"—we're being jolted through traffic and roughed up by thugs and very nearly arrested, not to mention made the object of an evangelical sermon in two dead languages simultaneously."

"Trying to protect me from what?"

"Trying to protect you from the kind of people who gave me this extra opening on my left cheek."

"I can protect myself, thank you very much."

"Can you indeed?"

"Yes I *bien certainment* can, you pretentious, exasperating, egotistical WASP. My virtue was never in peril."

"Who said anything about your virtue?"

"That is what you were talking about and do not pretend otherwise. I have already pointed out that you are a poor liar."

"Is that French for 'thank you'?" Thomas asked.

"It is English for mind your own affairs."

"What's that supposed to mean?" Thomas demanded.

"It is supposed to mean that you have been meddling in matters that concern only me, and I want you never to do so again."

"How can you say that?"

"I can say it in French, German, English, or Latin. How would you like to hear it?"

"Very funny."

"Thank you. Do you have any other questions?"

"Just one."

"Ask it quickly, please, and leave."

He leaned forward and rested both of his fists on her desk.

"When was the last time you were spanked?"

She didn't bat an eye or back up an inch.

"Three years ago, during an amateur performance of *Tartuffe*." She leaned forward, put her own knuckles on the desk, and brought her nose to within a smidgen of his. "The actress who played my maid had roughly twice your muscles—which was essential to the plausibility of the scene."

Thomas rocked back and his right bicep flexed and for a

second I thought he was actually going to hit her. Then he did an about-face just the way they teach them in basic training, whipped out of the office, and slammed the door behind him.

I opened the door. It was a psychological gesture, a subtle suggestion that I was in control of the situation and everyone who was left should follow my example of calmness and steadiness. I would have brought it off too, but as soon as I opened my mouth, Mrs. Valbach came charging over with information that couldn't wait.

"Mr. Singleton is on your line, Mr. Furst," she said, implicitly censuring me for not being where I could answer my own telephone. "He says he is returning your call."

Chapter 26

You know, when events speak strongly and you agree on
fundamentals, you can be very flexible about methods. . . .

—Charles de Gaulle

As I picked up the phone to talk to Geoffrey Singleton, I
was shaking my head and talking to myself. Singleton was humming "On Wisconsin."

"Hello?"

"Theodore," Singleton boomed jovially. "Just wanted to
touch base with you on that little matter you asked me to
check on."

"What've you found out?"

"Only this: There has been no significant piece of litigation
involving any company called Frampton Electronics or any
plausible variation on that name pursued in state or federal
court in Milwaukee at least since the first of this year and
probably not for a long time before that."

"You sound very sure."

"I may be in error but I am not in doubt."

"I don't think you're in error either. Okay. Thank you,
Geoff."

"Whenever, Ted. Look me up the next time you're—"

I said "Right" distractedly and hung up without consciously
listening to the rest of his sign-off. It must have registered sub-
liminally, though. About once every five minutes for the next
half-hour I caught myself humming "On Wisconsin."

I sat at my desk, feeling lost and discouraged. One more blind
alley.

For want of anything more useful to do, I decided to have a talk with either Thomas or Sandy to try to get them over their quarrel. I didn't have especially high hopes for this undertaking, but since they were apparently too young to behave sensibly and too old to send to bed without supper, talking to one of them was the only thing I could think of to do.

I flipped a coin and it came up tails. Thomas.

I knew exactly where to find him. Everyone in the firm did. This wasn't the first time he had stalked out of Curry & Furst's precincts after a sharply worded disagreement, and whenever he did he invariably went six floors up, to the library of Leverett, Lodge & Means.

LL&M was an insurance defense firm par excellence. It included 120 lawyers, a scandalously large number for the day. It occupied three entire floors of our building, and its very complete law library took up most of one of those floors. LL&M gave library privileges to us, in exchange for an occasional referral and a few other lawyerly accommodations on our part. Its library was where Thomas went when he got into a snit and didn't feel like a drink.

I found him in a remote corner, reading desultorily through the eightieth volume of the Second Series of the Federal Reporter—80 F.2d for short. You might think this choice of reading material conclusive proof of a personality disorder, but you'd be wrong. Plenty of opinions are as dull as dishwater but a respectable number are filled with inside jokes and coy allusions, and Thomas knew which judges produced each kind and understood the code they used. For him, paging through 80 F.2d was the equivalent of a Cornell English professor working an *Atlantic Monthly* acrostic to decompress after a particularly futile committee meeting.

I pulled 78 F.2d off the shelves, sat down opposite him, and opened the volume on the table between us. He glanced up and gave me his archest, there's-mistletoe-on-my-coattail look.

"Are you still angry?" I whispered.

"No, I am not angry. I'm furious."

"I think you should apologize to Sandy."

"That's the wonderful thing about this country. Everyone's entitled to express his opinion, no matter how idiotic it is."

"That's the problem with young lawyers. They're very sound on the law, but they keep wanting to change the facts."

"You must have renewed your subscription to the Louis Nizer Quote-of-the-Month Club."

"Try to understand how it appeared to her, Thomas. She didn't just fall into an unpleasant situation, as we did. She planned the whole thing very carefully. She never viewed herself as being in any physical danger, and she probably wasn't. She deployed considerable ingenuity gathering what I expect will prove useful information. Then, instead of being congratulated or even given a chance to tell us what she's found out, she finds herself upbraided because she wasn't clairvoyant enough to hang around Cleveland's apartment until we could trip over each other trying to rescue her from peril she was never exposed to in the first place."

"Very eloquent. My father might even be able to sell it to a jury. But I know when someone is gratuitously insulting me, and I don't propose to be understanding about it."

"Of course she was insulting you. But it was hardly gratuitous."

"What do you mean by that?"

"Put yourself in her position: knowing what she knew but not knowing anything about your visit with Lieutenant McShea and that tape he played for you."

"I don't follow the argument."

"Why would you think she was in danger just because she was talking to Cleveland? To her, it had to look as if the thing that sent you scurrying down to the Village was your fear that she was going to interrogate Cleveland from a supine position." This earned me a sharp glance, so I knew I was making progress. "That particular apprehension wasn't well founded, and wouldn't have been any of your business even if it had been."

"You're saying that I insulted her by directing a clumsy rescue effort at her maidenly virtue rather than her physical safety."

"I'm saying that's the way it looked to her, in the heat of the discussion that you two allowed to get out of hand very quickly. Besides," I addeded off-handedly, "there's the subconscious frustration."

"Meaning what?"

"I keep telling you that she's probably as crazy about you as you are about her. She's done everything but announce it to UPI. She correctly deems herself a pretty fair piece of work and she keeps waiting for you to make a move, and all you do is dither in feckless detachment."

"Do you really think that? About her waiting for me to make a move, I mean?"

"Would I sit here and say it if I didn't think it?"

"Of course you would, as long as you thought it'd help prove your point."

"Fair enough. All I can say is test the hypothesis. Apologize to her. Show a little class. You did threaten to strike her, after all."

"Only implicitly. And I was provoked."

"No purely verbal provocation can possibly justify a gentleman's striking a lady."

"Elvis Presley did it in *Blue Hawaii*."

"I rest my case."

"All right," he sighed, pushing 80 F.2d away from him. "Maybe you're right. I'll go tell her I'm sorry."

"Good."

I was feeling pretty good about things. I felt as if I might actually have accomplished something. I stood up to put 78 F.2d back on its shelf. I started humming.

"What's that trite and overdone melody?" Thomas demanded.

I had to stop and think for a second.

" 'On Wisconsin,' " I told him then.

"Try *'Eine Kleine Nachtmusik.'* "

I was in such a good mood that I was actually about to comply when I heard Sandy's voice.

"Thomas," she said, "I have decided that I owe you an apology."

We both looked over at her. She was standing about six feet away, ramrod straight, her face set hard and her hands clasped behind her back.

"I shouldn't have called you a WASP," she continued. "That is a demeaning racial, ethnic, and religious epithet, and it was ill-mannered of me to use it with reference to you. I would have been deeply offended if you had called me a Jansenist, and calling you a WASP is in the same category. I am sorry I did."

I suspect that Thomas spent a moment wondering what in the world a Jansenist might be. I'm not sure because I wasn't paying close attention. What Geoffrey Singleton had said to me at the conclusion of our telephone conversation was struggling to get to the surface, and I was giving it all the help I could.

"Calling me pompous, egotistical, and exasperating, of course, was in a different league altogether," Thomas said.

I think that he was only trying to inject a lighthearted note into the exchange, but Sandy wasn't in a lighthearted mood.

"I am sorry for calling you a WASP," she said. Stiffly, carefully, and precisely.

The light went out of Thomas's eyes and his face went flat, as if you'd pulled a sheer mask over it.

"Very well," he said. His voice was as formal and bloodless as hers. "I accept your apology. No offense taken. I apologize for threatening to hit you."

"Accepted," she said. "I did not view it as a serious threat."

If I had had any mental energy available to follow this dialogue, I would've been more disturbed by it than I had been by the original fight. But I was too concerned with pinning down the maddeningly elusive notion about "On Wisconsin" and Singleton's conversation that was trying to formulate itself in my overworked imagination.

"What are the lyrics to 'On Wisconsin'?" I blurted.

"I have no idea," Thomas said.

Sandy whipped out a pen and wrote the title down.

"I can probably still reach a sheet-music store before five o'clock," she said.

"I don't think that should be necessary," Thomas said.

He searched languidly on the shelf behind him until he found the index to the Wisconsin Statutes. After glancing briefly in that, he pulled out the first volume of the statutes themselves. And there it was, in section 1.10 of the officially engrossed laws of the sovereign state of Wisconsin:

> The Wisconsin state song is "On, Wisconsin", music by W.T. Purdy, the words to which are as follows: "On, Wisconsin! On, Wisconsin! Grand old badger state! We, thy loyal sons and daughters, Hail thee, good and great. On, Wisconsin! On, Wisconsin! Champion of the right, 'Forward', our motto—God will give thee might."

"Excuse me," I said, distractedly and more to myself than to them. "I have to make some arrangements."

"Arrangements for what?" Sandy asked. "I really should tell you what I learned from Cleveland."

"Tell Thomas," I said over my shoulder as I began to move briskly away. "Have him tell you about the answering machine tape. I have to see if I can manage to fly to Milwaukee tonight and be at the courthouse by first thing tomorrow morning."

"What are you going to be looking for?"

"I don't know," I said. "But I'm rather sure I won't find it here."

I didn't hear what came next. Which was a good thing.

"Do you see any obstacle to our continuing to work together efficiently on a professional basis?" Sandy asked in stilted, formal terms.

"No."

"Very well. I will have a written report of my discoveries this afternoon available for you first thing tomorrow morning."

"Actually, there may be something tonight on which we can work efficiently. On a strictly professional basis, of course."

"Thomas, if you please, I am not in the mood for banter."

"I'm not bantering. Just before I came in here I called Olivier Giraud. I told him that I wanted to buy the painting of the old woman walking past the billboard. We settled on seventy-five hundred dollars. We have an appointment at eight-thirty to close the deal. I thought you might want to come along."

"I would like that very much. Unfortunately, I promised Mr. Furst—"

"— that you wouldn't make arrangements to meet with Giraud until we'd all had a chat about the whole thing. I know. But you haven't made any arrangements or collaborated in any. I have. That's a contingency Theodore didn't think about and concerning which he didn't extract any promises from you. You wouldn't be coming along to meet Giraud but just to keep an eye on me and make sure I didn't foul everything up."

"You are right," she said, after a few seconds' analysis. "I will meet you tonight at ten after eight—outside our building."

Chapter 27

I finally obtained the inspection, but on the condition that the results remain secret. They did remain secret, even from me. . . . Although I was a member of the government, I was never able to obtain a copy of the inspection report, nor even a summary. It was more than a State secret: it was a bureaucratic secret. The government itself didn't have access to it.

—Alain Peyrefitte

"The consensus at Foggy Bottom is that we'd just as soon members of the French Communist Party not serve in the French government. Although a vocal minority maintains that it would damn well serve them right if they did."

Fletcher Hamilton's voice brought this assessment to T. Graham Curry from Washington, D.C., courtesy of AT&T.

"The operative assumption, I take it, is that there are unlikely to be Communists in the French government as long as de Gaulle is president of the republic," T. Graham said.

"That is my understanding. He had some Communists in the government he formed after liberation. I believe that he did not regard the experience as a positive one."

Fletcher Hamilton's once-pure Brahmin accent—to get an idea of a Brahmin accent, imagine someone with overactive adenoids whose underpants are too tight but who's too polite to let anyone know that he's uncomfortable—had been softened by his frequent sojourns in Washington, where the dominant tone for decades was an unhurried southern drawl.

"May I ask," Hamilton said, "exactly what it is that provokes your interest in your government's present attitude toward Charles de Gaulle? Or more precisely, what it is that makes you think your government would have an attitude toward him that might lead to friction between the Departments of State and Justice?"

"Your question assumes a fact not in evidence."

"But nonetheless a fact. If there weren't something like that going through your mind, why would you have called me? I'm hardly the most important political contact you have. Therefore I must be the most pertinent."

"The immediate occasion for my question is an observation my son shared with me—or at any rate with my partner—about a rather dramatic episode they were involved in earlier today."

"Dramatic in what way?"

"This afternoon, my son and my partner surprised a couple of thugs in the act of burglarizing the flat of a young and justifiably obscure artist named Arthur Cleveland."

"Quite stimulating for those involved, I'm sure, but hardly unusual. I have it on good authority that there are eight million stories in the naked city."

"Entirely true. What struck me was the police reaction to the incident."

"That's odd," Hamilton said, "I must be more worldly than I give myself credit for being. I thought that a general attitude of police indifference to such matters was proverbial in the urban jungle."

"The thing is," T. Graham continued, "it wasn't indifferent at first. Even before Furst and my son got the facts across to the first officers on the scene, there seems to have been some extraordinarily energetic police work. Specifically, they tell me that two individuals were apparently taken into custody by plainclothes officers while they—the individuals arrested, not the plainclothes officers—were in the process of leaving the building in some haste."

"Remarkable. Before the uniformed police officers got there, you say?"

"Yes."

"Remarkable. What do you infer from that?"

"I infer that the building was under surveillance, before the burglary, by a law enforcement agency other than the New York City Police Department."

"A reasonable inference."

"Even more suggestive is the fact that no record appears to have been made of the arrest of these two individuals, no report about it appears to have been made to the New York authorities, and there is every reason to believe that the two have been released."

"Leading you to believe what?"

"That the two were collaborating in some way with the United States government."

"Unless something is going on that I don't know about— something that would make the Bay of Pigs look like an exercise in diplomatic restraint—they were not."

"I accept that," T. Graham said. "Still and all, the affair smacks of improvisation but not of chance."

"Speaking hypothetically, Curry, wouldn't you agree that if it becomes clear that two people who have been arrested cannot be prosecuted and that their continued detention is potentially inconvenient from the standpoint of another department of the government, the expedient thing to do is to release them with as little fanfare as possible?"

"Yes, I would," T. Graham acknowledged. "Tell me something," he said after a moment of silence. "What in the world would the French government be doing having a couple of toughs with diplomatic immunity running around New York City breaking into people's apartments, manhandling my partner, and pistol-whipping my son?"

"Gracious," Hamilton said. "Who said the French government was doing anything like that?"

"No one. I was asking hypothetically."

"Oh. Hypothetically. Have you heard of the OAS? Organisation Armée Secrète?"

"That the outfit that tried to knock off de Gaulle?"

"Back in the fifties, yes. French-Algerian army officers.

They're very cross with de Gaulle because when he took power they had the distinct impression that he was going to save Algeria for France, and it turned out that his plan was to save France from Algeria, by cutting the ties between the two countries as fast as he decently could."

"I see."

"They started out just writing 'OAS' on walls all over Algiers and no one paid much attention. Then they moved on to blowing things up and trying to put bullets in people. You can hardly blame the French government for being interested in them, can you?"

"In New York?"

"A number of the wealthier French-Algerian expatriates ended up here, as well as in Quebec. New York is relatively close to Quebec and has the virtue of not being in Canada, whose government doesn't have quite the obsession we do with civil liberties, especially the civil liberties of French-speaking people."

"It's a long way from Paris."

"There's money and talent here. You can always fly to Paris."

"That doesn't explain the surveillance."

"You're right. That doesn't and I can't."

"Can't or won't?"

"May not and will not."

"Understood."

"If you'll forgive my saying so," Hamilton said, "you seem unaccountably relieved."

"I am."

"You must learn not to get so emotionally involved in the affairs of your clients."

"It's not a client. It's my son."

"Oh?"

"Yes. I was afraid that this matter reflected some kind of continuing investigation into—into the disreputable Algerian activities that apparently forced him to resign from the U.S. Attorney's staff and from the bar."

"I beg your pardon?"

"Forgive the circumlocution, Hamilton, I—"

"It's not the circumlocution that astonishes me, Curry, it's the facts. You are misinformed. I might even say radically misinformed."

"Am I indeed? Then by all means fill me in."

"Curry, your son resigned from the U.S. Attorney's staff because he sharply disagreed with his government's treatment of a gangster named Telly Formolo, who was shot nine times by FBI agents a very few moments before he would have made a serious attempt to end your son's life."

"Why would my son react so negatively to activity as wholesome and productive as that?"

"I believe he felt that Formolo had been set up, and that he had been used to bait the trap. Formolo had made a clumsy effort to suborn young Thomas in his official capacity, using the Algerian activities you referred to for that purpose. Your son surmised that Formolo must have learned about Algeria by way of a calculated government leak, intended to entice Formolo into doing precisely what he did. After resigning from the U.S. Attorney's staff, he surrendered his law license in order to minimize the chance that anyone would ever think he could be subjected to pressure such as Formolo tried to employ."

"Is that a fact?"

"No, it's an analytic inference. You can take it for what it's worth."

"Well, by God. You know, Hamilton, by the time someone's thirty-two, lack of judgment may be something you can still correct, but lack of character is irreparable. The boy is an ass, there's no getting around it, but there's one thing I've been wrong about for over ten years: He has got character. Despite everything, despite all of my foul-ups, despite his sainted idiot of a mother going off and getting herself blown apart in China, despite everything, he might actually turn out to be not totally worthless after all."

"Always the incurable optimist," Hamilton said. "Always."

Chapter 28

It's the orders you disobey that make you famous.

      —Colonel Arthur MacArthur

"**S**eventy-five hundred dollars, I think we said."

"Sold. I'm too distracted to bargain. I hope you're not disappointed."

"My only disappointment is that I didn't start at five thousand."

Giraud offered a brief suggestion of a smile at the comment.

"Well," he said, "permit me to show you into my study and I'll try to make you comfortable while I draw up the papers."

Thomas and Sandy followed the small, delicately framed man through a rear door, down a short hallway, and into a windowless room, wainscotted floor to ceiling. A Persian carpet, its design intricately woven in luminous reds and blues, each strand of its fringe ending in eight knots, accented a parquet floor. It seemed to Thomas that every stick of furniture in the room could have come straight from an Edwardian gentlemen's club.

"There are Marlboros and Gauloises in the box on the table," Giraud said, gesturing carelessly as he crossed to a cabinet on the other side of the room. "I'm afraid my selection of potables is a bit on the thin side. I'm not an aficionado of alcoholic beverages myself. I do have scotch but if you don't care for that the only alternative is apple juice."

"Scotch," Thomas said, firmly and instantly. "With soda if you have it. Otherwise on the rocks."

Sandy's most recent experience with scotch was less than

encouraging, and before Thomas spoke she had been inclined to ask for apple juice. With Thomas's decision, however, she reversed her own and asked for two fingers of scotch, neat.

Giraud fixed the requested drinks and distributed them. He took apple juice for himself and ambled over to the rolltop desk. There was an Olivetti manual typewriter on top of it. Seating himself, he fetched three preprinted pages from the top left-hand drawer and rolled the first of them into the typewriter.

"You'll want the bill of sale signed by the artist himself, of course. I'm sure I can get that taken care of within forty-eight hours. I'll provide for the payment to be held in escrow until then. Cash?"

"You will please provide for a deposit to be held until then, in the form of a check dated two days from today. Balance at closing, when I receive the painting and the bill of sale, executed, witnessed, and notarized in my presence. Exactly the same as an escrow and less complicated."

"My word. Something in me seems to bring out the lawyer in you, Mr. Curry. Very well. A deposit. Why don't we make it a thousand for the sake of round numbers?"

"Ten percent would be seven hundred and fifty dollars, which is quite round enough for me. And I'll need a receipt."

"Of course. If you don't mind my saying so, you are remarkably close with your pennies for someone worth four million dollars."

"Take care of the pennies and the dollars will take care of themselves. Or so I've always been told."

"No doubt correctly," Giraud answered, but he said it distantly as he concentrated on the staccato rattle he was making with the typewriter.

Thomas glanced over at Sandy. He caught his breath. In the subdued lighting he thought she looked as lovely as she did by candlelight, her beauty enhanced now by his certainty that she was irrevocably lost to him.

He hadn't expected her to return his glance, and she didn't. She focused instead on Giraud, following with lively interest his rapid, seemingly effortless typing.

"Tell me," Thomas said to Giraud, "have you been able to lend a hand to the police in their inquiries into Mr. Tyler's recent demise?"

Not a muscle on Giraud's face moved, but Thomas and Sandy both saw the sudden, reflexive tensing that ran through his shoulders.

Giraud removed the page he'd been typing from the Olivetti, laid it beside the machine, and rolled the second page into it.

"If you wish to examine that it may save us some time," he said. "It's a standard form, prepared by the American Art Dealers and Brokers Association, so I don't suppose I could agree to change anything, but you might as well know what it says."

"You know," Thomas continued, "when we met outside Tyler's flat, I was sure you told me that you had an appointment to see him."

"This bill of sale won't take a moment," Giraud said. "Just a matter of filling in some blanks. Then you said you wanted a receipt also, didn't you?"

Giraud took the second page out of the typewriter, laid it on top of the first, and rolled the third into place.

"You have quite a bit of experience with papers, haven't you?" Sandy asked.

"I have quite a bit of experience with interrogation, also," Giraud said. "The Gestapo had me for three hours once. They didn't get anything out of me, and they were better at it than you two are."

He pulled the third page out, put it together with the first two, and tendered the package to Thomas.

"Please look those over to the extent you feel necessary. Then we can sign the ones that require signing, you can give me your check, and you and Mademoiselle Cadette can be on your way."

Thomas accepted the proffered documents.

"Not talking, eh?" he asked, smiling at the self-parody.

"Mr. Curry, I only went fishing once. I only caught one fish. As I looked at the pathetic creature, lying there on the riverbank, the thought that went through my mind was 'He'd be alive at this moment if only he hadn't opened his mouth.' "

"That suggests that you feel you have something to fear," Sandy said.

"At the moment I fear boredom. Let me see if I can short-circuit this unpromising discussion. Arthur Cleveland has been to see me today. Late this afternoon, in fact. He was rather incoherent, but from what I could gather of his blatherings, I surmised that you induced him to confess that it was he who tried to turn Mr. Tyler's last painting into confetti, and that he then effected an escape from the apartment in a manner strongly suggesting consciousness of guilt. I can appreciate that you might not have thought him the most plausible suspect before that revelation, but you must certainly put him in that category now. You apparently want me to say something that you can use to reinforce the case against him, and I am not going to do so. It's as simple as that."

"You have things front to reverse," Sandy said. "Before seeing Mr. Cleveland this afternoon, I was inclined to believe that he was the one who had killed Tyler. After my encounter with him, I am quite certain that, whoever killed Tyler, it was not Cleveland."

"Mademoiselle Cadette, you disappoint me. You remind me that France is populated by fifty million Cartesians who haven't read Descartes."

"But I have read Descartes, and I have also read Cocteau, from whom you stole that quip."

"Then why don't you apply him to this perfectly straightforward problem? Descartes, I mean, not Cocteau. Cleveland has acknowledged in the same breath that he was present at the scene of the crime and that his behavior betrayed a powerful motive for murder. The conclusion is obvious."

"It is indeed, but it is the opposite of the conclusion you suggest."

"I find it impossible to follow your reasoning."

"Cleveland's destruction of *Badger Game* was an irrational act of blind fury, the hyperemotional frenzy of a temperament in a transport of passion."

"I ask for logic and you give me poetry."

"The killing of Tyler, on the contrary, was the product of a calculating intelligence. It was deliberately planned, carefully set up, and cold-bloodedly executed. The very fact that Cleveland vandalized the painting is the clearest evidence that he didn't kill the painter. Tyler's killing required an entirely different mentality—the type of mentality required to live by one's wits and seek out entrepreneurial opportunities in occupied wartime France."

"If you imagine that that sally gives you some moral advantage in my eyes, you're mistaken. I'm not ashamed of my activities during the war. The twenty-nine people that I brought safely from France to Switzerland were quite happy that there was someone available with my entrepreneurial instincts."

"The uncounted scores that you left behind because they couldn't afford your fee perhaps had a different view of things."

"I never said I was an altruist. I didn't claim to be a hero of the Resistance. I risked a session with rubber truncheons and piano wire every time I took a group across the border. I insisted on being paid for that risk. Once I was paid, though, I delivered. I never betrayed anyone that I agreed to help. Everyone who paid me got where I said I'd take them."

"And if someone you counted on betrayed you, you killed him."

"That is your theory, mademoiselle."

"Insofar as the war is concerned, it is a documented fact. Insofar as Harrison Tyler is concerned, it is at least a plausible theory, is it not?"

"No, mademoiselle, it is not."

"Why not?"

"Because Tyler's murder was too complicated. Do you want to know what a cold, calculating, perfectly disguised way to murder Harrison Tyler would have been? To drag him into an alley, smash the back of his head in with a blunt instrument, and make off with his wallet and his watch. That would be the perfect crime, mademoiselle. Just another mugging. Another random, tragic victim of senseless New York street crime. Unless one were stupid enough to hang onto the murder weapon, the timepiece, or the billfold, there would be no way to solve the crime, and the police would scarcely try. The murder that took place was absurdly complex. There were a thousand things that could have gone wrong. Harrison Tyler's murder wasn't the work of a skillful, calculating criminal, such as you conceive me to be, but of a blundering amateur, too clever for his own good."

Sandy walked a few steps to the coffee table. She took a Gauloise from the box and lit it with a short, wooden match from a clay cylinder beside the box. She followed her first puff with a delicate sip from the glass of scotch she was still holding. She did all this quite deliberately, not because she was thirsty and still less because she particularly wished to smoke but because she wanted a few moments to think.

"Your argument has considerable force," she said when the little ritual had run its course. "The fact remains that someone did kill Harrison Tyler, not in a dark alley but in his flat, and not in a violent rage but in cold blood. Wisely or foolishly, whoever did it pursued an elaborately calculated plan to accomplish his end."

"And you persist in believing that Arthur Cleveland is incapable of calculation?"

"I am perfectly confident that the man who lashed out in a mad frenzy at *Badger Game* is not the same one who induced Harrison Tyler to drink a drugged cocktail and then carefully if ineptly set up his murder to look like a suicide."

"If you wish to marry logic, Mademoiselle Cadette, you will find it an unforgiving spouse. It demands absolute fidelity. You must follow it to the end. You cannot take it so far and then abandon it in favor of intuition when you think you don't like the conclusion it is leading you to."

"But a different metaphor leads to a different injunction. I have no experience with marriage, so I do not think of logic as a spouse. It seems to me to be more like scotch: It is a useful and talented servant, but a cruel and pitiless master. You must use it. You must not let it use you."

She put her glass down on the table.

"Thomas has your check for you, and we will be going. Au revoir."

Despite the valedictory, she stood where she was for a moment and Giraud's gaze met hers and held it. He had never heard about the Northman who had founded her family in the fourteenth century while selling his blade to whoever would buy it. But as he stared at her his expression froze in sudden and chilling realization, just as Thomas Andrew Curry's had on a plateau in the Algerian *bled* seven years before, and Arthur Cleveland's had in his apartment that afternoon. Behind the elegant words and the cultured rhetoric he saw, mocking him down through six centuries or so, the icy blue eyes of the barbarian killer.

Thursday

Chapter 29

It thus happened that political democracy [in classical Athens] was associated with cultural conservatism, while those who were cultural innovators tended to be political reactionaries. Somewhat the same situation exists in modern America, . . . [b]ut the enlightened are politically weaker in America than they were in Athens, because they have failed to make common cause with the plutocracy. There is, however, one important and highly intellectual class which is concerned with the defence of the plutocracy, namely the class of corporation lawyers. In *some* respects, their functions are similar to those that were performed in Athens by the Sophists.

—Bertrand Russell

"Thank you for meeting me here on such short notice, Geoff."

"My pleasure, Ted. No problem at all."

Geoffrey Singleton and I walked through the east entrance of the Milwaukee County Courthouse, up some steps and down the long first-floor corridor.

"And thank you for sending that earnest young man to pick me up at the airport last night. You really didn't have to. I could easily have taken a cab."

"Nonsense. That's why God created associates."

We reached the Clerk of Circuit Court's office.

"Here we are," Singleton said. "I'm not sure what you're looking for that you couldn't more easily have had someone here look for on your behalf, but whatever it is I presume that our search begins here."

"That's the whole difficulty, Geoff. I'm not entirely sure what I am looking for. That's why I had to come out myself. A young lawyer came out here several weeks ago and wandered around this courthouse. While she was here, she saw something that made her realize something about a different matter that apparently involves my firm. I have to see if I can wander around and manage to see the same thing."

"Highly qualitative and nonrigorous, Ted. Doesn't sound like your sort of thing at all."

"You're actually to blame. It was that exit line of yours on the phone yesterday that started me down this path."

"All I said was to look me up the next time you were in the Badger State."

"Precisely."

"I'll take your word for it. Where shall we start?"

"Where do I look to find out what cases have been filed since, say, the first of the year?"

"By name of parties?"

"By approximate name of one of the parties?"

"That would be the record room. Follow me."

He led me into the clerk's office, then down a massive, internal stairway and pointed me toward an array of mismatched filing cabinets with drawers sized to accommodate three-by-five index cards. I pulled the B to Bax drawer open and dove in.

I was prepared for Wisconsin, being the Badger State, to have a lot of companies with "Badger" in their names. I wasn't prepared for as many as I found. Flipping despairingly through a thick pack of cards I saw Badger Awning, Badger Boat Motor, Badger Carpets, Badger Diesel, Badger Electric, Badger Furs— you get the idea. And then, suddenly, there it was: *Badger Game Corporation, f/k/a Johnson Industries, Inc.* v. *Omicron Instruments Ltd.*

"Bingo," I said.

"Found something?" Singleton asked with mild interest.

"I think so. How do we find out what happened in this case?"

"Write down the case number and come with me."

Singleton led me to one end of the long counter and opened

a huge binder. He paged through the book and then stood aside, pointing to the docket sheet for *Badger Game Corporation* v. *Omicron Instruments Ltd.*: Suit filed February 10, 1962. Motion for temporary injunction filed one week later. Answer filed. Hearing on injunction motion held March 1, 1962. Motion denied same date. Defendant's motion for summary judgment made same date and taken under advisement.

"Hm," I said. "What do you think?"

"I think the plaintiff got surprised."

"I do too. Can we look at the file?"

"Right this way."

Singleton strolled behind the counter with me in his wake and began wandering up and down the aisles between the shelves stuffed with manila folders. They were filed in numerical order by case number and we came soon enough to the place where ours should be.

It wasn't there. In its place was a long card labeled Out at the top and with various places written in and crossed out on the lines below. The bottom place written in wasn't crossed out, and that read "Br 14."

"Branch Fourteen," Singleton read. "The judge has it. He must be about ready to get a decision out on the motion that's pending."

My heart sank.

"Does that mean we can't lay our hands on it?"

"Certainly not." Singleton snorted. "Where do you think you are, New York?"

We took the elevator to the fourth floor. Branch 14 was in Courtroom 406. It was comforting to know that Milwaukee followed the same kind of logic in identifying courtroom locations as New York did. If clients get to the point where they don't need us for anything else, they'll still have to hire us to find the courtrooms for them.

Say "courtroom" to the average person and he'll think of a place packed with spectators watching a trial or a hearing. In most courtrooms, however, nothing is going on most of the time, and they're next to empty. Branch Fourteen was like that when we got there. Apparently they'd just wrapped something up. The judge, still robed, was standing up behind the bench, chatting with a balding man who had every earmark of a court-house regular. The judge's clerk sat in front of the bench sorting papers, marking file jackets, date-stamping documents, and oth-erwise giving every evidence of frenzied activity. The secret to being a good judge is knowing how to delegate.

Singleton nodded briefly at the others as he ambled up to the bench. I hung back near the bar. I was an out-of-town lawyer, a highly dubious species in the best of circumstances.

"Dolores," Singleton said to the clerk, "do you suppose we could get a look at this one?" He handed her a scrap of paper with the case number written on it.

"Which one is that?" Dolores asked without glancing at the paper.

"Badger Game against Omicron."

"It's on the bailiff's table. Help yourself."

We helped ourselves. Singleton found the file and brought it over to the nearer counsel table. Standing with our backs to the bench, we opened the file on the table and took a look at it.

I started by looking at Badger Game's brief in support of its temporary injunction motion. Badger Game, formerly known as Johnson Industries, was upset because Omicron had stolen Badger Game's design for an electronic swim-meet lap-timer. This design was a Badger Game trade secret, one that Badger Game had developed itself at immense expense and taken ex-tensive measures to protect. Omicron, the rascal, had gotten the design by hiring away a faithless Badger Game employee, despite the covenant not to compete in his employment con-tract. The device represented a large part of Badger Game's intangible corporate value, and there were in fact delicate ne-gotiations under way even as suit was filed over purchase of the design by an outfit known as Frampton Electronics. Hmm.

"Looks good to me," I said as I finished the fifteenth page. "I wonder why they lost."

"Here's why," Singleton said. He handed me Defendant's Exhibit One.

Exhibit One was a copy of an article that had appeared in *Trade and Engineering News* the week before suit was filed. It described in detail the design for an electronic lap-timer, capable of employment in aqueous environments. I just love the way engineers write.

"So much for that trade secret," I said.

"Mm-hmm. Omicron could have gotten it by burgling Badger Game's offices, cracking its safe, and photographing the blueprints with a Minox, but it stopped being a trade secret when a third party independently published a substantially equivalent design."

"Tough luck for Badger Game. It's a good thing Frampton Electronics had the energy to send a bright lawyer out here to monitor the hearing." And a tragic coincidence that that lawyer happened to be Katherine Colleen Ferguson, I thought.

"You fellas finding what you need?" the judge asked from behind us. He had come down from the bench and was about to go into his chambers.

Singleton turned around and assured him that we were. I turned around to keep from seeming impolite. That's when I saw it.

The judge had been blocking it when we came in, but when I turned around the mural immediately behind the judge's chair hit me full force and without warning, in all of its up-close hideous magnificence. I was looking at the original of *Wisdom*, the painting that Harrison Tyler had slammed in *Badger Game*.

Chapter 30

Much inquiry having been made concerning a gentleman,
who had quitted a company where Johnson was, and no
information being obtained; at last Johnson observed, that
"he did not care to speak ill of any man behind his back,
but he believed the gentleman was an attorney."

—Boswell's *Life of Johnson*

While I was disporting about the Milwaukee County Court-
house in the company of the unflappable Geoffrey Singleton,
T. Graham was in earnest, face-to-face conversation at the Sixth
Precinct with the even less flappable Lieutenant McShea. T.
Graham was in the process of trying to flap him, but he wasn't
making a lot of progress.

"I wouldn't be bothering you with this, Lieutenant—"

"You wouldn't like hell."

"—but the chap was a client of my firm. Not by my choice,
of course, but in a firm you're stuck with your partner's decisions
as well as your own."

"So what?"

"Well, I suppose we have some responsibility to act on behalf
of his estate, until we can get ourselves relieved of that chore. It's
a nuisance, but someone has to inventory the household goods,
collect the mail, get the odd painting appraised and so forth."

"Go see a judge."

"Lieutenant, I'm not asking for a great deal. I only want a
key to my client's apartment, an authorization to pick up his
mail despite the hold order you sent to the post office, and a
list of his safe deposit boxes."

"The answer is no, counselor. Accept it. I don't like your attitude and I'm not going to change my mind."

"To be precise, actually, you don't like my son's attitude."

"Same difference."

"Well, no, really, it's not the same thing at all. You see, I have a great deal more experience than my son, and you'll find me much more cooperative than he has been. Now—"

"What was that again?"

"I merely said I have always thought it best to help the police in any way that I could. So—"

"So you might actually share some information with me if I let you continue to stick your collective noses into this criminal investigation?"

"Just tell me what you'd like to know," T. Graham said, smiling beatifically.

"I would like to know everything you know."

"That seems reasonable. I—"

"You better believe it's reasonable."

"Quite. I am going to be having a meeting this afternoon with everyone at my firm involved in this matter for the purpose of tabulating exactly what we do know about it. I solemnly assure you that I will impart to you first thing tomorrow morning every bit of data we have."

"There's only one more thing," McShea said.

"What's that?"

"I want this information because I'm a police officer and you are all citizens with a duty to give it to me. I don't want it because I've bribed you to give it to me by letting you rummage around a dead guy's apartment playing detective."

"Then you're only willing to give me the mail and the safe deposit boxes?"

"Who said anything about safe deposit boxes?"

"Just the mail?"

"The mail I'll do for you. Not because there's anything says I have to but because it gives me a carrot and a stick."

"A carrot and a stick?"

"Right. You say I'm going to get a report tomorrow morning.

You get mail today. That's the carrot. If I do get a report to-morrow morning and it really is everything you know, you get mail tomorrow. Another carrot. If I ever even suspect there's a scrap of relevant information that you haven't told me about, you don't get mail any more. That's the stick."

"Very elemental I'm sure," T. Graham said, opening his briefcase. "I have the authorization right here."

Chapter 31

The French people have maintained an exceptional talent
for making something out of nothing and creating dramatic
events that are then commented on indefinitely.

—Raymond Aron

"**M**iss Cadette, you seem to be the only one here who has
been taking notes carefully. Perhaps you would be good enough
to summarize what we have collectively learned since the last
meeting that brought us all together."

"Very well," Sandy said in a crisp, efficient voice. She glanced
up at T. Graham, who had given this instruction, then over at
me, then, very briefly, at Thomas.

"We have learned that Harrison Tyler painted a small portrait
of Katherine Ferguson, when she was still Casey O'Rourke,"
she began. "This portrait in my judgment suggests at least the
possibility of an intimate relationship between them. Mr. Furst
has determined that, shortly before her last call to Thomas,
Mrs. Ferguson had the opportunity to see the original of the
mural that Harrison Tyler satirized in his painting *Badger Game*.
There is possibly, perhaps probably, a connection between her
seeing this mural and her call. She was apparently in Milwaukee
because of a possible transaction with a company now named
Badger Game, which was the same company involved in the
scandal that broke out over the, *comment dit-on, fuite*—"

"Leak," Thomas said. I glared at him.

"—leak, thank you—"

"*Du rien.*"

"—of information about the tender raid. We have learned

that Arthur Cleveland admits being the one who destroyed *Badger Game*, but he denies having killed Mr. Tyler. We have learned, what else, let me see, yes, that Tyler himself removed his footlocker from his apartment and saw to it that it was thoroughly demolished with all of its contents. Finally, that Olivier Giraud was a gangster of some kind in occupied France and in postwar Europe and claims to have come to this country to pursue a career originally in pornography, which, however, he seems to have done anonymously. That covers it, I believe."

"Thank you very much," T. Graham said. "Very thorough."

"A wealth of data," I put in, mostly to keep Thomas from opening his mouth again, "but I can't see any meaningful pattern to it. Except that people seem to be taking art much more seriously than I ever have."

"There is one intriguing pattern," T. Graham said.

"What's that?"

"Confidential information. Johnson Industries when Thomas and this recently deceased Hibernian female were clerks with the same firm downtown. The same company under a different name a few months ago, shortly before the female in question went to her final reward."

"If that pattern were any more intriguing it'd be totally opaque," I commented. "Where does it get us?"

"Well," T. Graham responded, "let's see what we can come up with. What is it that makes information confidential?"

"Not being generally known," Thomas said.

"No, without more that only makes it obscure. The date of the Battle of Resaca de la Palma isn't generally known, but it's hardly confidential. You can look it up in any history of the Mexican War. To be confidential, information must be known only to a limited number of people and not readily ascertainable. In addition, and this is the key, the people who know it must want to keep other people from finding it out."

"Very illuminating," Thomas said dryly.

"Now," T. Graham continued, "the fact that those who know confidential information don't want others to find it out gives that information an intrinsic financial value. An outsider who obtains the information may be able either to persuade those who don't know the information to pay him to reveal it to them, or to induce those who already know the information to pay him not to reveal it to others."

"Extortion," I said.

"In the latter case," T. Graham agreed. "Trafficking in stolen information in the former. But one way or the other, a way to make a dollar."

"A provocative hypothesis," Sandy said.

"It's not a hypothesis yet," T. Graham remarked. "We've identified two ways of making money by exploiting confidential information. But there are problems with both methods. If you want to make money by selling the information to those who don't have it, their own use of it tends to be readily identified, and the chance that you will be fingered by the authorities therefore is great. You can't make money on inside stock information without making stock trades, which are all matters of record. You can't exploit a purloined trade secret without putting a product on the market that employs the secret, thereby revealing your theft."

"That leaves the converse method," I put in. "You get the people who don't want the information revealed to pay you not to reveal it."

"In which case you run an even graver risk. Namely, that they might dispense with paying you off, and kill you instead."

"If the stakes are high enough," I said.

"If someone's willing to pay you for the information, then the stakes are by definition high enough."

"Those risks are both quite real," Thomas agreed. "But they would seem to be unavoidable."

"Suppose, however, that someone found a way to avoid them. Suppose this person specialized in obtaining information that someone would pay him to reveal, not to the person paying him, but to the world at large. Or to some smaller, but large and innocent group."

"Like market-makers," Thomas said.

"Or people who read engineering publications," Sandy offered.

"Yes," T. Graham said. "Like them."

"That's quite elegant," I commented. "The information about the Johnson Industries tender offer was leaked to short-swing profit-takers, but benefited the incumbent management of the corporation, by killing the tender offer. The information about the Badger Game timer was leaked to trade publications, but indirectly benefited Omicron."

"Not to mention Frampton Electronics," T. Graham said, "which didn't have to buy the design once it was judicially determined that Badger Game's trade secret wasn't secret."

"Hm," I said.

"Hm," Thomas said.

"How did this get Harrison Tyler killed?" Sandy asked.

"Always the spoilsport," T. Graham responded. "I'm not sure. On the other hand," he added, brightening, "we have accumulated an impressive array of information to share with Lieutenant McShea, pursuant to my promise to him this morning."

"What was that?" Thomas asked. His tone was ominous.

"I had a chat with Lieutenant McShea this morning," T. Graham said offhandedly. "I wanted some things from him, to tell the truth. He seemed to attach considerable importance to evidence of a spirit of cooperation on our part, so I naturally undertook to make a complete disclosure to him."

"Naturally. I trust you got something monumental in exchange?"

"Oh, I don't know." T. Graham shrugged. "I got the hold order on Tyler's mail released in our favor." He gestured toward the top of his desk, where a stack of unpromising envelopes with windows and a small, bright yellow, rectangular box rested.

"Are you entirely sure that was wise?" Thomas asked. This was Curryese for "That's the most idiotic thing I've heard today."

"I did my best."

Thomas stood up.

"Thomas," I hissed, "act your age."

"Gentlemen, Miss Cadette, if you'll excuse me, I have a pressing engagement."

"At five-ten?" T. Graham asked, glancing at his watch.

"Good evening."

Thomas turned and walked out of his father's office.

T. Graham indulgently watched his son's exit. He winced slightly as the door slammed, then turned his attention back to Sandy and me.

"Apropos the problem at hand," he said, "what do you think?"

I held my peace and puffed on my pipe.

"We need more information," Sandy said without hesitation.

"We need more information," I agreed.

There was a knock on the door, followed immediately by Mrs. Valbach's entrance.

"There's a Conrad Marek who wishes to see you," she said disapprovingly to T. Graham. "He says he has some information for you."

Chapter 32

[A] cavalryman was found guilty of sodomy. "Will he be hanged?" the king was asked. "No," he replied, "transfer him to the infantry."

—Robert Asprey, describing
Frederick the Great

Thomas of course wasn't around to share the promised information, because Thomas had stalked out in a huff. As far as I was concerned, that served him right. I imagined that he'd go back to his apartment, cool down, think things over, and begin feeling sheepish just about in time to do something useful in the case.

This shows that with age and maturity comes the opportunity to make more and different kinds of mistakes.

Thomas was angry because T. Graham, having elbowed himself into Thomas's case, had chosen to commit us to disclose information to the police, which he knew Thomas wouldn't approve of; and had done this without consulting Thomas; and worst of all had gotten practically nothing in return.

Thomas wasn't in any condition to recall that he himself had invited T. Graham into the case, and that the first assignment given his father had been, precisely, to extract information from his "police contacts." Or that, if T. Graham hadn't been given express permission to exchange data with the authorities, no one had said that he couldn't do so if that seemed like the best way to get something useful from them. Thomas didn't recall any of that because, as I said, he was mad.

My mistake was in thinking that Thomas had left the meeting

because he wanted to sulk. The fact was that Thomas had the same opinion the rest of us did: What we had was fine, but we needed more information. More important, Thomas had a precise idea of what information we needed, and he intended to get it without meddling from his father, ironic commentary from Sandy, or dubious assistance from me.

As soon as he got into his apartment, Thomas whipped off his suit coat and flung it over the back of his couch. He loosened his tie and unfastened the top button of his shirt. He strode into his kitchen, flipping on the light as he came in. From his refrigerator he took a quarter of ham, a jar of Hellman's mayonnaise, a slab of Swiss cheese, and a loaf of Wonder enriched white bread.

Counting from the moment he got the ham unwrapped, it took him seventy-five seconds to make the sandwich. He cut it in half, slapped the two triangular halves on a small plate, opened a bottle of Heileman Special Export from the refrigerator, and carried the meal into the living room. He set the plate down on top of his stereo cabinet. He took a modest swig of the beer. Drinking beer wasn't Thomas's idea of drinking. He did it strictly to slake thirst.

He picked up a sandwich half and took a generous bite from one corner. He started thinking. He let the scattered bits of data about Gloria Monday come to the surface of his mind and form their own pattern there: tall; blond; low, soft voice; typist; too much makeup; good at hiding and staying hidden—either that or dead.

He took another bite from the sandwich and gazed through the window without seeing anything as he chewed contemplatively. He thought about the case and what Sandy had told him yesterday evening and about the conference he had just stalked out of: Badger Game; confidential information; Harrison Tyler; Gloria Monday; Olivier Giraud; Gloria Monday; Arthur Cleveland; Gloria Monday; confidential information; Badger Game.

What did it all mean? He was pretty sure he knew.

He took a last bite from the sandwich and a final swallow of beer. As he stood at the window, the crumbs from his sandwich sprinkling his shirt and tie, mayonnaise smearing his chin, he figured out what he was going to do.

Leaving the beer and food where they happened to be, he turned abruptly toward his bedroom. He left his tie and shirt on the living room floor, kicked off one shoe on each side of his bedroom door, and threw the rest of his clothes on his bed. His shower took four minutes flat. A towel around his neck but otherwise naked, he padded back to the living room for his beer, leaving wet footprints on the hardwood floor.

He took the beer back into the bathroom, drinking perhaps a quarter of it along the way. He shaved. He used the towel to wipe the fog off the bathroom mirror so that he could see what he was doing. He used a Gillette double-edged safety razor to shave and he took unusual pains with his efforts.

He brought the beer with him back into the bedroom and drank some more of it. He picked up the telephone beside the bed and dialed nine.

"Yessir, Mr. Curry."

"Would you have Alfred bring the car around in—" he picked up his watch from the bed and glanced at it—"twenty minutes?"

"Jimmy'll be happy to do that for ya, Mr. Curry. Alfred's just about to go off."

"I need Alfred tonight. I'll make it up to him."

"Yessir, Mr. Curry. Twenty minutes."

He thought, briefly but carefully, about every item of clothing he now put on: undecorated white jockey shorts; black knee-length socks; a white shirt with French blue pinstripes; twenty-four-carat gold cuff links set with black onyx stones; dark blue trousers. He paused in a moment of longer indecision over what tie to wear. Then, smiling, he picked one that was solid crimson except for a white representation of a chubby, fatuous pig. He added the tie tack that matched the cufflinks and put on an oxblood belt.

It took him a minute or so of digging in his closet to find the shoes he wanted. He asked himself out loud at one point where they were, referring to them in a mutter as his "fuck shoes."

His tone as he asked this question was puzzled rather than exasperated, for the term in question was an adjective, not an expletive, and would probably have been momentarily baffling to anyone who wasn't a member of a fraternity at an American university between 1945 and 1965.

He soon found the pair of Italian loafers he was looking for and put them on. They were handmade, each upper formed from a single piece of shaped leather. They matched the belt. The jacket he chose was all wool, its gray the color of fine cigar ash.

He got a money clip and a key from his top dresser drawer. Then he squatted, opened his bottom dresser drawer, and used the key to unlock a sturdy metal box wedged into one corner of it. He took two hundred-dollar bills, two fifties, and ten twenties from the box and folded these into the money clip, along with the currency from his wallet. He put the black-and-gold clip into the right side pocket of his trousers.

Reaching again into the metal box, he removed a hand-sized device of no obvious function, made of black rubber, with an elastic band attached to it. Then he pulled from the box a .38-caliber Smith & Wesson snub-nosed revolver. He broke the cylinder out to make sure that it wasn't loaded. He snapped the cylinder back into place and dry-fired the trigger twice. He broke the cylinder out again and loaded four cartridges into the weapon, although it was chambered for five.

He fit the revolver into the hard rubber device. The gun nestled smoothly into the network of clips and openings.

He rolled up his right pant leg. He pulled the elastic band over his shoe and attached the skeleton holster to his right ankle. He rolled his pant leg down over it. He stood up, walked over to his closet door, and looked at himself in the full-length mirror there. The trousers were full—you didn't wear close-fitting trousers in 1962 unless you were female or under twenty-one or both—but Thomas thought he could detect a bulge on the outside of the right ankle. You had to be looking for it to see it, but if he didn't expect anyone to be looking for it he might as well wear a shoulder holster. He rolled up the pant leg again and shifted the holster to the inside of his right ankle. He rolled the pant leg down and examined himself again in the mirror. Better.

He put on his watch and left the apartment. He had two minutes to spare.

Chapter 33

The life of the law has not been logic but experience. . . .
A page of history is worth a volume of logic.

—Justice Holmes

When Mrs. Valbach ushered him into T. Graham's office, Conrad Marek had the look on his face you'd associate with a hayseed walking for the first time into the lobby of Chase Manhattan: intimidation poorly concealed by affected indifference. Replacing the patronizing joviality and sense of quiet superiority he had radiated at the Ackley reception was a hair-trigger wariness commingled with awe.

"Very good of you to come, Mr. Marek," I said, leaping up to greet him. I shook his hand warmly and he smiled in pleased reassurance. "Mrs. Valbach, would you please see if you can find Mr. Marek a cup of coffee? Or—" turning to him—"would you rather have tea?"

"Coffee will be fine," he murmured.

I led him over to the jade-green Chesterfield sofa that dominated one wall of T. Graham's office. I moved a file and three open volumes of the *New York Reports* out of the way to make room for him to sit down. He thanked me and sank gratefully into the inviting leather.

T. Graham gave Marek five seconds to enjoy the illusion of comfort that my skillful ministrations had created. Then, without moving from behind his massive, blond oak desk, he boomed a question across the office at Marek.

"So some new information has come to your attention in the last day or so, Marek, is that right?"

Marek started and looked over at T. Graham.

"Ah, well, no, not new, exactly. And not really in the last day or so," he stammered.

"Oh. Then you must've already told the police but now you've decided to tell us too, is that it?"

"No. I haven't told the police. I've come to you first."

T. Graham leaned forward, planted his right elbow on the desk, pressed his thumb against his first and second fingers, and held the now-clawlike hand absolutely still as he asked his next question.

"Am I to understand, then, that you have information material to the homicide of Harrison Tyler, a client of this firm, that you have had such information for several days, and that you have failed to disclose that information up to now?"

"You don't understand," Marek said defensively. He looked toward me.

"I daresay I don't," T. Graham snapped. "Perhaps you could enlighten me."

"Graham," I interjected in a placating tone, "he's trying to explain. Give him a chance. Go ahead, Mr. Marek. You must have a good reason for waiting until now to come forward."

Marek looked at a point halfway between my head and T. Graham's.

"I answered fully and truthfully every question the police asked me," he said, recovering a bit of dignity. "I haven't concealed anything from anyone. If there's information that I haven't volunteered, it's because I didn't see what it could contribute to any useful purpose, and I thought it might create pointless problems for—other people."

"And now that you have changed your opinion on that score and decided to create those problems," T. Graham demanded, "why have you come to us instead of going to the police?"

"I doubt the police would be interested," Marek said. "They've already decided who killed Tyler. And they've got the wrong man."

"You?"

"No."

"Who? "

"Arthur Cleveland. He's been practically a fugitive for almost twenty-four hours."

"Do you mean a warrant's been issued for him?" T. Graham asked, adding a note of alarm to the bullying tone of his earlier questions.

"No, not a warrant, as far as I know. But Lieutenant McShea's been seeking him rather insistently since early yesterday evening. Ostensibly for further questioning, but it was clear from the questions the lieutenant asked me that he's decided on Arthur as the suspect to pin this murder on."

T. Graham got up from behind the desk and walked over toward the couch. He clasped his hands behind his back and stood there, towering majestically over Sandy, Marek, and me.

"If Mr. Cleveland is in fact not guilty," T. Graham pontificated, "then he should by all means stop avoiding the police. At trial, the prosecutor could well argue that innocent men don't flee or hide."

"Take it easy, Graham," I said in a stage whisper. "The man has come to this office voluntarily and in good faith."

"I don't wish to seem overbearing," T. Graham said, in the most overbearing manner imaginable. "I'm merely stating facts. If Arthur Cleveland didn't kill Harrison Tyler, then he has little to worry about. We don't use the strappado or the rubber hose in New York City. Police here are sometimes sloppy and occasionally overzealous, but in murder cases tried by competent counsel, juries in this city seldom convict innocent men."

"You don't understand Arthur Cleveland," Marek said, shaking his head. "If they subject him to serious interrogation, he'll give them exactly what they're looking for."

"You think he'll deliberately talk himself into the electric chair?" T. Graham demanded. He used his jury voice and it was chilling. For a split second I imagined that I was in the death house at Sing-Sing. "We still have one in this state, you know, and we actually use it now and again."

I summoned up the most soothing, coaxing tone I could manage and addressed Marek.

"Explain Cleveland to us," I said. "Tell us what you mean."
Marek sighed and began.

"Someone once said that Oscar Wilde made his life a work of art. You could say the same thing about Arthur Cleveland—if the work of art you had in mind was *The Wreck of the Medusa*. Psychologically, Arthur's a disaster. He puts on a front of cool egotism but he's fundamentally a submissive personality."

"When you say he's submissive," I asked, "do you mean guilt-ridden? Masochistic? That he has a need for punishment?"

"Not at all. He has one of the least developed concepts of personal guilt of anyone I've ever encountered."

"Then what are you trying to say?"

"It's hard to express. He reminds me of a young German officer I helped interrogate back in 1944. He—"

"You fought in Europe during World War Two?" I blurted. I was stepping out of role but I couldn't help it. I was genuinely astonished.

"Oh, yes," Marek assured me. "Well, maybe 'fought' isn't the right term. They gave me a gold bar and put me in intelligence. G-2 was the inevitable slot for anyone with a college degree and a passing knowledge of any European language."

"I know." I nodded, having been subjected to the same fate on the same rationale.

"About the young German officer," T. Graham prompted.

"Yes. We were using a technique called 'Mutt and Jeff' on him: One of the interrogators would come on very tough and sinister and the other would be reasonable and nonthreatening, almost pleasant with the soldier, as if he were taking the soldier's part. It's a fairly unsophisticated approach, but it works sometimes with subjects who are suggestible and not overly intelligent."

"Fascinating," T. Graham commented.

I sank my teeth into the inside of my lower lip until I felt the blood flow. It worked. I didn't burst out laughing.

"Anyway," Marek continued, "at first he was like a stone wall. They all were, at first. Usually, though, the wall either stayed intact or it began to crumble, bit by bit. This officer's wall just collapsed instantly, as if it had been vaporized, as soon as the nice-guy interrogator got to him. One second he was sitting there, not even giving us name, rank, and serial number, and the next second he was pouring out details so fast we couldn't write them all down: unit strength, casualties, objectives, everything. It was a torrent."

"A torrent that was possible only because he actually knew the facts he was telling you," T. Graham said.

"No, that was the funny thing," Marek said. "That was what I was driving at. You see, we'd gotten the prisoner's unit wrong. We were asking him about stuff he couldn't possibly have known. So, naturally, when he started talking, the information he gave us was a mishmash. One statement contradicted the next. None of it made any sense."

"You mean he was deliberately giving you false information to try to thwart the questioning," I said.

"No again. He was too rattled and too unimaginative to try anything like that. It was a sincere and total breakdown. He wanted to cooperate with us. He just didn't have any of the information we were asking him about."

"Then what's your explanation for what happened?"

"As I indicated, he was a submissive. Once he'd gotten that one-two, the hard guy and then the nice guy, he desperately wanted to tell the nice guy whatever the nice guy wanted to hear. He wanted to please him. He figured out what kind of information the nice guy was looking for, and he just made things up that fit into that category. Arthur Cleveland in his present condition will do the same thing with the police."

"Present condition?" T. Graham asked.

"He's badly shaken. I don't know what it was, but something happened that deeply disturbed him. He'll be putty in McShea's hands."

"So shaken that he'll confess to a murder he didn't commit?"

"I'm not saying that he's going to say he did it," Marek answered. "But he won't have to. You have to understand how the police operate once they've convinced themselves that they've got the right suspect. They'll feed him the details they need to build a circumstantial case against him, and in his present frame of mind he'll parrot those details right back to them."

"Thank you for explaining to me how the police operate," T. Graham said. "It's the kind of knowledge that comes in handy in a practice like mine." I didn't have any trouble picking up the sarcasm, and I don't think Marek did either.

"Graham, give the man the benefit of the doubt," I lectured my senior partner. "I find his analysis very plausible. He's come down here on his own to give us additional information, and the least we can do is listen to it."

"Very well," T. Graham said, as if his attitude reflected infinite indulgence. "What do you have to tell us, Marek?"

Marek was so anxious to answer that you'd have thought we were doing him a favor by letting him tell us what he knew.

"I can tell you where Gloria Monday is," he said. "Or, that is, I can tell you where you can find her, anytime between nine and midnight tonight."

"How is that you know that?" T. Graham asked.

"I'm not at liberty to say."

"You know, Marek, I had the most remarkable intuition that you were going to answer in precisely that way."

"Never mind that," I said, waving in feigned impatience at T. Graham. "Where can we find her?"

"At a clip joint in Brooklyn called Piccadilly Bird. She operates there Thursday through Saturday nights."

"Does she indeed?"

"Yes."

"You know what, Marek?" T. Graham asked after a few moments' pause. "I'm going to show you something. I think you'll find it quite interesting." He picked up the bright yellow box from the pile of Tyler's mail and began to walk toward the door. "I hope you don't mind, Miss Cadette. I took the liberty of having the apparatus set up in your office. I thought it would be too cumbersome in here. Come along, everybody."

We followed him docilely out of his office, down the corridor that separated lawyers' offices from our modest typing pool, and into the windowless space I'd wangled for Sandy. Along the way, I wondered what the mysterious apparatus he had mentioned could be. An electronic swim-meet lap-timer?

We filed into Sandy's office, and there it was: a Bell & Howell slide projector. It was set up on top of Sandy's desk, focused on the bare wall a few feet away.

T. Graham opened the bright yellow box he had brought along and began fitting the cardboard-mounted slides into the slide tray from the projector. Anyone who's ever done that can tell you that you have to watch what you're doing or half the slides will end up upside down. T. Graham, however, slid the slides rapidly into the tray, like someone who had put those particular slides into that particular tray once or twice already.

"There we are," he said when he had the tray loaded. He slipped the tray into place on the projector, turned on the fan and then the lamp, and gestured to Sandy.

Sandy killed the fluorescent light overhead. We all looked toward the bright, white square projected onto the wall opposite her desk. T. Graham punched in the first slide. A colorful image appeared where the bright square had been. Sandy took her breath in sharply. Marek gasped.

"*Badger Game*, if I'm not very much mistaken," T. Graham said.

"Yes," Sandy whispered.

"Good Christ," Marek breathed.

It was the first time I had seen it, and I was dazzled by the thought of what the finished painting must have looked like on canvas before Cleveland mutilated it. The impact was almost physical, hitting me like an emphatic punch in the chest.

It reminded me of the first time I saw a Jackson Pollock canvas. I'd seen pictures of them in magazines and I'd had the same reaction to them a lot of people had: a five-year-old child with a box of crayons could have produced the same thing. When I actually saw a full-size canvas, though, I realized I was wrong. There was something extraordinary there. I didn't know what it was. I couldn't explain it. I couldn't analyze it. Every attempt to analyze it that I heard or read struck me as baloney. But something was there and whatever it was reached out and grabbed me. I felt the same thing when I saw the projected slide of *Badger Game*.

"I think this is the best picture of it in the lot," T. Graham said blandly. "All the slides are of the painting. I think he must have tried at least six different lens apertures and three different shutter speeds, to be absolutely sure he got one decent representation of it. And I'd say he succeeded."

"How did you know you'd find it?" Sandy asked.

"I didn't, to tell the truth. I was just struck by your report of the conversation you and Thomas had with that cabbie."

"About how Tyler went to so much trouble to get rid of the footlocker?"

"That was certainly curious, but that wasn't what most piqued my interest. I just couldn't get my mind off that last little nagging detail: He'd stopped at a mailbox on the way back to deposit a small, yellow envelope."

"But that could have been anything," Sandy protested.

"Not just anything. It had to be something fairly important to engage his attention at that particular time, given what was apparently on his mind."

"Important to him, you mean."

"Exactly. And the only common object I could think of that met the little yellow envelope description was a mailer, the kind you use to return film to Eastman Kodak for processing. That was the only interesting thing I really expected to find in Tyler's mail. From the way you and Thomas described him, he didn't strike me as the epistolary type."

"And you didn't know what the slides would show?"

"No. I had my suspicions, of course. I rather expected them to show blueprints or technical specifications or identifiable people in compromising positions or at least sensitive memoranda. I was actually somewhat surprised when they all turned out to be the painting."

"Well," I said, "we wanted more information and now we

have it. We at least know what the finished painting looked like."

"We know more than that," T. Graham said. "For example, Marek, I surmise that the Amazon up there with the firearm looks a great deal like the much-bruited Miss Gloria Monday. Right?"

None of us moved in the second of silence that followed as we waited for Marek's response.

"I can't answer that question," he said at last in a strangled kind of voice.

"You have answered it, Marek," T. Graham said jovially. "Oh, by the way. You may be excused now. Thank you for coming and all that, but I'd appreciate it if you'd take this opportunity to buzz off."

Taken aback by this abrupt dismissal, Marek looked around for a moment in confusion. He glanced at me, as if expecting some more support from my quarter. He didn't get any. Finally he moved with shambling uncertainty toward the door. T. Graham waited until Marek actually had the door open and was in the doorway before he spoke again.

"One more thing," he called.

Marek looked back over his shoulder.

"I'm not entirely sure whether you've actually been scared into betraying the redoubtable Miss Monday, or whether you revealed her supposed whereabouts in an effort to set a trap for my son Thomas. I just want you to know that if Thomas should fall into the East River, or hang himself in a frenzy of moral crisis, or walk in front of a speeding cab on Madison Avenue, or have a crumbling cornice fall on his head, or otherwise come to casual or suicidal harm of any description, I'm going to see to it that you wish fervently that you'd never been born."

I don't imagine Marek even thought about the response he made to this comment. Without realizing it, he'd been conditioned by uncounted dozens of movies and television programs to make it.

"Is that a threat?" he asked.

"Yes," T. Graham said. "That's a threat."

*   *   *

"We know something else we didn't think we knew," I said as soon as Marek was safely out of our firm's suite. "I—"

"Let me anticipate you," T. Graham interjected. "Thomas lacks judgment, but he's not without intelligence. If Gloria Monday was a typist at Caldwell and Ichabod the same summer he clerked there, he had to know what she looked like. My recollection is that there were very few unmarried females on Manhattan Island at that time whose appearance he wasn't familiar with." T. Graham suddenly remembered Sandy and he blushed. That was worth the price of admission all by itself.

"Anyway," he continued after a moment's flustered confusion, "he had to know what she looked like. If the top figure in the painting Tyler showed to Thomas and Sandy had looked like Miss Monday, Thomas would have noticed that and commented on it. Conclusion: Tyler changed the painting between the time he showed the unfinished work to Thomas and Sandy and the time he finished it and made these slides of it."

"Your logic is unassailable," I remarked. "However, that wasn't the point I was going to comment on."

"I apologize for stepping on your lines, then, Furst," T. Graham said. "What were you going to say?"

"I can't be absolutely certain, but I'm rather sure that the face of Wisdom in the lower half of Tyler's painting there is different from the face Wisdom had in the mural I saw in Milwaukee. The face on this painting looks vaguely familiar, but I can't quite put my finger on it."

"It's Marianne," Sandy said, her voice quiet and far away.

"Marianne who?"

"Marianne, the woman in Delacroix's painting *Liberty Leading the People*. Marianne, the woman on half of France's coins and most of her currency. Marianne, the symbol of republican France."

"My word," T. Graham said.

"I liked this case better when we only had a little information that we didn't know the significance of," I said. "Now we've got a lot of information that we don't understand the significance of."

"Nonsense." T. Graham snorted, all business again. "I think we know everything we need to know to solve the whole puzzle. We have all the pieces. It's just a question of putting them together."

"Imagine being dismayed over a detail like that."

"Sarcasm doesn't become you, Furst. You've far too straightforward a personality for it."

"Let me be speak straightforwardly then. We began with three plausible suspects in Tyler's murder: Cleveland, Marek, and Giraud. Sandy has opined, on grounds I find quite convincing, that Cleveland couldn't be Tyler's killer. We now have strong evidence that Marek likewise didn't commit the murder."

"Why do you say that?"

"Because he served as an officer in the United States Army during World War Two. Therefore, he was trained to use and care for the Colt forty-five automatic pistol. Hence, he knew that that particular weapon has a squeeze safety. For that reason, he wouldn't have made the mistake that Tyler's killer made: setting up the murder to look like a suicide, but setting it up in such a way that Tyler couldn't have fired the gun in the way it would have had to have been fired if he had killed himself. Conclusion: Marek isn't the killer."

"Marek didn't come across as particularly military," T. Graham observed. "I can imagine that there might have been quite a few details in basic training that he failed altogether to grasp."

I shook my head. "There are certain experiences in life that make an indelible impression on the memory. Learning how to fire a Colt forty-five automatic is one of them. It has a kick that you feel right down to your ankles. I'm not much more military than Marek is, and I haven't touched a weapon in seventeen years, but I'm confident that if you put a forty-five in front of me right this minute I could fieldstrip it in sixty seconds."

"Very well then," T. Graham said. "If all you say is right,

the conclusion is ineluctable: Either Olivier Giraud killed Harrison Tyler, or nobody killed him and he's still alive."

"Very droll," Sandy said.

"I do my best. At any rate, we have two immediate questions before us. I have a moral obligation to report to Lieutenant McShea first thing tomorrow morning on everything we've learned. We have reason to believe that a key actor in this drama, Gloria Monday, can be found at the Piccadilly Bird this evening. It may be a trap and it may not. I take it we are agreed that we should at least go by this establishment tonight, see what we can see, and consult about further measures based on our observations."

"Yes," I said.

"Yes," Sandy said.

"And I take it we are agreed that none of us should under any circumstances intimate to Thomas that anything of the slightest interest is possibly to be found this evening in the vicinity of the Piccadilly Bird. Agreed?"

"Yes."

"Maybe ensure."

Chapter 34

A Revolutionary-Socialist woman told me that at Saratov, where the whole municipal council was made up of Socialists elected in perfectly regular fashion, the Bolshevik troops opened fire without any explanation immediately upon their arrival. It was their way of starting negotiations.

—Marcel Semblat

"**W**hat about this place?"

"I think not, sir. That establishment caters to gentlemen who prefer other gentlemen."

"That doesn't sound very likely for our purposes, does it?"

"No, sir."

"How about here?"

"A remote possibility, Mr. Curry. The management there has always enjoyed a reputation for impeccable probity."

"This is turning out to be more of a challenge than I anticipated."

"I would counsel patience, Mr. Curry," Alfred said to Thomas. Alfred swung the limousine through an effortless left turn. "We are still within a two-block radius of Broadway and Seventh. We shall see at least forty more bars, saloons, and night spots before we get outside the plausible range."

The limousine crept along the street. Alfred serenely ignored the angry honking behind him. Thomas peered through the smoked glass windows, trying to read basement and first-floor signs through the crowd surging nonstop, gutter to property line, along the sidewalk.

A red-and-black neon sign caught Thomas's eye. It depicted

a twenty-five-cent piece that had sprouted arms and legs and was vigorously shaking a pair of maracas. The twisted-wire letters above it spelled out The Latin Quarter. Thomas already had his mouth open to call attention to the place when Alfred spoke.

"Yes, that does seem a rather likelier candidate. Shall I pull around the corner to avoid making your entrance unduly conspicuous?"

"By all means. Pity my only pink suit was at the cleaner's or I could have achieved total inobtrusiveness."

"Quite, sir. By the way, sir, based on my limited experience, if it is going to happen at all it should do so within twenty minutes."

"No doubt."

Thomas slipped out of the limousine and moved back up the sidewalk. He went down eight steps to a landing. The landing had been covered with textured vinyl that was supposed to make it look as if it were made up of dozens of small red, black, green, and yellow bricks. It didn't.

He stepped through the door of the Latin Quarter into harsh orange light and music that might have passed for Latin in Dubuque. The orange light lasted for two steps. Then he was in semidarkness. The place seemed crowded, but that was because people were pressing around the bar on one side and the booths on the other. Only one couple moved on the dance floor, and they looked as if they were paid to be there.

Thomas moved toward the bar. He didn't make it. A cocktail girl—that's what they called them—intercepted him.

"What'll it be?" she asked as best she could around a generous pouch of Wrigley's spearmint.

"Heineken, draft."

"We don't have that. How 'bout a whiskey sour?"

"Bar booze and generic fruit." Thomas winced. "I'm too young to be nostalgic for Prohibition."

"What's 'generic' mean?"

"The opposite of specifically named—for example, Lowenbrau."

"We don't have that. How 'bout a champagne cocktail?"

"You do have beer, don't you?"

"Sure. Just tell me what you want."

"Maybe things will go more swiftly if you tell me what you have."

"Sure, tiger. Lessee. We got Falstaff and Busch Bavarian."

"I thought you said you had beer."

"We got Falstaff and Busch Bavarian."

"You know something, Tex Guinan? You just sold yourself a whiskey sour."

The cocktail girl hustled off without asking what Tex Guinan meant. Thomas looked toward the back of the dance floor and spotted the band. It consisted of three instruments, all brass. The three guys playing the instruments looked about as Latin as the Boston Celtics.

"That'll be three seventy-five." The cocktail girl was back.

Thomas accepted an old-fashioned glass full of murky liquid with a lemon slice floating in it. He took out his money clip. He put the glass back down on the cocktail girl's tray and fumbled at the bills in the clip. He extracted four singles. He dropped these on the tray and picked his drink back up.

"Keep the change."

"Thanks a lot, big spender."

He took a sip from the drink and headed again for the bar. He thought it over as he worked his way through the crowd. Bar or booths? Bar, surely.

He was right.

"How's the drink?"

The purring, female voice came from over his left shoulder. He answered without turning around.

"You know, I believe a hard-shell Baptist could drink this on Good Friday without the slightest twinge of guilt."

"You talk funny. Anyone ever tell you that?"

"I don't know. I never listen to what anyone else says."

The woman who had spoken circled around in front of him. She stood quite close. She was black, smooth-skinned, wearing a pageboy wig. She puffed delicately on a small cigar and coyly turned her head to blow the smoke away from him.

"You want a date, big fella?"

"That depends."

" 'Pends on what?"

"What do you think it depends on?"

She put her arms around his waist, laid her head against his chest, and squeezed tightly.

"My name's Twyla," she said. "What's your name?"

"Thomas."

"Whadda your friends call you, Thomas?"

"Mr. Curry."

She giggled.

"You want a date, Mr. Curry?"

"I'm still waiting, Twyla."

"You ain't a cop, are you, honey?"

"Do I look like a cop?"

"Sure don't. Do I look like a hooker?"

"That's not a question a gentleman would answer."

"Shee-ut, honey." She giggled again. "I'm askin' you."

She raised her arms so that they were circling his chest and squeezed again. She thrust her groin up to his and rubbed vigorously.

"I guess if you was a cop I'd be in the tank by now. How does twenty for an hour and fifty for all night sound to you?"

"Your place or mine?"

Twyla's place, as it turned out, wasn't far from the intersection of Broadway and Seventh Avenue. It was a single room in a seedy hotel, not much different from the one Katherine Colleen Ferguson had plunged out of. It had a bed, a nightstand, a sink, a closet, and one straight-back wooden chair.

Thomas just had time to close the door before Twyla slipped her dress off and dropped it on the floor. She was more careful with her champagne pink slip, easily the nicest thing she was wearing. She took it off deliberately, folded it neatly, and laid it on the seat of the chair.

She had already kicked off her heels. She unfastened the

garters on her black knit hose and slid the nylons down her legs. She kept her legs straight and bent over at the waist as she did this, giving Thomas an unencumbered view of her bottom, framed by her garter belt. This accomplished, she removed her brassiere and the garter belt with rather less ceremony, lay on her stomach on the bed, and looked kittenishly over her shoulder.

"Don't keep me waitin', honey," she said. "I'm ready."

"Well," Thomas said. "Now we'll see how I perform under pressure."

He doffed his jacket, cuff links, tie tack, and tie. He did this without wasted motion but not with undue haste. Twyla squirmed impatiently and contributed a few moans in the bargain. Thomas put his money clip onto the nightstand next to the cuff links, and that seemed sufficient distraction for Twyla to procure a minute or so of silence from her.

Thomas had now reached one of the great divides separating American male college graduates of the period. The proper sequence in which to undress oneself when preparing to give amorous attention to a young lady was a subject of sharp debate between two schools of thought. One faction, drawing its inspiration from Louisiana State University, maintained that, having reached the point Thomas had, one should then remove one's shirt, so that one was stripped to the waist, before proceeding to trousers, then shoes, then underpants, and then socks. The other faction, sponsorship of which was disputed between Yale and Dartmouth, held for removing shoes, socks, trousers, and underpants, leaving the shirt for last. If you ever see a picture of someone from the era stripped to his skivvies but still wearing shoes and socks, you'll know where he stood.

True to the tradition in which he had been raised, Thomas followed the Yale/Dartmouth line. He sat down on the bed, rather near Twyla's head, and slipped off his shoes. He left his socks on.

"Hurry up, honey," Twyla moaned.

Thomas rose and turned around. He stood very close to the

bed, so that Twyla couldn't see below his knees. He looked down at the prone woman, who arched her neck to gaze up at him.

He dropped his pants to his ankles and stepped out of them. He bent, picked them up, and tossed them carelessly behind him, more or less in the direction of the chair. He repeated the procedure with his jockey shorts, making sure that Twyla could see them as he flung them over his shoulder.

"Oh, honey," Twyla shouted, her voice much louder than it had been up to now, "you can come on in."

"Do you mean it?" Thomas asked.

A sudden and insistent drumming on the door interrupted his question.

"You in there, Twyla?" an angry male voice demanded through the door. "You open up this door, you cheap slut, you hear me? Open up this door!"

Twyla rolled over to prop herself up on her right elbow. She looked wide-eyed toward the door. She raised the back of her left hand to her mouth and a little yelp escaped from her.

"You hear me, you two-bit whore? Open up this door! I told you I'd kill you if you went hustlin' again and I meant it."

"No, Sawtooth," Twyla yelled at the door, her voice sick with fear. "I ain't been hookin', honey. I was asleep. I'll be right there, soon's I get my robe on."

"You open up this door right now." The battering on the door picked up in volume and intensity.

"Get in the closet," Twyla hissed at Thomas. "Hurry! Please hurry. That's Sawtooth, my boyfriend. He find you in here he'll kill us both. Hurry!"

"What'd I tell you, woman?" Sawtooth asked again, punctuating his query with repeated hammerings on the door.

Thomas sprang, not toward the closet, but toward the door. He snatched it open and Sawtooth, in mid-hammer, stumbled over the threshhold.

Thomas grabbed the back of Sawtooth's collar and encouraged his progress into the room. He encouraged it vigorously enough that Sawtooth lurched forward, barked his shin on the corner of the bed frame, and sprawled on the floor beside the bed.

"The contemporary version of the badger game, if I'm not mistaken," Thomas said to Sawtooth, who was white, five-nine, and weighed about 150 pounds.

Sawtooth jerked his head around to look at Thomas. He started to spring to his feet. Then he saw the .38 Thomas was holding and changed his mind.

"You sure messed this up," Sawtooth said to Twyla.

Twyla lay wearily back on the bed.

"Look who's talkin'." She sighed. "You get your silly white self taken by an overgrown college boy who couldn't find his way around the block."

"Now, now," Thomas said. "Let's not quarrel. I don't necessarily have to call the police."

"You mean you're not the police?" Sawtooth demanded.

"I read Crimestoppers' Textbook faithfully every Sunday, but I don't think that's enough to qualify. So the answer is yes, this is your lucky day. Answer my question correctly and you don't have to go to jail. Give the wrong answer, on the other hand, and it's summer on Riker's Island for you."

"We're saying nothing," Sawtooth spat.

"Shut your mouth before I shut it for you," Twyla instructed Sawtooth. Rather calmly, her action suggesting irritation more than rancor, she reached down with her right hand and smacked Sawtooth briskly on the back of his head. "Listen to the man. He's saying something important."

"The question is this: Where can I find the tall blond white woman who was pulling this little racket in this neighborhood up until a few weeks ago? The name I have for her is Gloria Monday, but she may have used a different one."

"Don't know her," Sawtooth said.

"Beep-beep. Wrong answer, Sawtooth. Looks like you get the buzzer."

"It's the truth," Sawtooth insisted.

"Makes no difference. It's still the wrong answer. The deal is, I walk out of here with an address for Gloria Monday or you two get a police escort to the Tombs."

"She didn't work here regular," Twyla said.

"Shut up!" Sawtooth hissed.

Twyla sighed and swung her feet to the floor, so that she was sitting on the edge of the bed. She gripped Sawtooth's cheeks firmly between the thumb and fingers of her left hand and turned his face toward her. Among other things, this gesture made it clear why Sawtooth had gotten his name.

"Sawtooth, honey," she said, "I want you to shut up." She smacked him on the side of the head with her right hand. "Do you understand that? I said do you understand that?" She smacked him again. An ambiguous noise came out of Sawtooth's mouth. "Good. Now this is to make sure you don't forget." She smacked him once more, this time on top of his head.

Twyla let go of Sawtooth and swung her feet back up onto the bed, sitting cross-legged on it. She rested her forearms on her knees and looked at Thomas.

"Like I said, she didn't work this part of town regular. Just now and then. No one had the nuts to scare her off when she came because the word was she had some pretty good muscle behind her, you know what I mean?"

"I think so."

"Anyway, 'long 'bout six weeks, two months ago, things got too hot for her around here. I mean police hot. She ain't been back since then. Don't know where she come from, don't know where she went."

"But Twyla, that's just what I need to know."

Twyla closed her eyes for a minute and thought things over. "Sawtooth," she said then, "go make some phone calls."

Sawtooth looked warily at Thomas. It was Thomas's turn to think things over. He went with his instincts. He gestured impatiently with the barrel of the gun.

"You've got twenty minutes," he said. "Use the pay phone on the corner that I can see from the window."

Sawtooth sprang to his feet and began circling toward the door. Thomas moved slowly out of the way to let him through.

"Sawtooth," Twyla called just before he walked out, "you not back in twenty minutes, honey, I'm gonna get mad."

Twyla looked up at Thomas as he moved toward the window.

"Mr. Curry," she said, "if you can handle that gun with just one hand for a second, I surely could use a smoke."

Sawtooth was back in seventeen minutes and thirty-four seconds. He found Thomas fully dressed, Twyla still naked, leaning contentedly against the headboard of the bed and enjoying one of Thomas's cigarettes.

"The word is that Gloria Monday's at a place in Brooklyn called the Piccadilly Bird tonight," he reported.

"If that isn't true," Thomas said, "I know where to find Twyla, and Twyla knows where to find you."

"It's true."

"In that case, I'll bid you a pleasant evening."

Thomas stood up, left a fifty on the nightstand, and walked toward the door. Twyla glanced at the currency and then grinned in Thomas's direction.

"A contract is a contract," Thomas said.

Chapter 35

What a setup—
Holy cow!
They'd never believe it
If my friends could see me now!

> —"If My Friends Could See Me Now,"
> from *Sweet Charity*, music by
> Cy Coleman, lyrics by Dorothy
> Fields

"**W**ell, here we all are," I said to T. Graham. "What's the plan?"

T. Graham extracted a heavy gold pocket watch from his vest and consulted it gravely. If it kept time as well as the sober and unostentatious but quite expensive Rolex on my wrist, he learned that it was almost eight-fifteen.

"My suggestion is this. We will each engage a cab. Each of us will note the numbers of the cabs the others have engaged. Each cab will drive around a two- or three-block area, periodically coming back to this street. One of the cabs will be on this block at all times, so that one of the three of us will always have the Piccadilly Bird in sight. If we spot something, we have our cab flash its hazard lights to alert the other two when they drive up."

"How can we be sure that one of the cabs will always be here?"

"Whichever cab starts here won't leave until the second cab comes back. Then that cab won't leave until the third cab comes back. Then the third cab stays until the first cab returns, and so on."

"Why don't all three of us just find a comfortable place somewhere on the block here and sit tight?"

"That's called static observation. Carried out by amateurs, which we are, it is highly conspicuous to those who know what to look for. In other words, if there's anything for us to see here, we'll be spotted if we try it that way. If there isn't anything for us to see, then of course the entire exercise is academic anyway."

"That's very impressive, Graham. I didn't realize you were so conversant with sophisticated surveillance techniques."

"Some of my clients have become familiar with them in the way that Floyd Patterson's last two opponents became familiar with left hooks."

On the pretext of giving the proposal deep thought, I glanced surreptitiously at Sandy, seated beside me in the cab where we were having this conversation. More precisely, I glanced surreptitiously at the Greenwalds Drugstore sack on the seat beside her.

I know that it's not particularly gallant for a male to steal peeks at what a woman has bought in a drugstore, but I had an honorable motive. I thought it a little odd, when I stopped by in the taxi to pick her up, that she was uncharacteristically two minutes late because there was something she just couldn't put off popping into the drugstore to buy. I wouldn't have put it past her to hide a weapon of some kind in that innocent-looking sack and to try to sneak it along on this expedition. If she had I wanted to know, because I intended to put a stop to it. In my considered opinion, we already had one cowboy too many involved in the enterprise.

Fortunately, the mouth of the sack was open and I had no trouble seeing what was inside: a family-sized bar of Dial soap and a pair of nylon hose. I shrugged mentally. People handle stress in different ways, and obsessive attention to quotidian routine is one of the more common.

"What you are proposing seems sound," Sandy said, "but—"

"Thank you."

"—but what are we going to do if we actually see Gloria Monday walk up to the Piccadilly Bird?"

"The most promising thing to do at that point," T. Graham said, "would seem to be to go in and ask to speak to her. I suggest that when and if Miss Monday puts in an appearance, we join forces forthwith and either approach her or, if the situation seems to warrant it, consider some alternative, such as summoning Lieutenant McShea."

"Sounds good," I said.

"*D'accord*," Sandy said.

T. Graham and Sandy got out to find their own cabs, leaving me with the one Sandy and I had ridden over in. To tell the truth, I felt pretty good about things at that point. T. Graham's idea made sense. It was hard to see how anything could go wrong.

In 1962, there were at least two Brooklyns in America. One was located on a back lot at MGM and consisted entirely of tenements full of wacky, colorful Brooklynites, friendly bars where happy-go-lucky male customers who all said "toid" instead of "third" traded wisecracks with worldly-wise bartenders, and Ebbetts Field. The other was located in New York City and included everything you'd expect to find in what, if New York hadn't annexed it around the turn of the century, would be the third-largest city in America. The Piccadilly Bird was in the real Brooklyn, just off Fulton Street, about halfway between the Brooklyn Navy Yard and Prospect Park.

The west side of the block, as I came to realize over the course of the next hour, was eight storefronts long, with the Piccadilly Bird roughly in the middle. Flanking the Piccadilly Bird's garish neon and blinking white lights was an alley on one side and an arcade on the other. Taking up the rest of the block was an array typical for this kind of neighborhood in Brooklyn: a working-class diner, a bar and grill, a drugstore and soda fountain, a dollar-a-night hotel, a dry cleaner, and a pizzeria. There was a news and magazine stand on each corner and a steady flow of pedestrians ranging from Johnny-Lunchbucket-and-Katie-Keypuncher couples out on dates to guys in sailors' uniforms looking for dates of a slightly different kind.

I've done things that were more tedious than driving down the same block every six minutes for an hour, but I really can't remember what they were. After the first two passes, the exercise was monumentally boring. By eight-forty, no one in the world was hoping more than I was that Gloria Monday would show up so that we could move on to something—anything—else.

As the cab I was in pulled onto the street once more shortly after nine, I longingly searched the sidewalk on the Piccadilly Bird side of the block for a tall, blond woman. I didn't see one.

I looked along the opposite curb for T. Graham's cab. And my heart leaped.

The hazard lights on T. Graham's cab winked at me. Then they winked again.

"Pull over," I instructed the cabbie.

He slipped in behind T. Graham's cab and I clambered out. I leaned through the window of T. Graham's cab on the curb side, so that the cab shielded me from the Piccadilly Bird's entrance across the street.

"She arrived at nine-oh-three," T. Graham said calmly. "She got out of a cab in front of the main entrance, then walked down the alley on the side of the building, presumably to a staff door."

"Working girl," I commented.

"Let's not jump to conclusions. I guess we've reached the consultation stage. What do you think we should do?"

"I think—Good Lord. Look at that."

I straightened up and looked over the roof of the cab to see better what I had glimpsed through the street-side window. T. Graham leaned over to the window to see what I was exclaiming about.

"My sweet—" he muttered.

"Thomas Andrew Curry," I said.

"Dressed like a Boston College pre-med student on spring break."

"How do you suppose he got here? Followed her?"

"I don't know. Followed us is more likely—and unless I miss my bet engaged in static observation for some time."

Thomas was coming from the south end of the block, strolling down the same side of the street the Piccadilly Bird was on, glancing around casually and taking no particular notice of us.

"Do you think he saw her go into the Piccadilly Bird?" I asked.

"I don't see how he could have missed her," T. Graham said. "He has probably been waiting to make sure she'd show up, just as we have."

Thomas stepped without hesitation through the main entrance of the Piccadilly Bird.

"That settles it," I said. "I'm calling McShea. This couldn't get any stickier."

"That's what you think," T. Graham said.

I looked back up. I saw Sandrine Cadette smiling insouciantly and walking toward the Piccadilly Bird from the north end of the block, swinging her small paper bag.

The man who greeted Thomas when he stepped inside was wearing a rental tuxedo. It wasn't a rented tuxedo, for the man owned it. It was a rental tuxedo, however: It had been made to rent and had in fact been rented many times before the man bought it for twenty-four-fifty. This told Thomas a great deal about the Piccadilly Bird.

"Good evening," the man said to Thomas. His voice didn't go with the tuxedo. On the other hand, it went rather well with the knotted muscles on his shoulders that threatened to swallow his neck. This told Thomas a little more about the Piccadilly Bird.

"Hello," Thomas said in a freshly scrubbed kind of voice. "Nice place you have here."

"We think so and we hope you enjoy yourself. There's just one thing."

"What's that?"

"No firearms allowed in the establishment. You'll have to check the rod here at the door."

Thomas opened his jacket wide and smiled winningly. The man smiled back, though not as winningly. He nodded toward Thomas's right ankle.

"Oh," Thomas said as if in sudden revelation, "you mean my thirty-eight."

"That's the one," the man said evenly. "I knew we'd communicate eventually."

That told Thomas everything he needed to know about the Piccadilly Bird. But he went ahead anyway.

Stooping, he took the weapon gingerly from its ankle holster, broke the cylinder open, emptied the four cartridges into his hand, and tendered the revolver, cylinder still swung out, to the smiling bouncer in the rental tuxedo.

"You can pick this up on your way out," the man told him. "Enjoy yourself. As we say here, if you don't have a good time at the Piccadilly Bird, it's your own damn fault."

"Elegance itself," Thomas said, and moved past the man toward a decor of Union Jacks and dart boards that represented the only apparent nod toward the establishment's name.

It was a classier place than the Latin Quarter had been. They let him get all the way to a tiny table and sit down before a smoky-voiced woman hustled up to extract his drink order. This was an important detail. It made her a cocktail waitress instead of a cocktail girl.

"What'll ya have, sport?" she asked.

"Pabst Blue Ribbon," Thomas said, assuming that Heineken was a lost cause a priori but not resigned to consuming another two ounces of fruit juice flavored with lighter fluid and masquerading as a whiskey sour.

"On tap or bottled?"

"You mean you actually have it?"

The waitress nodded matter-of-factly, grasping instantly the subtext of his question.

"Those homos over in Manhattan'll drink anything you put

in front of 'em, but here in Brooklyn if you don't have real beer to give someone he'll change your face for ya."

"A thoroughly wholesome attitude." Thomas nodded. "Pabst Blue Ribbon on tap."

"Two-drink minimum. Four seventy-five each, payable in advance."

Thomas pulled out his money clip. He worked a twenty out and tossed it on her tray.

"Two Blue Ribbons on tap, and one for you, and bring me a roll of nickels for the juke box, and keep the change if you can get the whole thing back here in less than three minutes."

"You really are a sport, aren't ya?"

While Thomas was having this stimulating conversation, Sandy was speaking in her turn to the man in the rental tuxedo.

"Here alone, miss?"

"I'm meeting someone."

"Do you mind if I take a look in that sack?"

"Certainly not, if it amuses you." Sandy smiled.

The man in the rental tuxedo inventoried the family-sized bar of Dial soap and the pair of nylon hose.

"Enjoy yourself. As we say here, if you don't have a good time at the Piccadilly Bird, it's your own fault."

Sandy smiled again, slipped by him, and headed for a table along the front of the building, diagonally across the room from Thomas.

"Two Blue Ribbons, a roll of nickels, and no change from a twenty."

"Well done."

The waitress shrugged and moved away. Thomas had time to sip from one of his beers before another woman, wearing a red wig and a skintight dress that came to her ankles, approached him.

"You looking for company?" she asked.

"As a matter of fact I am," Thomas said. "I'm looking for a particular kind of company."

"I'm very particular." The woman sat down, or came as close to it as she could, given the dress she was wearing. The waitress reappeared instantly.

"What'll ya have?"

"I'd recommend Pabst Blue Ribbon," Thomas said, drinking some more of that product himself. "It's robust, full-bodied, and every bit as good as that fancy-schmancy stuff they sell in Europe."

"Oh, I don't care for beer," the woman said in a tragic voice.

"What'll it be?" the cocktail waitress repeated.

"I like champagne," the woman said.

"I'll tell you what," Thomas said. "I came here because I want to see Gloria. Why don't you get Gloria out here and I'll spring for champagne?"

"No one named Gloria works here."

"I don't care what name she's using now. You know who she is. Tall, blond, almost as lovely as you are. The last time I talked to her she was calling herself Gloria Monday. I don't care if it's Nancy Saturday or Phyllis July these days, she's the one I want to have a drink with."

"What'll it be?" the cocktail waitress reiterated. "I haven't got all night."

"It'll be nothing," Thomas said, the joviality evaporating from his voice. "The young lady was just shoving off. Weren't you, sweetheart? When Gloria Monday sits down at this table, you get the young lady a glass of champagne and bring me the tab."

"I'll see what I can do."

The woman in the red wig levered herself out of her chair and tottered off toward the bar. The cocktail waitress shrugged again and went away again.

"What'll ya have, sister?" a different cocktail waitress was asking Sandy at about the same time.

"What kind of beer do you have?"

"Pabst on tap, Miller, Schaeffer, Pabst, Schlitz, and Narragansett in bottles."

"Bring me a Shiltz, if you please, in the bottle still."

" 'Sa matter, honey, you don't trust us?"

"I just like it better straight from the bottle."

"Takes all kinds. Two-drink minimum. That'll be four seventy-five each, payable in advance."

Sandy winced as she put a five, four ones, and a half-dollar on the table.

Thomas finished his first beer. Gloria Monday had had five minutes to show up at his table and she hadn't made it yet.

Sandy took a halfhearted swig from the first bottle of Schlitz the waitress had put in front of her.

Thomas noticed that it seemed to be getting a little crowded around the entrance to the Piccadilly Bird. Three men had come in, and stayed for the moment in the entry area. They seemed intent on taking lessons in suave from the man in the rental tuxedo.

There are limits to what you can hope to accomplish with disguises, Sandy thought. Pour gin into a 7-Up bottle and you might fool someone. Put a bottle of whiskey in a brown paper bag, though, and it looks like a bottle of whiskey in a brown paper bag. Put a longshoreman in a blazer and you're still not going to find anyone who'll mistake him for Pierre Mendes-France.

She took the family-sized bar of Dial soap out of the Greenwalds Drug sack and unwrapped it. She opened the package of nylon hose. She pulled one of the stockings to its full length. She dropped the soap into the stocking and worked it down to the toe. She allowed about six inches of free stocking above the toe. She gripped the stocking at that point in her left hand, then tied the rest of it securely around her left wrist.

If you're outnumbered, Thomas thought, fight in close quarters if you can. He decided he'd better go to them before they came to him. He wrapped his right hand around the roll of nickels, stood up, and started for the door.

Sandy stood up when she saw Thomas stand up. With her right hand she took one of the bottles of Schlitz by the base. As she moved deliberately toward the door, she turned the bottle upside down and let the sudsy beer pour down her skirt and leg and splash onto the floor.

No one was paying attention to her. The three newcomers at the door were intent on Thomas. She slowed down slightly so that she'd arrive at the entry area just behind Thomas. She turned the now-empty bottle right side up and let it slip through her hand so that she was holding it by the neck.

Thomas saw her. She searched his face, afraid that she'd see alarm and worry there. Instead she saw satisfaction. For a moment, but only for a moment, she smiled.

Thomas reached the entry area.

"Excuse me," he said to the first tough blocking his path.

"Hey, the night's young," the tough said. "Someone wants to talk—"

He never finished that particular sentence. The punch Thomas hit him with was not a Princeton punch. It was a Fort Benning, Georgia, punch. It was short, savage, and twisting. It had the added, concentrated weight of forty nickels behind it. And it hit the tough in his testicles.

The tough's knees buckled. As they did, Thomas landed the jab version of the same punch—straight from the shoulder, wrist twist at the end—on the tough's right temple. The first tough didn't thereafter contribute materially to the evening's proceedings.

This took one and three-quarter seconds. That was enough time for the second tough to get up a full head of steam and launch himself headlong at Thomas.

Thomas turned in time to receive the full force of the onslaught, straight on. The second tough wrapped simian arms effortlessly around Thomas's torso. Thomas felt his hands go numb, and the second tough was certain that there was no way Thomas could hit him.

That was why he was surprised, for the flicker of an instant in which he remained capable of cerebral reaction, at the massive, stunning pain that struck without warning at the spongy tissue on the back of his head, just above his neck. He heard a brief whirring, as if a weighted nylon stocking were being swung through the air like a Balearic sling, and a second, vicious blow smashed into his abused skull.

He fell to the floor, pulling Thomas with him, but his deadly embrace of Thomas's torso relaxed. His hands and arms were no longer receiving useful signals from his brain.

Without waiting to watch the second one fall, Sandy turned toward the third tough. His hand had already darted inside his blazer.

Sandy brought her right arm around in a fast, compact circle. She struck the bottle with all her strength on the corner of the partition defining the entryway. The brown bottle shattered. The third tough jerked backward at the startling noise.

His gun had almost cleared his coat. Sandy thrust the jagged remnant of bottle still in her hand at the tough's throat. Reflexively, the tough raised his hand with the gun in it toward his neck.

Faceted shards of glass buried themselves in the back of his hand. He screamed. The gun dropped from his spatulate fingers. His hand forced the broken bottle upward and it splintered again on his face. The lower half of his face seemed to explode in blood.

He raised both arms to cover his face and head. Thomas had rolled out from under the second tough and was on his feet moving toward the third, who was by now a pathetic, bloodied, and helpless figure. His condition wasn't something to which Thomas could be expected to be especially sensitive under the circumstances, however, and Thomas had already buried his nickel-laden fist in the man's solar plexus before he realized that he was out of that fight and any other fight that might occur that evening.

Thomas looked up to see the man in the rental tuxedo. The man was holding a gun. It was Thomas's gun. He smiled and held the unloaded weapon out, butt first, to Thomas. Having collaborated in what had turned into a first-rate fiasco, and having determined that he himself wanted no part of either Thomas or Sandy if he could avoid it, the tuxedo man had evidently decided to try to create at least the appearance of strict neutrality.

"This gentleman seems to have a remarkably flexible attitude toward the possession of firearms in his club," Thomas said to Sandy as he accepted the revolver.

"Obviously a believer in situation ethics," Sandy said crossly. "Now stop playing the clown. We have no time to waste." She began pulling him toward the door.

They stepped out onto the sidewalk, and Sandy looked around urgently for T. Graham and me.

"Wait a minute," Thomas said.

"*Merde!*" she snarled, her blue eyes snapping. She saw me and Lieutenant McShea hurrying across the street, and she again grabbed Thomas's arm and began pulling him toward us.

"I said wait a minute," he repeated. He seized her wrist and pulled her hand from his arm, a trifle less gently than he had to. He kept hold of the wrist.

She looked directly at him, fury rolling across her face.

"Why do you insist on dealing with me in this childish, overbearing, obstinate, exasperating, arrogant, asinine way?"

"Because I love you," he said.

"What?"

"I love you."

"You manhandle me on a public street when for all we know an entire gang of thugs might be lying in wait for us to tell me you love me?"

"I didn't manhandle you until you womanhandled me. But no. I didn't stop you out here to tell you that I love you. I told you that I love you because you asked me a question and that was the answer to it. I stopped you to tell you something else."

"What, for the love of all that is sacred?"

"You were magnificent in there. Thank you for saving my life."

Sandy's face instantly softened. The mercenary barbarian retreated back into the centuries for the moment and a young woman capable of hopes and disappointments took his place.

"Thank you for saying that," she said.

"You're welcome."

She paused uncertainly and looked away. Then, as if with an act of will, she jerked her head around and looked directly at him.

"Did you mean it when—when you said you loved me?"

Thomas grinned.

"Maybe ensure."

Chapter 36

$(A \propto B) \propto (\text{-}B \propto \text{-}A)$
(If A entails B, then not-B entails not-A.)

— DeMorgan's Theorem

"**W**here's Alfred?" Thomas demanded of McShea and me, when he and Sandy had finally finished their touching confabulation.

"Your father appropriated him, along with the car," I explained.

"Bloody hell."

"It looked like the only reasonable thing to do under the circumstances," I said soothingly. "Sometime between five and ten minutes after you waltzed into this den of iniquity, a tall, blond woman whom we have reason to believe was Gloria Monday came out of the alley there and took off for parts unknown. It seemed best to follow her. Lieutenant McShea hadn't arrived yet and the only effective way to follow her was to make use of Alfred and the car."

"You mean we flushed her?" Thomas asked, excitement and boyish delight coloring his voice.

"It might be as accurate to say that she flushed us, so we'd best not risk congratulation just yet. The important thing is that she's been spotted and unless Alfred has lost his touch she should still be in sight."

"You said she took off. On foot?"

"Only for a block, until she could flag a cab."

"She took a taxi?"

"Sic transit Gloria Monday."

"Theodore, you set me up for that."

"And Thomas, you walked right into it."

"How will we know where she ends up?"

"Graham will use the phone in the car to call Lieutenant McShea's precinct. The precinct will radio Lieutenant McShea's car."

"You've thought of everything."

"Not quite everything. I didn't think that you'd figure out some way to trace Miss Monday to the Piccadilly Bird. And it didn't occur to me that Miss Cadette might give us the slip and help spring the trap that was apparently set for you."

"We can talk about that later. Right now I'd—"

McShea's partner interrupted Thomas's comment by trotting up to our group.

"We just got an address called in on the Monday individual, Lieutenant."

"Let's go," McShea said.

McShea agreed to let Thomas, Sandy, and me ride along in his car, probably because he figured it was less dangerous than having us try to follow him in a cab. His siren didn't make much impression on the New York drivers clogging the streets, but he knew what he was doing behind the wheel and it didn't take him long—by interborough driving time standards—to get us down Fulton to Brooklyn Heights, across the Brooklyn Bridge, and back over to lower Manhattan, and then uptown to an address on Seventy-third, three blocks from Central Park. I'd never been there so I didn't make the connection, but Thomas and Sandy of course spotted it instantly.

"Giraud's brownstone," Sandy said.

"Another stunning coincidence," Thomas commented.

T. Graham was standing on the curb, leaning up against Thomas's limousine and gazing over its roof at the brownstone across the street.

"She got out of the cab around the corner and walked the rest of the way," he said as the rest of us joined him. "She must not have realized we were following or she would have left the cab farther away. She went in there just before I called and she hasn't come out."

"What about the back door?" McShea asked.

"Alfred is in the service drive that runs behind that entire block. He'll let us know if she comes out that way."

"You could conceivably get out on the near side of the brownstone into the alley running alongside it, couldn't you?"

"Only if you hadn't eaten recently. I suppose it could be done, at that. But if she did that, she could come out of the alley only on the street in front of us or on the service drive in back. If she'd come out on the street I would've seen her, and if she'd come out on the service drive Alfred would have spotted her."

"Well then," Thomas said, "why don't Sandy and I go pay a visit to Mr. Giraud? After all, we're scheduled to close the purchase of a moderately expensive canvas tomorrow. It wouldn't be entirely amiss for us to check on the status of things."

"Would you mind very much if I sort of tagged along, as long as I'm in the neighborhood?" McShea asked.

The trio walked across the street. They walked up the three steps to the brownstone's doorway. Thomas rang the bell. They waited expectantly.

Nothing happened.

Thomas rang the bell again. They waited expectantly again. Nothing happened again.

Thomas banged on the door with his fist. Nothing happened.

They stood there for a minute, looked at each other, then turned around and walked back over to where T. Graham and I were standing.

"What do we do now?" Thomas asked.

"I'm open to suggestions," McShea said.

"I must ask Mr. Giraud who his lawyer is." T. Graham yawned. "When the police deal with my clients they don't take no for an answer quite so easily."

"Whaddaya want me to do?" McShea shrugged. "I haven't got a warrant to arrest her or to search the house. I'm looking for her because I'd like to talk to her, but I'm not in hot pursuit of someone I think has just committed a crime. I don't see how I can break the door down just because you tell me she's in there."

"Somehow I think that if that house were in the Bronx and the owner's last name ended in a vowel, the door would be off its hinges by now and you'd have the owner lying face down with his hands cuffed behind him while you tried to think of something to charge him with."

"Maybe with some guys," McShea said, not in the least provoked. "Not with me. I play it by the book."

"Any other ideas?" I asked.

"As a matter of fact," Thomas said, "I have one."

It took a good forty minutes for Thomas's idea to bear fruit. It did so in the form of the deputy United States marshal who had served the grand jury subpoena on Thomas. His name was Elmo Brock.

Thomas remembered that Gloria Monday was one of the witnesses being sought by the grand jury and that she had managed so far to avoid service. The United States Marshals Service in the Southern District of New York was quite clear on the proposition that the only way a living witness should be able to avoid service was by leaving the free world. When he reached Brock, Thomas wondered out loud whether there was still a subpoena out for Gloria Monday and if there was whether Brock would like to be the one who tagged her with it. Brock's answers to both questions were emphatic affirmatives.

"You sure she's in there?" Brock asked when he arrived.

"I'm sure," T. Graham said.

"Let's go."

This time we all walked over.

McShea's partner detached himself as we reached the opposite sidewalk so that he could keep an eye and a flashlight on the passage by the side of the building. The rest of us trooped up to the front door. We were going to feel very foolish if we ended up just turning around and walking back to the cars again.

Brock repeated the bell-bell-knock sequence that Thomas had gone through. It proved just as effective for Brock as it had for Thomas.

Then Brock rapped on the door again, louder and more heavily than he had the first time.

"U.S. Marshal!" he yelled, in a voice that must have penetrated every corner of the house. "Open up! Open up or I'll break down the door!"

He knocked one more time and was in the process of repeating the injunction when we heard bolts being thrown behind the door. The door opened and Olivier Giraud appeared, looking vexed but making an ostentatious effort to exhibit grace under pressure.

"What can I do for you?" he asked.

Brock identified himself and displayed his credentials.

"I would like to speak with Miss Gloria Monday," he said.

"There is no one here by that name."

"Tall, white, blond, adult female, late thirties to mid-forties."

"There is no one here meeting that description."

"I'm afraid I'm going to have to come in and have a look for myself."

"Do you have a warrant?"

"No sir. But I've got a subpoena, a material witness who's evading service, and probable cause to believe that witness is in this house. I don't need a warrant."

"I should like to consult counsel."

"You go right ahead, but we're not going to stand here and wait while your lawyer gets out of bed."

"Are you saying you're going to force your way in?"

"Unless you let me in, that's what I'm going to do."

"I'm obviously in no position to resist you, but I want it understood that I'm only letting you in under duress."

Giraud stepped back and we all spilled quickly into the little foyer.

"I view this as a violation of my civil rights, and I intend to pursue every remedy that the law affords me," Giraud said, as he retreated still further.

Brock was busy making sure no one was in the closet off the foyer.

"Talk to Mr. Curry here," Brock said distractedly. "Maybe he knows a good lawyer."

Gloria Monday wasn't in the closet off the foyer.

Brock turned around and pointed toward the front room where Giraud had first shown Thomas three of Cleveland's paintings.

"We'll start in there," he said.

Giraud's brownstone was typical of the genre. Three floors and a small attic. No basement. On each floor, two rooms front and two rooms back.

You might think that in such a place there'd be dozens of nooks and crannies and odd places for someone to hide. But there weren't. There were curtains to sweep aside, occasional closets and cabinets, pieces of furniture to look under and behind, and a chimney to gaze up. That was it. It didn't take us long to conclude that Gloria Monday wasn't on the ground floor.

We trudged upstairs. How was it going to happen? I wondered. Were we just going to open a door and see her sitting there? Was she going to try to dart past us and escape? As I asked myself these questions, the possibility that we'd actually find her began to dim a little for me. It's not going to happen, I thought. She's not here. We're not going to find her.

On the second floor, we looked first in Alison Giraud's bedroom. Alison Giraud wasn't there. Neither was Gloria Monday. She also wasn't in the master bedroom.

We paused outside the bathroom. The door was closed. Giraud grimaced in distaste. We all looked at each other in momentary confusion. Finally, Brock raised his hand and knocked on the door.

"What is it?" a girlish, exasperated voice called.

"That's Alison," Giraud explained, and Thomas nodded.

"Excuse us," Brock said, "but—"

"There are some people outside who need to look around in there, pet," Giraud called through the door.

"I'll be out in one minute." Alison sighed.

Giraud looked toward Thomas.

"Please try to make these gentlemen understand that Alison is the most important thing in my existence. If there is some way that you could contrive to make this tiresome business a bit less traumatic for her, I'd very much appreciate it."

We all moved several steps down the hall. It seems absurd today, but there was a quite extraordinary delicacy back then about bathrooms and what went on in them. All I could think was that we were rousting a fourteen-year-old girl out of the bathroom in her own home. What were we going to do if she stayed in there another twenty minutes? Break the door down?

We heard the toilet flush loudly. We heard water running in the basin. The door opened and Alison Giraud stepped out in a powder blue robe and white cotton pjs decorated with delicate drawings of ballerinas. I felt like a child molester, except that child molesters presumably enjoy themselves.

"What's going on?" she asked, surveying us with cool disdain.

"Building inspection," Giraud said. "Don't worry about it. You run along to bed."

"I'll run along to my room," she said, and glided off down the hall.

Thomas, Brock, and McShea stepped into the bathroom ahead of the rest of us. I noticed a heavy scent that smelled like a combination of cloying, cheap perfume and Right Guard, but I didn't think anything about it. Brock made sure the bathtub was empty. Thomas and McShea looked at the open window well up on the wall next to the toilet.

"It'd be a pretty good drop," McShea said. "And Sam woulda spotted her when she hit the ground anyway."

"I suppose she could be hanging outside the window," Thomas speculated dubiously.

"Hollywood stuff," McShea said. "You see too many B movies. Go ahead and have a look if you want to, though. Couldn't hurt."

Thomas walked over to the window. His nose came just to the sill.

He glanced down at the toilet. White terrycloth covered the lid. He raised it and stood on the toilet seat itself. As he climbed up, I thought I saw his gaze linger for an extra moment on the bowl, and I allowed myself a little excitement.

Perched precariously on Olivier Giraud's toilet, Thomas put his head out the window and gazed down. Shaking his head, he pulled it back in and leaped nimbly to the floor.

"Nothing," he said. Superfluously.

We abandoned the bathroom. It's fair to say that our uneasiness was growing.

"What'd you see in the toilet?" I asked him as quietly as possible as we headed for the guest bedroom—the fourth and last room on the second floor.

"A cigarette butt," he said.

Great, I thought. We've caught an adolescent sneaking a smoke in the bathroom. That puts us on a par with the average high school assistant principal. And we didn't even catch her red-handed.

The guest bedroom was stale and anonymous, just as you'd expect a guest bedroom to be. Brock opened the closet, which contained an old-fashioned black leather Gladstone bag, but no fugitives.

"All right," Brock said. He was a bit testy now. I didn't blame him. "We'll look on the third floor."

"You go ahead," Thomas said. "I'm afraid the night's exertions are beginning to tell on me. If no one minds I'll just wait out the rest of the search here."

I was surprised at Thomas letting his side down like that. You don't drop out of the game just when it looks like your team's going to get its pants beaten off. I almost remonstrated with him about it. Everybody else was exiting in disgust but without comment, however, so I decided to let it go. Everyone except Giraud, that is.

"I think young Curry is showing excellent judgment. I'm going to join him here while the rest of you blunder about on the third floor. You know where the stairs are. Help yourselves."

"I think that I will stay also," Sandy said.

Thomas sat down on the bed and let a half-smile play at his lips as he heard the feet tramping upstairs. Giraud stood near the door. Sandy walked across the room, put her arms across her chest, and looked out the window at the service drive behind the building.

"Curry," Giraud said, "have the grace to acknowledge that you at least entertain some doubt that I killed Harrison Tyler."

"On the contrary," Thomas said, "I don't have any doubt whatever on that score." Giraud paled and Sandy's eyebrows rose slightly. "I am perfectly certain that you did not kill Harrison Tyler."

Sandy turned around. Giraud broke into a narrow smile.

"I'm pleasantly surprised by that statement, though I suppose it's tactically obtuse of me to admit it. Do you mind telling me the source of your certainty?"

"Very simple. You weren't there."

Chapter 37

The maxim "let justice be done though the heavens fall"
is honored more in the breach than in the observance.
When the skies begin to fall, Justice lifts her blindfold and
tips the scales.

—Corbin

"**O**f course," Sandy said thoughtfully. "It is as simple as a
children's puzzle."

"Then perhaps you could explain it to me," Giraud said.

"Whoever killed Tyler had to be in the flat with him when
the fatal shot was fired," Sandy said.

"I'm with you so far."

"The shot could not have been fired until the music started,
because the music was used to drown out the noise of the shot."

"All right."

"The first piece of music played loudly enough to be heard
in the coffeehouse downstairs from Tyler's flat was the 'Ode to
Joy' from the fourth movement of Beethoven's Ninth Symphony."

"And so?" Giraud asked.

"Cleveland said that he got to Tyler's building by two o'clock
but kept watch for twenty minutes or a few minutes more before
going up to the flat. The 'Ode to Joy' was still playing when he
went up."

"Ah, I'm beginning to see." Giraud took off his glasses and
began chewing absently on one earpiece. "Please continue. I
find this fascinating."

"The fourth movement of Beethoven's Ninth Symphony is

less than twenty-five minutes long. Since it had not ended by the time Cleveland got inside the apartment, we may conclude that Cleveland had the place under surveillance during the entire time that it was possible for the shot killing Tyler to have been fired."

"Ergo—" Giraud prompted.

"Ergo, if whoever fired the shot had left by the front door of the apartment before Cleveland entered it, Cleveland would have seen him—or her."

"Agreed."

"If Cleveland had seen you leaving Tyler's apartment, he would certainly have mentioned it when I—when I spoke to him about the matter."

"I like the way she put that, don't you?" Giraud asked Thomas. "Yes, I daresay he would have mentioned it at that."

"Therefore, you did not leave Tyler's apartment by the front door before Cleveland started up the stairs."

"So far we are certainly in agreement."

"The same thing would of course be true a fortiori of the possibility of your leaving the apartment by the front door between the time Cleveland started up the stairs and the time he himself fled. While Tyler's painting engaged most of Cleveland's attention once he got into the apartment, he would not have missed someone passing within a few feet of him, which is what you would have had to do to go out by that way at that time."

"Hard to argue with that."

"Insofar as the front door is concerned," Sandy continued, "there remains the possibility that you concealed yourself in the flat until Cleveland had decamped and then left yourself. Had you done that, however, the young man in the coffeehouse would have spotted you."

"But we're reasoning at length to a conclusion we could reach by a much shorter road. If the beatnik would have seen me go down, had I gone down, he would have seen me go up, had I gone up. And he didn't."

"Not necessarily. There is no reason in principle that you couldn't have been in Tyler's apartment long before the young man ever began watching—no reason that you couldn't have been there from six o'clock that morning. For that matter, just because he was attentive enough to notice Cleveland going up, we are not entitled to assume that he noticed everyone who went up even after he got to the coffeehouse."

"Then why are we entitled to assume that he noticed everyone who went down?"

"We are not. The significant point, however, is that he noticed, not everyone who went down, but the fact that no one went down after Cleveland went up. He mentioned that someone, who turns out to have been Cleveland, went up and had not come back down by the time Thomas and I went up and met you on the landing. He was unable to describe the person he meant. Therefore, to be confident that that person had not come back down, he must have been sure that no one had come back down."

"And we may be confident of the same thing?"

"Yes. Indeed, although it is not strictly entailed by the known facts, we may justifiably surmise that the young man was being particularly attentive, because he had noticed something about Cleveland's manner suggesting that his meeting with Tyler might be unpleasant, and he wanted to be in on the fun."

"I see. So we've ruled out the front door?"

"Yes. That leaves the roof."

"The exit Cleveland chose."

"Quite, and very foolishly."

"Why foolishly?"

"Because, while it is certainly bad to be found in the apartment of a man who has just been killed, it is much worse to have been seen going into that apartment and not be seen coming out, or to be seen coming out in a surreptitious way."

"I see what you mean."

"We can be confident that you did not leave by the roof and fire escape before Cleveland started up the steps because traipsing around on a rooftop and a fire escape in broad daylight is not the hallmark of a carefully planned crime."

"So if I left that way it would have had to have been because something unforeseen—namely, Cleveland's arrival—had forced me to improvise?"

"That is exact. If you left in that way, it had to be after Cleveland arrived at Tyler's apartment."

"And why do you exclude that possibility?"

"Because if you had left by that way at that time, you would have known two things: one, that Cleveland was in the apartment in proximity to the murder engaging in incriminating conduct; and two, that the tar on the roof was hot and sticky, likely to adhere to one's shoes."

"True. But so what?"

"Knowing that Cleveland was in the apartment under incriminating circumstances, you would have done one of two things: one, find ways to invite the attention of the police to Cleveland's compromising behavior, and thus shield yourself from suspicion; or, two, conceal this knowledge, either to protect Cleveland, because of the value to you of your relationship with him, or to use it to blackmail him, forcing him to behave to your advantage."

"What a bloody-minded concept."

"You did nothing to put the police onto Cleveland. This leaves protection or blackmail. For either to be effective, you would have to have exclusive possession of the pieces of evidence implicating him. Knowing, as by hypothesis you would have, that someone crossing the roof that afternoon would have had tar stick to their shoes, you would not have left Cleveland's incriminating shoes in his closet for me to find when I did."

"You've certainly convinced me."

"In sum, in order for you to have been in Tyler's place at the time he was killed, at least one of a number of things would have to be true. None of them is true. Therefore, you were not there. Q.E.D."

"I am in complete agreement."

"Did I get it right?" Sandy asked Thomas. "Is that the way you analyzed it?"

"Not exactly," Thomas said. "The way I figured it was that if this were a carefully planned crime and Giraud here had planned it, then he wouldn't have left a threatening telephone message on Tyler's answering machine shortly before the murder was scheduled to take place."

"Threatening message?" Giraud asked.

"Yes. About asking Tyler to lend you a hand. Absolutely evil thing to say to an artist who's already lost one hand."

"Well, it's a good thing in that case that you reached the conclusion you did. It's clear that I wouldn't be able to count on either of you as character witnesses if I were forced to defend myself in court."

"No," Thomas agreed, "if I were you I'd stick with a defense on the merits. You're guilty of extortion, blackmail, at least petty theft, and procuring confidential information by unlawful means. I'm not altogether sure that last one is technically a crime. They could probably get you for it under some theory of criminal conspiracy. Nonetheless, although you are a criminal and a thoroughly despicable human being, you are not guilty of murdering Harrison Tyler."

"You know," Giraud said, "you impress me. You have impressed me from the time I first spoke with you. You obviously don't reciprocate my esteem, but I'm able to be objective about these things."

"Objectivity is a secondary virtue."

"Perhaps. I nevertheless view it as a great pity that your talents can't be deployed to their full potential. I've looked into the circumstances of your resignation from the bar. I can't help admiring your action and what I surmise to be its motivation. I am convinced that it would be an unalloyed benefit if some way could be found to permit you to practice law without being subject to the pressures that the record of your conduct in Algeria could generate."

"You could get a pretty good argument over that from a number of people."

"I'm not interested in persuading those people. What if you were to receive a full presidential pardon covering the entirety of your Algerian adventures? What would you think of that?"

"Not much."

"I'm not saying it could happen next week or next month. I'm not pretending that I could pick up the phone this minute and bring it off. I haven't looked into it. I don't know exactly how I'd do it. But I know that I could do it. It might take a couple of years. But it would get done. What would your reaction be?"

"Negative."

"I wouldn't ask for anything in exchange, of course. I hope that goes without saying. Just the privilege of doing a favor for someone whom I view as a valuable resource that his native and my adopted country cannot do without."

Thomas looked up at Giraud and smiled coldly.

"No sale," he said.

"Let me ask you something," Giraud said to Thomas, offering him the same kind of chilly smile. "What conceivable right do you have to go around making moral judgments?"

"None."

"I make no claims to sanctity, but I never killed anyone just because I couldn't think of anything else better to do with my life."

"No one said you did."

"Those people you were flying guns to in Algeria weren't soldiers, they were terrorists. They killed unarmed women and children. Nothing I ever did compares to that in terms of sheer moral irresponsibility."

"You're right," Thomas said.

"Then by what right do you judge me? By what right do you pretend to stand in moral judgment over me, say what I have done is blameworthy, and high-mindedly resolve to help the police bring me to justice?"

"By what right do I breathe?"

"That strikes me as evading the question."

"Then you're missing the point. I must either breathe or not breathe. I have the choice of one or the other, but I don't have the option of not choosing one or the other."

"The analogy eludes me."

"I have acquired certain information and reached certain

conclusions about your behavior. I can choose to reveal it or I can choose not to reveal it. But I can't choose not to make a choice between those two possibilities. The question isn't whether I have a right to make a moral judgment. I have to make a moral judgment. Either choice is a moral judgment. The only question is which judgment I should make."

"You have an excellent mind, Mr. Curry," Giraud said slowly. "An excellent nineteenth-century mind."

"Thank you very much," Thomas said.

The rest of us rejoined the conversation at that point. We were not in the best of spirits.

"We have searched the entire third floor and the entire attic," Brock said in a frigid, disappointed voice. "We have searched them thoroughly. We have not found Gloria Monday."

"As I assured you you would not," Giraud said, rising. "I hope—"

"Try in there," Thomas said. He gestured toward the Gladstone bag.

I gulped. It was a pretty grisly suggestion.

"Are you serious?" Brock demanded.

"Mm-hmm."

"I thought you were supposed to be a lawyer," Brock said.

"Why do this evening's conversations keep coming back to that?" Thomas asked, a trifle petulantly.

"I don't have a search warrant," Brock said. "I have a subpoena to serve on a human being, specifically a tall, adult female. I can't look for a machine gun in a matchbox, as you're supposed to have learned your first semester in law school, and I can't look for a tall adult in a suitcase that wouldn't comfortably hold a two-year-old child."

"All right," Thomas said. "Have it your way. I'll look."

He got up and walked toward the closet.

"I absolutely forbid you to lay your hands on my property," Giraud said. "This farce has gone on long enough. You have invaded my house without the slightest justification. You admit that you can't find the person whose supposed presence was the flimsy pretext for your forced entry. Now I must insist that you all get out."

Thomas picked up the bag from the closet floor. He carried it over to the bed.

"Lieutenant," Giraud insisted, "as a legal resident of this city and state, I demand that you protect me from this man's mishandling of my property and invasion of my privacy in my own home."

Thomas laid the suitcase on the bed.

"Sue him," McShea said with a shrug.

Giraud sprang toward Thomas. Thomas stood up straight. He towered over the short, precise man. Giraud stopped, then grabbed under Thomas's arms, trying to reach the bag.

Thomas snapped open the catches on each side. Giraud seized the luggage. Thomas let him have the lid but held onto the bottom. Giraud tugged. The suitcase burst open and fell flat on the bed.

A drop of cold water fell from my diaphragm to my stomach and splashed. The splash reached all the way back up to my diaphragm.

I saw Gloria Monday's dress, the dress I'd seen her in for a few moments tonight. I saw Gloria Monday's hair, a handmade wig of blond, human hair, striking in its quality, dazzling in its beauty. And I saw Gloria Monday's complexion, her eyebrows, her lips, stuffed into jars and tubes and cans that seemed to fill the other side of the case.

"A tall blond woman," Thomas said, nodding toward Giraud. "A short blond man: Height is relative. A man who types extremely well. A man who has a straight-edge razor that he uses painstakingly to shave as close as he can. Serve your subpoena."

I've never seen anyone move as fast as Giraud did. He sprang off the bed and plunged between us as if he were a scatback and we were a bunch of lead-footed defensive linemen who'd been sent out by mistake to try and stop a kickoff return. He was through the door and to the top of the stairs before any of us could move a muscle in reaction. McShea and then Brock finally sprinted after him.

"Once they run him down," Thomas said, "they ought to get a proper warrant. They'll want to check the upstairs toilet for tissues that Giraud used to remove his makeup when he got back here tonight—tissues that I suspect clogged the toilet and prevented Alison's cigarette butt from going down. They might find some other interesting stuff too."

"Thomas," Sandy said, "should you tell them that Giraud did not kill Tyler?"

"If time permits," Thomas said, "but it's not a priority. After all, he did kill Casey Ferguson."

Chapter 38

The more a disagreeable phenomenon diminishes, the more unendurable what remains of it seems to be. Thus, any reduction in the level of violence is accompanied by an increased sensitivity to violence, therefore by a feeling of insecurity.

—Jean-Claude Chesnais

McShea and Brock cornered Giraud in the foyer. When I came on them, Giraud was lying on his right side, his torso propped on his arm, looking from McShea to Brock like a fox at bay surveying in turn the hounds that have treed him.

Brock had his .38 leveled at Giraud in the classic federal officer's stance: both hands gripping the gun, arms almost fully extended, body bent slightly at the waist, gun barrel level with his eyes—straight out of Quantico. McShea was kneeling on his left knee, his revolver held casually in his right hand, his right forearm resting on his right knee. For some reason, he actually looked more menacing than Brock did.

"All right," Giraud said. "I'm ready to make a deal."

I was the only one who laughed.

"The questions began to converge," Thomas was saying.

Thomas, T. Graham, Sandy, Alfred, and I were sitting in the all-night diner seven blocks from Giraud's brownstone. Sandy was eating a grilled cheese sandwich and the rest of us were eating large, greasy cheeseburgers with everything. They were delicious. We were all very hungry, and none of us was hungry for veal cordon bleu.

It was thirty minutes after McShea had arrested Giraud, charging him for the moment with conspiring to conceal physical evidence material to the homicide of Harrison Tyler. It seemed to me like a pretty thin charge. Thomas was explaining why something more substantial could be expected.

"For example," Thomas continued. "How did Giraud get out of France in the late forties when both the French police and the Mafia were gunning for him? How could he have been involved in pornography without anyone in that line of endeavor remembering him? How, without capital or connections, did he manage to develop a successful underworld enterprise in this country? How could Gloria Monday keep popping up and then disappear without a trace? And most important, what did he do to make money, and how did that tie him to me and Tyler and Casey?"

"You mean," I said, "that Giraud was a transvestite. He disguised himself as a woman. He used that guise to get out of France alive, and later to operate criminally in this country."

"Yes, but he was more than a transvestite," Thomas said. "He was a female impersonator, and an extremely talented one. And he didn't just disguise himself. He created a complete alternative identity, with her own set of papers and her own history. It was the same kind of thing he sometimes had to do to smuggle people out of occupied France during the war."

"When he got here," T. Graham said, "he did indeed become involved in the smut trade. But he did it at a very low level. He wasn't an owner or producer or distributor. He was a model—a female model who couldn't easily be traced to Olivier Giraud. Bad Rug gave me the answer without either of us realizing it when he made that crack about anatomical verisimilitude."

"But why would he have gotten involved in that?" I asked. "Even if he had no prospects, he must have been able to think of something better than that. It can't have paid very well, and it's unspeakably sordid."

"It was precisely because it was unspeakably sordid that he sought it out," Sandy explained, the way you tell children how to tie their shoes. "Pornographic magazines are sold very discreetly, and were sold even more discreetly back then."

"What's more," Alfred put in, "the wealthier buyers, especially those with more unusual tastes, occasionally engage models for, ah, individual performances."

"That is exact," Sandy continued. "These customers include prominent people who would be harmed if it were known that they did so. Think of it. Having it known that you are gratified by seeing women tied up or seeing men ridden as if they were horses. It is not only against public morals, it is ludicrous. Involving himself in that activity was a way for Giraud to find out information that he could then disclose for profit."

"That was the unifying theme," T. Graham said. "That was what tied together everything he did. He looked for ways to find out things that someone would pay him to disclose or not to disclose to someone else. Think of the candidates for U.S. Attorney, federal and state judge, zoning commissioner, and so forth who are quietly passed over every year without any reason being given. One photograph in a plain brown envelope, delivered anonymously to the right two or three people, could kill someone's chances. If you have a reason to want another candidate to get the job, or a reason to want that particular candidate not to get the job, you call up Giraud, pay him his fee, and it gets done."

"Once he had developed the concept and established his credentials with the people in the market for that kind of thing," Thomas said, "he moved it onto a higher plane. For example, Giraud could type. Therefore, Gloria Monday could type. Gloria Monday used secretarial work as a way of getting access to information that could be marketed in the same way: One person pays you to disclose the information, not to him, but to someone else, in a way that benefits the person paying you."

"That was what happened to the Johnson Industries tender offer, and to the Badger Game trade secret," I said.

"Right. When Giraud found out about the anticipated tender offer, he went to Milwaukee and dropped some hints about it to incumbent management at Johnson Industries. They paid him to leak detailed information to inside players in the market. It was a zero-risk way of defeating the offer before it was made."

"But then he pressed his luck," T. Graham said.

"Right again."

"What do you mean?" I asked.

"During his dealings with Johnson Industries, while he was in Milwaukee at the courthouse—"

"At the courthouse?" I interjected. "Why there, of all imaginable places that he might have met whatever people he was dealing with?"

"Well, it had to be somewhere, didn't it?" T. Graham rejoined. "They certainly didn't want him on the company's property itself. The Milwaukee County Courthouse is a nice, plausible place for, say, the general counsel of a Milwaukee company to be, without anyone in particular knowing exactly why he happens to be there. And it has one overriding virtue that almost no other place you could think of shares."

"What's that?"

"It is virtually guaranteed not to be bugged."

"Okay," I said grudgingly.

"Anyway," T. Graham continued, "while he was there he spotted that mural, *Wisdom*. I suspect he took a picture of it."

"I wonder why *Wisdom* in Milwaukee made such an impression," Alfred said. "You can find representational paintings of allegorical subjects without ever leaving New York."

"Not as bad as *Wisdom*," I assured him. "Not out where people can see them."

"At any rate," T. Graham said, "it did. He saw to it that both Tyler and Cleveland saw the picture, hoping at least one would use it. As it turns out, both of them did, and Giraud realized he could use his knowledge of the source of their afflatus to play one against the other."

"How did that amount to pressing his luck?" I asked.

"Because one or more of the scoundrels he had dealt with at Johnson Industries—now called Badger Game—decided to offer one of the company's competitors an irresistible opportunity: to obtain the design of the Badger Game lap-timer by hiring away a key employee, while being insulated from legal liability for misappropriation of that trade secret. This required creative dissemination of confidential information. The scoundrel or scoundrels naturally turned to Giraud, a specialist in that field with whom they'd had recent, favorable experience. Giraud couldn't turn down the opportunity."

"Tell me about Giraud pressing his luck," I insisted.

"Patience, Furst," T. Graham said. "This amounted to Giraud pressing his luck because Tyler found out what was going on. Tyler was very taken with his idea for *Badger Game*. He wouldn't compromise it. On the contrary, he was determined to use it to free himself from any hold Giraud had over him."

"How did he propose to do that?"

"By including in the painting allusions to what Giraud had been doing. The title, the figures, and the subject of the painting all coyly suggested Giraud's criminal enterprises. Tyler would know the code. The painting was an implicit and rather dramatic threat that, if there were any controversy over the painting or if Giraud created any other problems for him, Tyler would spill the beans. By creating and publicizing that painting, Tyler hoped to give himself a club that he could use not only to keep Giraud's own mouth shut, but also to make sure that Giraud kept Cleveland from squeaking."

"How did Tyler find out about Giraud's activities?"

"He had, er—" T. Graham reddened, looked involuntarily at Sandy, looked down, and then stammered on—"uh, intimate relationships at different times with Casey O'Rourke and, I suspect, Arthur Cleveland. Some of Cleveland's more cryptic comments during his rather intense interview with Miss Cadette strongly suggest that. I expect Tyler's knowledge had something to do with that."

"Hold on a minute," I protested. "It sounds to me as if you pulled that one right out of left field. How did Katherine Colleen O'Rourke Ferguson know anything at all about Giraud?"

"She didn't," T. Graham explained tolerantly. "But she knew that the Johnson Industries leak—a crime threatening her own professional reputation and career—was the work of either my son or a blond typist named Gloria Monday. Tyler himself had had dealings with Giraud earlier in his career. These transactions were dubious enough that, according to Cleveland, Tyler very much wanted to stop having them. And they apparently went back at least as far as some portion of Giraud's involvement in pornography, because Tyler knew about that."

"And so?" I challenged.

"So," Thomas said, "if Casey told Tyler about the Johnson Industries episode, Gloria Monday, and me, Tyler had all he needed to surmise that Giraud had taken his exotic literature persona into a different field of operation."

"Then how did Tyler learn about Giraud's involvement in the trade secret business?"

"Through Cleveland," Thomas and Sandy answered at once.

"How did Cleveland know?"

"Ah," T. Graham said. I couldn't wait to hear what came next. "To answer that question, we have to figure out exactly what Giraud was using Cleveland for, after Tyler 'gave' Cleveland to Giraud, as Cleveland bitterly complained."

"What's your guess on that?"

"It's a bit more than a guess," T. Graham insisted. "Off-market sales to foreign buyers. Sales that Cleveland felt victimized to be involved in. Sounds like a way to cover shady money to me."

"And there would necessarily be shady money involved in the Badger Game/trade secret business?"

"Of course."

"Unfortunately from several points of view," Thomas said, "Casey happened to get the assignment of going out to Milwaukee to look in on trade secret litigation involving a company that had once been called Johnson Industries and was now called Badger Game. She saw the mural, she knew about the painting Tyler was working on, and she made the connection."

"And what connection was that, precisely?" I demanded.

"*Evidemment*," Sandy said, "the connection between Tyler and someone—either Thomas or Gloria Monday—connected in some way with the Milwaukee company involved in the tender offer leak. The name Badger Game and the location of the mural in the headquarters city of that company was more than anyone could have attributed to coincidence."

"That's why she called Thomas from Milwaukee?"

"Right," Thomas said.

"She knew that either Thomas or Gloria Monday had leaked the tender offer," Sandy said. "If it weren't coincidence, it followed that the same person had been involved in the trade secret disclosure. She started to ask questions. Hence, she tried to get in touch with Thomas. And presumably with Tyler."

"Why was there a record only of a call to Thomas, and not to Tyler?"

"Because she knew Tyler's number and could call it directly, rather than patching it through her office's switchboard. Indeed, she might well have preferred to do so."

"So why was she in the Broadway District Hotel late the following night?"

"Unless I am very much mistaken," Sandy said, "she was there because Tyler had told her, in reaction to her unsettling questions, that she could make contact there with Gloria Monday."

"Which she did," T. Graham said, "in the person of Olivier Giraud in full costume. It turned out to be the last mistake she ever made."

"But she had at least once meant something to Tyler," I protested. "Why would he lure her into a trap?"

"Because he didn't know it was a trap until too late," Thomas said. "He thought of it as a way to guarantee his hold over Giraud, by demonstrating concretely to him how perilous his position was. He didn't realize that with someone like Casey O'Rourke Ferguson there wasn't any turning back. Once she knew that something illegal had happened and could prove it, she was going to the cops."

"Something that Giraud couldn't afford to let her do," T. Graham interjected. "A serious official investigation aimed in his direction was something that Giraud couldn't risk, since everything he had ever done in this country, starting with his very presence here, was dubious in one respect or another."

"Giraud felt he had to act," Thomas said then. "He talked Tyler into luring Casey to a rendezvous with Gloria Monday. He probably told Tyler that the idea was to entice her away from her inquiries—buy her off. But Casey wouldn't be bought."

"Just as Thomas wouldn't," Sandy said.

"So he killed her. He knocked her unconscious and threw her out of a tenth-floor window. Tyler's complicity in that murder gave Giraud something much more serious than misappropriation of an artistic idea to hold over Tyler's head."

"That was why Tyler tried to get in touch with Thomas through me," Sandy said. "When the grand jury began investigating a possible connection between Casey's death and the Johnson Industries tender raid, Tyler had to find out whether Casey had told Thomas anything incriminating."

I wasn't convinced.

"All of this depends on Giraud being the source of Tyler's idea for *Badger Game*," I objected. "What basis do we have for that breathtaking leap into darkness?"

"Tyler's footlocker and the pains he took to destroy it and its contents; his preoccupation with what seems, on reflection, to be a rather improbable threat of litigation by Cleveland; and the fact that that looks like the most logical way to explain Tyler and Cleveland doing major works at about the same time on themes addressing contemporary art in terms of classical figures associated in an oblique way with the state of Wisconsin—a sovereignty heretofore known more for cheese and beer than as a source of significant artistic inspiration."

Thomas said this and I had the feeling that he'd prepared it ahead of time. It was his way of getting me back for sic transit Gloria Monday.

"I find that less compelling than Aquinas's first proof for the existence of God," I said. "And I'm not a Thomist."

"I'm not claiming that it's absolute, deductive proof," Thomas said. "It's a logical inference."

"It's an inference," I said.

"An analytic inference at least," Sandy commented.

"All right," I rejoined. "We've got Giraud, working in collaboration with Tyler, tagged with Casey Ferguson's murder. We've also established—or you and Sandy have, at any rate—that Arthur Cleveland didn't kill Tyler, because Tyler's death was coolly planned and executed, whereas Cleveland at the time in question was in a transport of passion. I'm convinced that Marek didn't kill Tyler because Marek wouldn't have made the mistake about the forty-five. You argue persuasively that Giraud couldn't have killed him because he couldn't have been at the scene of the murder at the time it occurred and wouldn't have recorded an obvious threat to him ahead of time. So who killed Tyler?"

"Tyler killed himself," Thomas said.

"But Thomas, you proved that he couldn't have killed himself, because of the squeeze safety on the forty-five's pistol grip."

"That was exactly the conclusion Tyler wanted everyone to draw. He wanted to kill himself in such a way as to implicate Giraud and Cleveland and get maximum publicity for *Badger Game*, which he regarded as his greatest work. He succeeded."

"But how did he do it?"

"He put a rubber band around the grip to hold the squeeze safety down. Then he put turpentine liberally on the rubber band. Turpentine is corrosive to rubber. The rubber band held the safety long enough for Tyler to fire the gun. Then the turpentine ate through the rubber band and, when it had gotten all the way through, the rubber band snapped off. The turpentine smell that McShea picked up was the most significant evidence in the room, even though none of us realized it. It wasn't a murder set up to look like suicide. It was suicide set up to look like murder."

"But why?"

"Why what? Why did he kill himself or why did he arrange this elaborate setup to try to hurt Giraud and Cleveland?"

"I presume he killed himself because he was overcome with guilt at his role in Mrs. Ferguson's murder."

"Something like that," Thomas said. "I think it might be more accurate to say that he was overcome with self-disgust. He'd had bouts of it before. He looked at himself and decided there wasn't anything there. He valued things like courage, integrity, authenticity. He viewed his artistic success as artificial and contrived. He viewed himself, once he'd been trapped by his success, as a poseur and a fraud."

"A hard man to please," T. Graham said dryly.

"He thought he'd found redemption in *Badger Game*," Thomas continued. "Then, when he saw how easily he could be pressured by someone like Giraud, the kind of person he viewed with contempt, when he saw that he could be manipulated into collaborating in the murder of an innocent woman without even admitting to himself that that was what he was doing, he viewed himself as gutless on top of everything else."

"He was pretty hard on himself."

"He wanted to throw a spotlight on *Badger Game* as a way of making things right. As Dad pointed out, *Badger Game* was more than a painting. It was a puzzle. That business about Gloria Monday pointing a rifle at the symbol of France wasn't an accident. It was a message that would have meaning for Giraud and perhaps for others."

"What was the message?" I asked.

"I don't know. I've been trying to figure it out and I haven't come up with anything," Thomas said.

"But Giraud viewed it as dangerous?"

"Yes. That was the reason for the phone message about Tyler lending a hand. Giraud was using that threat to try to prevent Tyler from showing the painting in that form."

"A dilemma for Tyler."

"Yes. He knew that he couldn't stand up to Giraud's threat. He couldn't live with the possibility of losing his other hand. But he wasn't willing to change the painting. His solution was suicide. In killing himself, he made sure that *Badger Game* would attract attention, and by making the slides of the painting he insured that it would survive in some form."

"But why all this indirection on his part?" I asked. "If he

wanted to hurt Giraud and Cleveland, why not just blow his brains out and leave a note, as any sensible psychotic would have?"

"Pretty banal, don't you think?" Thomas commented. "Remember, things didn't happen exactly the way Tyler hoped they would. It was Cleveland who locked the door, not Tyler. Ideally, Sandy and I would have come on the scene just in time to find Cleveland or Giraud or both in the vicinity of a dead body near an undamaged and triumphantly completed painting. By sounding the alarm, we would have provided the most dramatic imaginable unveiling of *Badger Game*, in the midst of the most incriminating possible circumstances for Giraud and Cleveland—and all of that with no need for Tyler to expose the sordid aspects of his own dealings with Giraud."

"Thomas," I said, "I sincerely hope that Giraud confesses or that the police find a lot of corroborating evidence somewhere. I think your theory's right, but I sure wouldn't want to be the lawyer who had to sell it to a jury."

"Are you kidding?" Thomas asked. "Can't miss."

Later

Chapter 39

History always repeats itself, the first time as tragedy, the second time as farce.

—Karl Marx

"I'm not the type who discusses Proust at the breakfast table," Thomas said to Sandy. "I enjoy classical music, but I can't abide most so-called serious music composed after 1905. I think ballet is lovely, but when I watch grand opera I tend to start laughing in inappropriate places. I have a sneaking suspicion that Picasso is a joke—that he paints those things and sells them for a million dollars and then goes home and laughs his head off."

"You are quite a dogmatic individual," Sandy said.

"I know. At the same time, I'm not absolutely horrible to be around and I have scads of money that—"

It was T. Graham who interrupted this self-evaluation. I could see what was going on as soon as we walked into the place—it happened to be the Rainbow Room—and I tugged at T. Graham's sleeve to restrain him. He heeded me, for once, and stopped his progress toward their table, but it was too late. Sandy spotted us and waved us over.

They stood up as we walked over. If Thomas was agitated, he covered it very well.

"Dad, Theodore," he said as we shook hands, "will you join us for a drink?"

"Why, thank—" T. Graham began.

"No," I said firmly. "We've got to get back to work. We came over because we've received a report from Lieutenant McShea and I thought you might be interested in it."

"By all means," Sandy said. "At least sit down."

We complied.

"Giraud wasn't joking when he said that he was ready to make a deal," T. Graham said. "He has been dealing frantically."

"What does he have to deal with?" Thomas asked.

"Information."

"What else? What information does he have?"

"The project that Tyler was hinting at in *Badger Game*."

"What's that?"

"A plot by the OAS, in collaboration with the Mafia, to assassinate de Gaulle."

Sandy didn't gasp but her eyes widened and her head recoiled a fraction of an inch.

"The money was coming from here," T. Graham explained. "Giraud learned about it because someone approached him about using sales of Cleveland's paintings to take dirty money from Italy and Spain, bring it here, and change it into clean money that could be sent to France. Giraud has been using privately arranged sales of Cleveland's paintings to launder European money for a long time."

"What did Giraud do about that overture?"

"He pretended to be interested so that he could learn as many details as possible, but he kept raising difficulties that prevented him from actually doing anything. Meanwhile, he did what he always did with sensitive information that came his way: He tried to figure out how he could peddle that data for his own profit."

"Had he come up with anything?" Thomas asked.

"So he says," T. Graham allowed, "but there's something a bit off about it."

"What do you mean?"

"He claims to have given a hint to the French government, which was sufficiently aroused that two of its more energetic representatives visited Mr. Cleveland's apartment in time to search it just before Thomas and friend Furst here got there. If he's telling the truth, however, the French government seems to have taken considerable pains not to reveal the fact or extent of its knowledge to anyone."

"Of course," Sandy remarked.

"Why of course?" I asked.

"*Evidemment*, if one discloses the plot, the conspirators will abandon it."

"I rather thought that would be the point."

"Certainly not. After abandoning that one, they will simply put together another one. If, on the contrary, one allows them to pursue the plot, while secretly taking measures to thwart it at the last minute, one discredits the plotters and makes it much more difficult for them to set up such a conspiracy again. The Mafia does not like to be associated with failures—particularly expensive failures."

"Sounds like Machiavelli."

"Richelieu, actually."

"If Giraud is telling the truth," Thomas said, "that explains why he was especially anxious to prevent Tyler from noising this thing about. Disclosure limited to the French government would be safe. Public disclosure would simultaneously irritate the French government and put him on the OAS hit list."

"In any event," I said, rising and prompting T. Graham to rise with me, "whether or not Giraud informed the French government of this plot, that government has now been informed of it. Perhaps time will tell whether Giraud was speaking the truth or not."

Thomas stood up and shook hands with us again and called his father dad again. I didn't really expect anything better to happen to me that day. I was wrong.

"By the way, Thomas," T. Graham said, "I don't think that I should let this case close without mentioning that, in my judgment, you turned in a first-rate piece of work on this matter. First-rate."

"Thank you," Thomas said. "I think Sandy's efforts were at least equally praiseworthy."

"They were," T. Graham said. "But I expect first-rate work from her."

T. Graham and I retired. Thomas was free to resume the conversation, or rather the semimonologue—that we had interrupted.

"Let's see, where was I?" he wondered. "Oh yes. I'm not an awful person to be around, and I have loads of money—"

The waiter appeared.

"Something more, sir?" he asked Thomas.

"I think not." Thomas sighed. "Now—"

"Check, then, sir?"

"By all means," Thomas snapped impatiently. He took the oblong sheet of stiff paper out of the man's hand and scrawled his signature across it, seemingly without looking at the numbers. The waiter bowed and retreated.

"Now—" Thomas said.

"Thomas, please do not tell me again that you have a great deal of money."

"Well, I do," Thomas said, "albeit fourteen dollars and seventy-five cents less than I had fifty-five minutes ago—but let me start over."

"*Bien.*"

"I have been unjust to you."

"How so? I have no complaints."

"I conceived of you as faultless. That was very unfair. Faultlessness is an impossible burden to put on another person."

"Yes?"

"Yes. You're not faultless. No one is. You have faults."

"I think that perhaps I was enjoying this conversation more when you were speaking about your money."

"One of your faults is that, like many extremely intelligent people, you don't realize how smart you really are. Comparatively speaking, I mean. You see things instantly that it takes those of us with ordinary intellects a lot of mental plodding to understand. You attribute misguided disagreement to bad faith or perversity, whereas it's often simply lack of exceptional intelligence."

"Thomas, if this is the way you criticize, what do you sound like when you flatter someone?"

"You see, you weren't letting me get to the point about my money, which was that nothing in the world would give me greater pleasure than spending it on things that make you happy."

"Thomas—"

"What's more, I love you very much, as I've already said. I'll never hit you—"

"Not more than once."

"—unless you hit me first, and I'll never be unfaithful to you, and—"

"Of course you will never be unfaithful to me. What in the world would you do with some little doe-eyed airhead who could not tell a writ of quo warranto from a plea in abatement?"

"Sandy," Thomas said, "will you marry me?"

Sandy smiled and a deep light seemed to make her blue eyes luminous.

"Maybe ensure," she said.

Epilogue

Thomas Andrew Curry and Sandrine Cadette were married on Saturday, June 30, 1962, at St. Denis Roman Catholic Church in lower Manhattan. One of T. Graham's crustier acquaintances commented that his Presbyterian ancestors must be spinning in their graves at the thought of a Curry kneeling before a servant of the Bishop of Rome. T. Graham responded with materialistic, lawyerly bluntness that his ancestors were dead and his son was alive. On the Monday following the wedding, Thomas and Sandy left for Paris on the first leg of their honeymoon.

Arthur Cleveland suffered a nervous breakdown and spent sixteen months at Thomas's expense receiving rest and therapy. At the conclusion of this period, he applied for and was offered a job as a design specialist / artist with Hallmark Cards in Kansas City, Missouri. He continued to paint, although his canvases after working hours were exclusively abstract.

Conrad Marek, when questioned, instantly told the police everything they wanted to know and a great deal that they didn't want to know. Much of what he told them was true, but much of it was known to be nonsense and the rest was so fantastic as not to merit further investigation. He dropped from sight for several years, turning up in the late sixties as an instructor in art history at a private girls' school in Connecticut.

Alison Giraud returned to Europe and the permanent custody of her mother.

In mid-May, 1962, François Rocard was pinged (or PNGed), in the diplomatic jargon. That is, the United States government

296

informed the Secretariat of the United Nations that Rocard, one of its employees, was no longer welcome in this country —persona non grata, or PNG for short—and would be required to leave because of conduct inconsistent with his diplomatic status. He was transferred to Geneva, where he took a position with another UN body, the International Labor Organization. His career as an ILO bureaucrat was satisfactory both to himself and to his sponsors in the Marseilles Mafia.

On August 22, 1962, the OAS unleashed a fusillade of bullets at a car taking Charles de Gaulle and his wife and son-in-law to Villacoublay Airport. The bullets riddled the car and shattered the rear window, but the only wound inflicted in the attack was a small cut suffered by de Gaulle on the back of his neck, as a result of flying glass. The edition of *The New York Times* for August 23, 1962, citing *L'Aurore*, quoted de Gaulle as telling the commandant of the airport, "These people really aim very badly." According to Anne and Pierre Rouanet, however, who describe the incident in detail in their book *L'Inquietude Outre-Mort du General de Gaulle*, what de Gaulle actually said was "They shoot like pigs." Whatever his exact words were, the OAS thereafter enjoyed no standing at all with the French Army, and never again presented a serious threat to the stability or policies of the French government. It should be emphasized that there is no evidence that the French government in fact had advance knowledge of the August 22 attack.

Oliver Giraud arrived at an agreement with New York and federal authorities, under which he would reveal everything he knew, plead guilty to specified crimes, serve no time in prison, and be deported to an unspecified country. Unfortunately, while he was in custody awaiting judicial approval of this bargain, a fellow inmate whose last name ended in a vowel took a lead pipe and beat his head in.

In early May, 1962, Thomas and Sandy traveled to Framingham, Massachusetts, and talked for four hours with Patrick

and Bridget O'Rourke. They spoke primarily about the circumstances of Katherine Colleen O'Rourke Ferguson's death.
Knowing as they did that their daughter didn't wear makeup,
Mr. and Mrs. O'Rourke were particularly interested in one detail
that Sandy had gleaned from a painstaking review of the medical
examiner's report: namely, that makeup mixed with flecks of
blood had been deeply embedded under all four fingernails on
Casey's right hand. They were grateful, as Celtic parents for
dozens of generations had had to be, for the information that
their child had died hard.